The Tracer

Alan Baulch

About the Author:

Alan Baulch is a multiple genre Author as demonstrated by his latest novel 'Finding Bridie' and previous works 'Mind Trap' and 'The Tracer' together with his first volume of short stories entitled 'Love, Life and Fantasies & Poetry'.

A British, London born retired former Businessman, IT professional and Foster Carer. At an early age heavily influenced by Dennis Wheatley, Aldous Huxley and further by the French writer Guy de Maupassant. Modern day favourites include Dick Francis, Patricia Cornwall and John Grisham particularly in style. He belongs to a Prose & Poetry group with the U3A (University of the Third Age) where he collaborates with other like-minded authors and writes both short stories and poetry.

He is currently writing the sequel to Mind Trap and lives with Janet his partner of 40 years in Woodhall Spa, Lincolnshire.

By the same author

Finding Bridie

Mind Trap

•

Love, Life, Fantasies & Poetry

(Volume One – Short Stories)

The Tracer

Copyright © 2015 by Alan Baulch
All rights reserved.

1 3 5 7 9 10 8 6 4 2

Printed by Amazon.
Available on Kindle

No part of this book may be reproduced in any form or by any electronic or mechanical means including information storage and retrieval systems, without permission in writing from the author. The only exception is by a reviewer, who may quote short excerpts in a review.

This book is a work of fiction. Names, characters, places, and incidents either are products of the author's imagination or are used fictitiously. Any resemblance to actual persons, living or dead, events, or locales is entirely coincidental.

To Janet

Chapter 1

With the late afternoon cold of autumn beginning to bite, his long ten hour shift was finally coming to an end, Ray Packer normally spent his days in the Roddrick Brothers bookmakers studying the form newspapers pinned to the walls against the next racehorse meeting.

Owing the brothers a great deal of money, they suggested he worked a few days at their scrap metal yard, it being the best likely option for his health. They had acquired the yard as result of someone else's payback of gambling debts, he did not exactly jump for joy at the prospect but it was not the first time he had been given the option to retain his kneecaps. They were selling the site for redevelopment and needed it cleared of old cars and general metal scrap before a deal with a prospective purchaser could go through and get the approval of the local council.

Their 'request' came with the implied threat recommending should he wish to continue walking he considered their 'offer' of work very carefully, Not realising it meant working on his own all day long.

   The scrap metal yard reeked of damp rust, oil with rotting upholstery filling his nostrils, grime everywhere, even the yard office an old metal porta cabin originally sent for scrap. With a makeshift kitchen and washroom the aluminium stank of grease and urine, long ago he had stopped retching, his gambling habit finding a way to cure him.

   This normally happened when he built up debts the brothers would find tasks he could 'help' them with, shifting scrap, driving, delivering packages, collecting payments from other debtors. They were clever and he was a mug they had him trained him in how to operate the cranes at the yard. Once when driving one out from a collapsing pile of metal the manoeuvring knowledge he'd learnt on the courses had served to save his life, with the skill developed over time the Roddricks took full advantage so whenever he built up too much debt, they kept "helping him out" in exchange for his health and reduced debt. He simply paid by crushing the odd stolen car or two, he also learnt to keep his mouth shut, with no option but to agree otherwise he'd be the one ending up in the bailer.

   Working the two rusty hydraulic Case cranes, one with the hydraulic grabs and one with the magnet suspecting once scrap themselves they were old enough. Throughout the day placing at least thirty cars into the bailer along with the piles of segregated scrap metal, he created as many as forty crushed metal bales rectangular in shape, each stack ready for the recycling plant. The bailer tired and due for scrap itself.

They had told him to clear an area of the yard not touched for many years it backed onto the river path. The local council had already sanctioned the sale as long as clearance of the scrap had been started making way for a new housing development. They also wanted to widen the path once the site had sold to the housing corporation, who had bid for the land in order to pass the planning application they needed to see at least a partially cleared site beforehand.

Clearing the old metal and cars he gradually moved inwards toward the centre of the pile of scrap, within the pile of raised cars he recognised an old black Humber Hawk from the 1960"s with huge back and front chrome bumpers, ice blue leather interior on its bench style seats surrounded by wooden veneer. Moving an old Ford and old Saab onto another stack in another aisle, he tugged at the Humber underneath with the crane grabs, breaking the already cracked glass and shattering both sides of the vehicle as the grabs invaded the interior. Pulling the Humber out and sat it on a small pile of cars sitting on top of a now visible old lorry. Carefully he lowered the Humber as an old friend listening to the painful groan of metal fatigue as he placed it on top of the pile ready for the magnet to attach itself.

Leaving the crane, he climbed the metal stack forcing open the driver's side door brushing out the broken glass from the light blue leather bench seat. He sat majestically inside with the car rocking precariously high on top of the metal pile clearing the facia and dashboard ledge of glass, holding the steering wheel with his right hand and column gear change lever in his left hand.

He began recalling years ago when he used to drive one just like this for a couple of weeks around the countryside, good times he thought sighing and climbed out of the car and back down to the crane. Backing up the hydraulic crane he parked and shut down with the grabs left closed high above the ground, he was so tired it was time he went home.

The magnet crane parked by the porta cabin and used for positioning on bonnets, roof or boots of the vehicles bring the old scrap around to the bailer for crushing and compacting. After mounting and still with an eye on his watch he drove the crane down one of the runways between the high stacks of cars toward the pile with the Humber sited on top. Yawning, adjusting the sticking cabs magnet levers forcing them forward awkwardly with both hands, he positioned the magnet above the car dropping it onto the Humber's roof and felt the magnet claim the metal beneath. Normally he would raise the car clear of the metal piles and swing it around high enabling the crane to drive towards and drop the vehicle into the open mouth of the bailer, this time he made a mistake he was losing his concentration and had not raised the car high enough.

He was rushing to finish the day. He hadn't placed the magnet on the edging of the Humber's roof for balance properly the car had started to swing forward and in doing so it bowed to the front with the weight of its engine beneath the bonnet hitting the top of the pile of cars it had just come from. His knee jerk reaction was to lever drop the strength of the magnet, the levers again stuck so impatiently he used both hands to push them forward, it was too much, immediately the magnet released the Humber making it crash down back onto the pile, the sound reverberating around the site.

Ray Packer swore hard and shut down the crane leaving the magnet on the ground, now it was definitely time for him to lock up and go home he was making far too many mistakes. He decided not to wash in the porta cabin in favour of going home he padlocked the gates to the yard and left not looking back.

Residents living in the neighbouring housing estate across the River Stour would often complain about the screaming sounds coming from inside the scrap yard especially at night. The local people were looking forward to the redevelopment of the site and had gotten used to the groans of metal fatigue that naturally came during the early hours of the morning as frost, and cold wind in winter. April breezes and in the summer heat gave little let up, the atmosphere dependant on the time of year made its way through recently positioned scrap, the night's air would bring with it more sinister sounds to enhance the eerie shadows within the site itself.

Earlier, Ray Packer had positioned the Humber Hawk badly its balance started to shift moments after he left the yard, it started to move no more than an inch or so an hour. With one side up to the lorry cleared the overall balance of the stacks had gone, the pile of scrap metal seemed determined to plug the gaps created by the movements just above the lorry holding up four cars including the Humber on top. It was unlikely the Roddrick Brothers knew what load the lorry had been carrying, when it was placed there many years ago, it was hidden well before they had ever acquired the yard.

Unknown to the brothers Ray had not bothered to return to the scrap yard the next morning he needed the rest. With the yard closed, wind and cold whistled through the rows of cars, today a different sound began emerging. The creaking and constant tapping of metal banging, slipping beneath the Humber Hawk layers above the old lorry took on an ominous tone with a gradual lean toward the cleared space of yesterday.

One moment a tapping then a screech of metal contact, a slight slip and a small movement was all it took. An eerie silence descended upon the yard, a split second before the spark from the metal voiced hard and loud into the night, puncturing then igniting two gas canisters, part of the previously hidden cargo of the open back of the lorry. The explosion raising the Humber majestically high into the sky as if airborne with wings before plummeting downwards and crashing into the other cars above the lorry, setting off ten more canisters that failed to ignite the first time around.

Metal began to fly inside and outside of the yard causing uncertainty among row upon row of stock piled cars. The metal appeared to target every area of the compound taking on lives of their own each piece flying around the whole yard and beyond breaking through the part of the yard where the wooden fencing erected thirty years ago had once stood.

The blast, firing wooden panels and metal struts out across the river like a machine gun toward the residential houses, hitting and driving a hole just above the water line into the green thirty-foot river barge moored permanently on the river bank directly opposite the yard on the residential side. By connection, the hits of metal set off the gas canister feeding the barge stove, itself blasting a hole upwards through its roof.

What metal and wood not halted by the barge headed directly into the housing estate leaving windows smashed, doors and fences forced to give way under the pressure of the gas blasts, raining wood and metal, splashing into the flowing current of the river washing down stream, debris searching out its own targets.

Inside the yard, a chain reaction car after car along the created runways tier by tier ignited in plumes of smoke. The flames sparking out like plume rays as each one contacted with any remaining oil or petrol left in the cars on site. The fire determined to claim and seek out every drop with upholstery blazing at will. Sadly, the light blue leather of the Humber's interior turning into sticky glue like substance as the blaze of heat intensified Ray Packer would never see the show he created. The explosive force pushed further continuing to blast onwards, shattered greenhouses, flattened sheds and scorched hedgerows in its wake.

Ray slept soundly in his one bedroom apartment in Ashford. The drink the previous night adding to his stupor in his subconscious somewhere the sounds of the emergency services coming to life, the Fire Station began responding to the early morning calls from the local residents, someone called an ambulance, there was a casualty.

Chapter 2

The LED monitors high on the walls around the busy service help desk office displayed details of the number of calls dealt with, calls abandoned, calls being worked on by the 14 operators on the early morning shift and calls awaiting pick up.

   Returning to his pod from a break, he placed the coffee down on the desk, looking around at the sea of operators taking calls from computer users throughout the southeast region of the National Health Service, he nodded his return to the duty manager, which meant a break for another operator. Pulling the headphones on automatically as he sat down signing into his terminal instantly becoming operator 15 'available' he pressed the call claim button on the telephone key pad. He looked at the problem whiteboard it was clear confident the call would be routine.

   "Good morning, East Kent Hospitals NHS Trust, IT Service desk, Daniel speaking, how may I help you today?"

   "Oh yes, thank you. This is the Ward Sister from Kings Intensive Care Unit Ward B2, William Harvey hospital in Ashford. I believe there is a problem with one of our monitoring machines. I'm not sure if you're the people to speak to, only I read your laminated card on the wall above the patient's bed," Sister Jocelyn said somewhat nervously. "Not actually sure whether it just meant the Television, Radio or our own computer equipment at the nurse's station."

"I can see how that might be confusing," he offered helpfully, already displaying on his computer terminal the hospital's IT profile. WHH, 473 beds, number of wards 23, single rooms 100, served by 230 machines terminals, personal computers, laptops, servers, blackberry's and printers plus additional equipment logged and not their responsibility.

"Are you able to give me the four digit number on the bottom right hand corner of the laminated card please, which will identify where you are and then I can begin to take some details from you?" He displayed in front of him on screen the full equipment for the hospital.

"Oh yes here it is, 6718."

"Thanks, I have it ICU, Kings B2 room 11, WHH. Who am I talking to?"

"Jocelyn Martin."

"And you're the Ward Sister?"

"Yes I am."

"I don't have any equipment registered for this room except for the TV and Radio, is this a piece of equipment that's on a two ledged silver trolley?"

"Yes it's a brain monitor which attaches to the patients head for traumatic injuries, strokes, coma's etc.," she was not keen on going into too much detail over the telephone.

"Does the equipment have a green metal label attached near the bottom right corner of the base?"

"It does, lettering and numbers are FH-ICU-BM-14," she offered before he asked.

"Thanks I now have the details on my screen, it's classed as a Neurodiagnostic system, is that right Sister?" He found it under medical specialist equipment.

"Yes it is."

"Unfortunately it's not covered as a piece of IT equipment however it's on our register and comes under the laboratory technicians remit. They would have initially taken delivery and made sure it was working properly for you so it will be natural to pass the problem onto them. Before I do that can you briefly tell me what you think is wrong with it, is there power to it for example?" he offered supportively.

"Oh yes but it's the trends which are erratic?"

"Sorry I don't understand."

"This particular machine monitors several trends in the brain and these are called envelope trends monitoring right and left hemispheres, spectrogram trends show frequency differences in each. We also have the raw EEG data, brain waves that is," she explained, suddenly appreciating the person on the end of the telephone she had been talking to, the poor man she thought.

"OK you've got me, I confess I didn't understand a word, but I've typed all that in the call log I have opened for you. You are suggesting that what is going on is not normal and you want to verify if the machine is working correctly?"

"Yes I do, because I've never seen the trends going so crazy and random in any one before," he heard the concern in her voice.

"Is that in any machine or patient?"

"Sorry, I do mean the machine, but it goes for both, unfortunately you can't help with the patient," she smiled to herself.

"We'll try and help you Sister," he emphasised. "I'll give you our call number and pass this onto the lab boys, I'm sure they'll get to you as soon as they can, I'll mark it urgent. The call number is 536224 if nothing happens in the next 24 hours come back to us quoting the number and we will chase them for you. Is there anything else I can help you with today?" Daniel proceeded to reassign the call into a queue on the service desk system where others would be alerted and pick it up on their screens. He shut down his own work part on the call.

"No, that's it thank you." Sister Jocelyn replaced the telephone back on its wall holder above the patient's bed and stood watching information provided through the electrodes placed around the skull and forehead. She sat on the edge of his bed, a good looking man laid in front of her no outwardly signs of harm except for the bruising around his temples, something severe happening inside his head the machine told a separate story.

The brain patterns were looping, flat lining, pulsing with jagged strokes trying almost to push themselves outside of the screen, only to collapse then start all over again. Mesmerised she tried to identify a common pattern but quickly gave up.

She had other patients, with six, six-bed wards and twelve side rooms, Sister Jocelyn Martin had forty-eight patients to care for, rotating constantly according to their well-being. At visiting times, her team had at least twice as many people coming through her ward doors with children running around uncontrolled, and getting into everything because of the boredom of the family and friends having to make the polite conversation they would not normally do. The visitors got in the way and disturbed her care for the patient's even they got tired of the falseness of it all. No one visited this man, with the exception of the Police.

The four nurses who supported her spent much of their time gossiping about doctors, male nurses, parties and currently dreaming up a make believe life for her patient with no name, her staffing never enough at times without porters, cleaners or administration staff, her team constantly deflected from providing real care for their patients. Same old story, same old NHS and same old Sister's battle cry, although she did wonder about him too.

At the nurse's station, one of her team was writing in the patient's notes folder the results of varying tests the many doctors had requested for the entire Kings ward. Another writing on the busy whiteboards the latest patients discharge and the likely new arrivals. Another ran off to deal with a patients 'accident' grabbing a cardboard sick tray and bedpan as she moved like lightning toward one of the six bed wards while Jessica her trainee nurse of two weeks awaited instructions in the kitchen and locker area just behind the station after supplying a welcome cup of tea for her Sister.

She wondered how they ever actually provided the care they should. Sadly, each day was the same except for the patient in room 11, his case was unusual something was happening to him and in her twenty-two years as a nurse, she had never seen the monitors go so crazy. She assigned Jessica to the pill dispensing trolley and gave her the medicine, stock cupboard key, so it could be prepared for patient rounds.

On their morning shift in the hospital's laboratory Kelly and Darren had their usual backlog of allergy, HIV, Hepatitis, Cancer, Kidney, Infectious, sexually transmitted disease, DNA or paternity blood testing. Both of them hunched over their microscopes assessing the plasma on their slides.

Kelly was bored she'd been stuck at her microscope for the past two hours and needed a break she removed her latex sterile gloves stroked her dark brown hair, wishing she'd washed it that morning. She adjusted the hair clip, which stopped it falling into her eyes. Carrying her blood sample bottles toward the refrigeration units housing further vials of blood awaiting testing, she spotted the red flashing circle at the top right of Darren's computer screen indicating a message had arrived she tugged on his ponytail as she walked by him.

They both liked to receive service calls from the IT department it got them out from day after day, testing blood samples, sputum and any other whim the doctors asked for.

Darren completed his tests and wrote down his findings. Kelly had already seized on the call by clicking on the red spot on Darren's screen.

"Problems with an electroencephalogram machine in Kings ICU, they want us to have a look, I'm sure we must have a manual for it somewhere." The team provide specialist advice on medical care equipment, making sure it was functioning.

"Come on, let's print off the call sheet and go, I

could do with the break" she suggested excitedly. "Better put on the white coats it'll mask our jeans and t-shirts," Darren's typically was unwashed and tea stained.

Two floors below and three corridors later, Sister Jocelyn Martin appraised the young oriental girl who introduced herself as Kelly and the blond lanky individual with facial youth spots and a ponytail. What is that about she thought to herself she never understood why grown men wanted to wear them she noted his name as Darren she took them into Room 11.

Grey room, a six inch floral border patterned its way around the room two thirds up the walls from the floor, above painted on the last third to the ceiling in a pale green colour giving off the intended hue of clinical cleanliness, the border, an attempt by the hospital management team to introduce a homely feel for its patients.

A corner armchair, movable trolley at the end of the bed for food, water and papers complimented the bedside cabinet bereft of 'wish you well' cards, flowers or fruit beside the bed which contained a middle-aged man no one knew, his four day beard stubble the only visible indication the patient was alive. His breathing supported by an oxygen mask making it difficult to get a clear impression of the man himself.

Wired up to a machine on a trolley with a small printer attached underneath. The machine itself purred its screen alive with furious activity. Kelly and Darren had never seen this type of machine go so crazy. Darren immediately took charge.

"Can you disconnect the electrodes from the

patient for me please Sister, I'm going to run some tests on the machine first before I do the tried and tested technique."

"What's that?" She began removing them from the patient's forehead.

"I switch it off and on again Sister," offered Darren keeping a straight face.

Kelly stifled a grin.

"What happened to him Sister?" Kelly asked considering the patient while Darren ran the diagnostics. It was rare they got close to a real one.

"Apparently he got caught up in a series of explosions at a scrap metal yard down by the river with a possible electricity charge to his body, hasn't woken up since, I'm not sure of all the details except the Police have asked to be kept informed so they can speak to him when he does wake up."

"Hey, I remember seeing something about that on the TV news, so this is him? Shaking houses as if a bomb had been dropped, causing flooding as well so they said."

"I hadn't heard anything, where did this happen?"

"Darren all you're ever interested in are your blood tests," Kelly scolded. "There's an old scrap yard by the side of the Great Stour River which runs through Ashford between the Milton and Fordwich bridges. The site, not before time, is due for redevelopment it is one of the last parts of an old industrial site, soon to be turned into a residential area. Always said the houses were too close to the river, the explosions apparently tore half of them apart according to the newspapers and flooded the other half on the opposite side of the river, where an old barge was damaged as well."

"Was he the only casualty?"

"Pretty much apart from cuts and bruises from flying debris, no one was working in the scrap yard that day either."

"The tests come out fine so far, the machine appears to be OK. I'll switch off and leave it for a couple of minutes."

"For how long has it been behaving like this Sister?"

"He's been here for four days now, the machine has shown abnormal brain activity ever since, yet he always looks so peaceful," suggested Sister Jocelyn getting them back to the task.
"I'll turn the machine on now if you want to reapply the electrodes to him please Sister."
The machine reacted immediately even more erratic as if it was trying to make up for the loss of connection.

"Sister could you remove the electrodes again please?" he turned off the machine, half expecting the patient to complain.
"Now would you kindly put them on me, Kelly could you stand by and be ready to switch the machine on again?"
Darren nodded to her once Sister Jocelyn replaced the electrodes on his own forehead.
"How's it looking Sister?"
"The reading is normal and very calm."
"Do you mean Darren's normal? I don't believe it Sister," Kelly joked.

"Is it working as you'd expect Sister?"
"Yes," frustration creeping in her voice, she did not have time for this.

"What's it mean Darren?" Kelly asked.

"It means that there's nothing wrong with the machine, it's the patient that's causing the machine to react the way it does," he deferred to Sister Jocelyn.

"I'm afraid it looks likely now," she accepted, agreeing with him.

"When we get back to the Lab we will close the call you placed if that's OK with you Sister."

"Yes that's alright, at least I know it's not the machine, thank you both," She ushered them both from the room and her ward. She was expecting the patient's neurological consultant and his band of interns at any moment.

Darren was unhappy he needed to mull this one over in his mind there was no reason for the machine to behave that way. A bit of research on his part needed and a look at the patient's notes, he would ask the sister for them later.

Right on cue, the stocky rounded imposing figure of Geoffrey Broadacre was at her nurse's station his eyes darting back and forth searching for every patient folder that might be his. A sea of seven faces in pristine white coats with new name badges and security passes on their breast pockets and newly acquired stethoscopes all attempting to impress and look experienced doctors they peered from behind the big man terrified of making a mistake in his presence. The interns always looked shifty why was that she asked herself.

"I have your patients file Mr Broadacre," she showed him carrying a blue folder with her automatically leading the way into room 11 assuming the consultant and his entourage would follow, pushing the door of the room wide open for him.

"Ah, I see our machine is still behaving erratically Sister?" She explained the process she had been through earlier for getting the machine checked out with the laboratory technicians.

"Mmm, good, good." he looked carefully at the patient in the bed and then at his group. "Can anyone tell me what's wrong with this patient?"

He noted a good deal of shuffling and coughing behind him, more and more he took great pleasure in these outings with a feeling it made these potential doctors all the better for it.

"He's in a coma Sir," Sister Jocelyn located the nervous young man attached to the voice.

"Very bright Mr Fordham, has anyone read the patient's notes, what is he doing here?" he questioned sharply.

"His injuries were sustained because of an explosion Sir, but we cannot ascertain the full extent of these as it depends on whether he had been under the influence of alcohol, some form of drugs or he may even be a diabetic."

"Ladies and gentlemen, in his notes it talks of electricity and the likelihood of a shock any evidence?"

"No Sir, nothing at all until he wakes up that is."

"Thank you, Miss Fitch, we have tested for diabetes and we can rule out drugs as well as any alcohol in the blood, which leaves us with what anyone?"

"He's had a severe head injury Sir."

"Well done, Mr Sloane, so with severe head trauma cases we are faced with what?"

The group paused seemingly lost for words.

"Come on ladies and gentlemen, its life and death answers please," he succeeded in making them panic even more.

"Bleeding, swelling and tissue damage which could be followed by seizures or haemorrhages, at best it's likely to leave the patient with a certain amount of memory loss."

"Excellent Mrs Benson, now what are the coma stages does anyone know?"

"It depends on how they begin to react to sounds, their reflexes or movements all have a bearing, right now he appears to be in a deep sleep."

"Good, good, Mr Turnball. Sister how long has this patient been in hospital?"

"Four days, Mr Broadacre."

"Mmm, not long, not long at all and how long can we expect him to be in a coma, group?"

"Sir unless we chemically induce him if he's going to come out of it naturally it should be no more than three to four weeks."

"Nice to hear from you Mr Marsh, so should the patient overcome his medical difficulties, wakes up, what's his likely outcome overall?"

The group chorused a likely loss of memory.

"Yes, yes in one form or another, amnesia, ladies and gentlemen, amnesia. Now Miss Hewson not wishing for you to feel left out of the group come forward please don't be shy!" he was adept at noticing those interns who tried to hide from him. "Perhaps you would be so kind as to talk to us about amnesia," He caught Jocelyn's eye and winked imperceptibly.

Jocelyn felt her face redden she noted the look of horror on the young intern's face at being pinpointed.

"Firstly," she stuttered. "The cause is to do with either a physical trauma like this patient or infection, drugs alcohol abuse, electric shock, anything that would likely be to cause a reduced blood flow to the brain."

Well done thought Jocelyn, one up for the girls.

Broadacre pleased with her explanation so far prompted her to continue.

"There are three types, one where the short term memory and recent experiences are lost, two where the patient doesn't remember anything before the trauma or three, confusion and forgetfulness on an ad-hoc basis.

"Very, very good, Miss Hewson, you've obviously done your homework, finally what do you recommend we do now?"

"Do nothing Sir and wait."

"Absolutely right Miss Hewson, let us move on people. Thank you very much for your help and time Sister," he said firmly, winking to her as he passed her on the way out of the door.

Sister Jocelyn watched the group leave the room and then looked closely at the patient he was no better for their visit. She straightened his bed covers and checked the monitor, still erratic.

Chapter 3

"Sam, are you ready with the broadcast camera, we are supposed to be on air in ten minutes?"

A muffled grunt came from her cameraman going through the connection tests outside the mobile TV van, Sam Cougar hated these types of assignments on a bank by a river the cold and damp did nothing for his expensive equipment, his last two jobs had been covering a Racehorse meeting and a Car racing derby, a million miles from here. All this fuss for the aftermath of a gas explosion and helping 'bambo' the office nickname for his presenter on this shoot due to her lack of charisma. The burnt wood and pungent metal rust smell was not pleasant either, the quicker this assignment was over the better.

He'd arrived earlier to try and plan the varied locations of his shots, the only person he'd needed to liaise with, their news presenter Jillie, who had only arrived ten minutes earlier, stuck a handkerchief on her nose to avoid the smell, ignored him and rounded up a couple of stooges for the camera take. He was working with bad light as the day itself was overcast the smouldering dust of the fire just across the bank of the river wasn't helping, any minute now it might just rain. Having just taken delivery of his new Sony camcorder DSR400K, although strong and rugged he did not want it damaged by the atmosphere, he liked its weight it was good for extended shoulder shooting. He stroked it lovingly.

"Hi to you," Bambo the news presenter said in her most 'girlie' voice to both the Police Inspector and the Chief Fire Officer standing alongside her. "We will be ready shortly, I'll do an intro and then turn to each of you and ask you questions that OK?" she giggled flashing her eyelids, it counted as the 'you're special' look.

She did not wait for a response, walking to the back of the mobile van to check on her hair and make-up in the reflective windows of its back doors.

Sam watched the airhead waiting for her to begin applying more lipstick and purposely banged hard on the side of the van to indicate he was ready, hoping it made her jump, it did.

"Two minutes," she shouted to anyone that would listen. She knew exactly what Sam had done and what those in the office thought of her, but right now, she had the looks and the balls to do this and did not care about anything. She was just passing through on her way up the ranks. Her intention is to do a few good interviews and move on leaving those at the regional news stations well behind, with their petty nicknames and smallminded mentalities, and would rise above it. She could feel her red high-heeled shoes sinking in the damp grass of the bank beneath her she was unprepared and unable to rise to her full height of five feet six inches in heels.

Everyone coughed to clear throats attempting to ignore the smell of hide roast and bad vegetable oil that many old car upholsteries were made of. Silence fell as all were watching for Sam's new camera red light to indicate they were "live" and recording. He noted the interviewees were well versed in presenting themselves to talk to the media, she was lucky.

"Hi there, this is Channel Five news I'm Jillie Grantham reporting to you live on the edge of the Great River Stour where four days ago this idyllic location was disturbed by a series of what we now know to be gas explosions causing injuries and severe damage to the surrounding homes. We are here to find out the latest on the injuries and the cause of the explosions themselves. We have with us today to help us both Police Inspector Paul Wyndham from the Ashford Police Constabulary and Chief Fire Officer Andrew Landen from the Ashford Fire Station."

She gestured for Sam to pan the landscape with his camera behind her taking in the blue and white tape that acted as a barrier to onlookers and then to focus on the two men standing either side of her. Sam took in the scorched overhanging willows and beyond touching briefly on the scrap yard panning towards the new housing development and the river barge showing a perfect example of what damage on this scale could do, scarred by the blast from the explosions. The noise of the Stour river at its height, on its constant journey from a tributary of the river Medway starting in Lenham and travelling at midpoint through Ashford and being joined by further tributaries passing under the Milton Bridge and onward to Fordwich Bridge where they were now. Eventually the river would make its way toward Pegwell Bay and enter the Strait of Dover where Sam presumed it linked to the English

Channel and beyond, he had done his homework in case she had needed it, not on this occasion it seemed. Quickly he came back to Jillie and her interviewees.
Jillie seemed irritated by the noise the river made running its course downstream, if she could have turned it off she would have done for the sake of good news coverage, Sam half expected her to ask someone such was his faith in the presenter.

He noted the mannerisms of the two men standing beside 'Bambo', the Police Inspector kept tugging at his eyebrows nervously and the Fire Chief was adjusting his balls, Bambo noticed. Both preening themselves like matadors in her presence, she was pretty he granted. He caught her eye as he adjusted the camera on his shoulder, a faint knowing wink between them.

"Inspector Wyndham, do we know how many people were injured in the explosions?" She pitched her voice just above the river noise.

"Only five houses of the housing estate across the river bank were affected," he pointed. "They took the full blast of the explosions, we were fortunate, because the explosions took place during the day. It meant only two people escaped with minor injuries with the rest being out either shopping or at work."

"There was some suggestion on an earlier newscast of flooding is this true Inspector?" She knew the answer and wanted to highlight another broadcaster's misinformation.

"Wide of the mark I'm afraid, could have been but didn't happen."

Jillie Grantham looked pointedly at the river barge listing toward the far bank and nodded for Sam to capture the shot.

"Oh yes, the river barge moored on the far side of the bank took the major force and as you can see it has started to list where most of the centre section is destroyed, ripped apart which has caused debris to litter the river."

Sam panned the wreckage with the camera the barge looked to be approximately sixteen to seventeen metres long with the timber-framed cockpit shattered. Unfortunately, the blast caused the kitchen gas canister to explode internally to create a perforated punctured hole into the side of its steel plated starboard side, just above the water line.

"Was there anyone on board at the time Inspector?"

"Again we were fortunate the owner was actually in the local Fordwich Arms, approximately a mile walk downstream from here." A smile crossed his face. "He's currently staying in one of the bed & breakfast rooms at the public house until we release the barge for inspection by the insurers."

"But there is a more serious casualty we gather who is currently in hospital who also took the full force of the effects of the explosions, we understand he's currently in a coma isn't that right Inspector?" she added the right weight of seriousness and concern in her voice playing to the camera.

"That's true, as far as we know he's the only serious injury we have," his smile disappeared. "We're very concerned about him as soon as he wakes we will maybe find out more."

"Have you identified him yet Inspector?"

"No not yet, he hadn't any identity papers on him so we are unable to inform relatives or friends at the moment," he pre-empted her next question. "We have of course, taken his fingerprints and are doing DNA testing to see if that will provide us with any clues about him.

"Fire Chief Landen, if I may turn to your investigations," Sam watched her pout at the camera and admitted to himself she was good. "Are you able to tell us exactly how these explosions were caused?"

"Yes, it appears that within the scrap metal yard several years ago and perhaps even as long ago as twenty five years. A stolen red or rust coloured BMC lorry bearing an old H registration plate, was purposely hidden under several old cars and general scrap to be destroyed but because of its load containing metal gas canisters, the lorry was left to one side until it could be cleared."

"Have we been able to trace when the canisters was put on the site Inspector?"

"Unfortunately no, whether the load was part of what was actually stolen we're also not sure of, in any event the load itself was never cleared. We need to determine how far their records go back it is likely they also went up in the blaze. As far as we can tell, gradually over time old scrap in the form of cars and corrugated iron were placed around it, gradually, they raised the surrounding pile to a level where the metal and cars could be put on top of the lorry ultimately making it disappear from view whether intended or not. The net effect was to lose visual sight of the lorry itself and its content, thus over time it appears it has been literally forgotten."

"Surely the H registered cars were in the early nineties?" she smugly said, counting the years to the present day believing she'd caught him out and would look good on the television news.

"I don't think you quite realise, a bit before your time I'm sure, but we are talking about a 1969 registered plate the old "H" displayed to the far right of the plate and not the left.

"Oh," Jillie heard Sam's snigger in the background.

"So what happened then?" she stammered trying to compose herself quickly.

"The site we understand is due for redevelopment and is in the later stages of the planning process, the current owners Roddrick Brothers are selling the site to Hall's Premier Housing Corporation, who are responsible for the other local builds in the area," Sam panned to the damaged explosion wrecked houses nearby.

"The owners decided to begin clearing the site. It's believed by starting to shift the metal around the site with their cranes particularly in the area nearest the river bank and above the old lorry which we can now see clearly behind us," he turned and pointed to the lorry's position, with Sam quickly swinging the camera around to the pointed view.

"The cars and scrap had unknowingly become unsafe, fortunately, the weight of the metal only gained its stress pressure gradually beginning to collapse after the brothers and staff had left the site," he emphasised. "They would not, could not have foreseen what has happened."

"What was the load on the old lorry, Chief Landen?" She already knew the answer but it was good TV news.

"Gas canisters 48-50 kilograms each and there were two dozen of them. This meant as the load collapsed, metal punctured one or two of them, with so much friction a simple spark could have set the whole batch to ignite, hence the series of explosions."

"Were the gas canisters that fragile Chief?"

"Of the fragments from the metal canisters we've been able to recover it appears like all the metal on site they've been subject to the rusting process in this case some twenty five years."

"Did all two dozen explode Chief?"

"No only twenty, we have controlled the release of gas from the others so it is now perfectly safe and under control."

"Thank you Chief Landen," Jillie turned back to the Police Inspector.
"What about the lorry itself, do we know who stole it originally?"
"I'm afraid that's a dead end, with age and with the fire damage itself it's impossible to extract any fingerprints or DNA whoever stole it or was involved over twenty five years ago, would be long gone, all it's good for now is a museum I'm afraid."

"Or scrap Inspector," she heard a titter from Sam.

"Quite, I also doubt it would be the best use of our resources to try and solve a twenty five year old lorry theft," he was not amused and tugged at his eyebrow hair.
"Do we know who owned it Inspector?"

Inspector Paul Wyndham bored with the interviewing and it showed. "According to our records they show the lorry belonged to a Midlands

Calor gas supplier to local caravan sites. We checked on the company and it closed down fifteen years ago. The surviving directors have supplied us with the documentation relating to the insurance company paying out on the missing vehicle, an investigation we understand took place at the time with our own records showing after seven years the case was closed due to lack of evidence without a satisfactory conclusion."

"Inspector thank you so much for the information, do we know any more about the man in hospital?" she asked pressing him. "Where's he from?"

"As I've said we haven't identified him yet, according to an eye witness account, he had been strolling along the river walk. One couple were walking with their two Labradors and noticed him passing wearing jeans, trainers and a hooded track suited top bearing the words "Old Navy" and "Varsity" underneath."

"Is that significant Inspector?"

"As it turns out no, those tops can be purchased in America, New York to San Francisco this one had markings linking it to Jacksonville to be precise but there the lead ends we cannot tell who or when it was purchased," he was now getting really tired of this interview Jillie noticed.

"Truly an international feel to this case then Inspector," flashing her eyes at the camera. "You could gather he was a travelled man?"

"Someone could have given him a present or he picked it up from a charity shop we've no way of knowing and it doesn't get us any nearer to his identity," dismissively he summarised for her. "Another witness from the other side of the bank some way from the explosions, stated they saw the shape of a man literally fly through the air, then hit the side of the river barge and bounce right back onto the wooden fencing of the scrap yard. Which happened to be housing the residential electrical substation serving the area including the housing estate across the river near where we are standing, he then appeared to fall to the ground, missing the river entirely."

Sam wished he had been able to get the shot of the man flying through the air, now that would've been a scoop.

"Ouch," she said for effect to the camera. "Do we know the extent of his injuries?"

"According to the hospital the man sustained heavy impacts to his head and shoulders," his voice deepened as he reflected on the state of the injury the man must have suffered. "His head particularly shows signs of both sides of his skull being impacted with a fair degree of force."

"No burns Inspector?" she asked surprised.

"Strangely no, appeared to have been blown free of any fire. However gathering by the damage done to the substation he could've received an electrical shock as well."

Fire Chief Landen interrupted. "In terms of electric shock it is more of a certainty there I'm afraid, the substation had become "live". To enable us to remove the man from the scene we first had to turn off the substation causing an outage to the residents across the river to the estate."

"I see, is the power for the residents back on now?" Jillie knew of course it was, but she had to ask.

The Fire Chief nodded.

"What do the doctors feel his chances are of survival Inspector?" She asked turning the conversation back to the main casualty of the explosion. "Likely to be brain damaged, would you say Inspector?"

"You have to get that information from the hospital to be more accurate, as I understand it by sustaining a blow of such force to one side of the brain can be fatal. It appears by sustaining the equivalent blow on the other side a split second later, which caused the brain itself to "rock" within the skull it is suspected any damage could have righted itself. The doctors are quite hopeful of a full recovery at this stage, although he is still in a coma. We don't have an assessment of the possibility of an electric shock though."

"Do we have any pictures of him we could show live on television in order for people to try and recognise him?"

"It's a good idea but not yet, we would prefer to wait until he wakes. In the meantime if a family, friend or anyone are aware that a man approximately forty years old, brown hair and around six feet tall is missing, please contact us at the Ashford Constabulary," he gave out the telephone number, Jillie Grantham made sure she repeated it correctly.

"May I thank the both of you for spending time with us, I'm sure you both still have much to do on this site," Jillie bowed to the two men as they each made their way back to their respective teams working behind them.

To the camera held by Sam she wrapped the discussion up for the viewers, unexpectedly she walked toward him kissed and thanked him hoping it would be played out by her TV news company for early evening broadcasting.

    Ray Packer was constantly jumpy he watched the news and had been waiting for the Roddrick Brothers to pay him a visit. He knew he'd caused the explosion tired and fed up working all day on his own he'd been monitoring on television and in newspapers, if only he'd been more careful placing the Humber back on the pile. Having just spent his last ten pounds on a horse as he was walking home from their Turf Accountants shop, they found him.
    The large black Chrysler 300 pulled up close to the kerb he was walking on, the door opened for him to get in.
    For Ray Packer life just got better, the brothers were happy with what he'd done they would get the insurance for the explosions as well as the site's development money, no-one needed to know who caused it. According to the insurers it had happened at other scrap metal sites, they accepted it to be natural risks of the work. They said it was the reason premiums were so high, not something, the Roddricks had concerned themselves with, if left to them they would not have been insured luckily for them their previous debtor who signed the yard over to them did worry about the risks involved. They agreed to write off his debts completely giving him some extra money and an address in Spain where they suggested he "rested" for a year or so. Who would miss him? He flew out from England the next day. No one would ever link him to the explosions and he was pleased his kneecaps were

still in one piece.

Chapter Four

For the three weeks that followed as instructed by her Inspector, Detective Sergeant Josey Rainbow had been visiting the patient in room 11 of Kings ICU ward in the William Harvey Hospital. She needed to wrap up an accidental injury case. For this she would need a statement from the "John Doe" they were unable to identify.

On each occasion, she became mesmerised by the monitoring of his brain waves. The tremendous activity recorded on the machine with no communication at all from him. She took a series of photographs of him, fingerprinted him for any likely identification with blood tests already arranged for the DNA matching.

The ward sister fortunately befriended her and spoke of the silent screams and inner torments the patient seemed to be having, at times his body arching in severe torment. It is was not uncommon for the patient to open his eyes wide and visibly scream for several minutes silently, the first time Josey saw it for herself it unnerved her completely. Tremors, rolling from side to side, head banging onto the pillows and shaking uncontrollably with his back arching were a normal, everyday occurrence with no sign of his coming out of the coma, after each attack he would be at peace for a while except for the bruises at his temple darkening on each side of his head. Josey found herself claiming him as a person he was alone no one except her and the medical staff visited.

Through his internal trauma, she would hold him tightly stroking his sweating head waiting for the tremors and screams to subside and when they did she would gently dab his brow with a wet cloth hoping to cool him down then kiss his lips very lightly, hoping one day he would return her touch. Lately becoming more daring in her approach toward him and began kissing him gently as a lover would. Once she felt him move and reciprocate and dismissed this as a contact reaction. It was in fact because she kept removing his oxygen mask.

There were moments of panic and moments of joy, small such as him breathing on his own, his monitor flat-lining for minutes only to fire back into life, muscle spasms often, his eyes would open a stared gaze only to close as if any information received had to be locked away.

During her daily visits Josey when alone, found herself fantasising over him, holding his hand, stroking and combing his hair she was deeply attracted to this handsome man. Each day she brought him something at first it was flowers and then hoping he would wake fruit, which she found herself eating to pass the time. She started to forget being a crime officer and instead, she had become a patient's moll, a groupie where she would be by his bedside reading herself and sometimes reading to him. This was followed by a get well card, some chocolate all without response, she soon gave up opting instead for a different approach where she always kissed his lips on greeting and would hold him in her arms for a few minutes each day careful not to interfere with the monitoring electrodes.

Almost caught by one of the nurse, because of the routine she had grown used to. Every few days she watched the nurses shave him, one day because of an emergency needing all the staff on the other wards within King College Hospital, she took the opportunity to take this task over from them, now she does it every other day herself.

It was on the final occasion when she finished his shave afterwards when as she kissed him fully on his lips he began to arouse from his coma. She felt a broad grin develop and her kiss properly reciprocated at last.

"That was nice," speaking his voice deep but faint before drifting gently into normal sleep. "God she thought she hoped she wouldn't be in trouble for what she'd done," Josey raised the nurses alarm becoming saddened at the intimacy she would inevitably lose she hoped a real relationship could develop instead.

The next few days the hospital team of nurses and doctors were in and out of his room. Any conversation Josey had about him was be told she was not a relative or they were continually running tests and not to be disturbed. She tried to adopt the Police approach but she could not get a statement from him despite her Inspector Wyndham's insistence. She would just have to wait.

Josey waited patiently feeling like a grieving widow unsure how she would react to the 'live' person she would soon face and whether he would know of the intimacy she'd had with him, embarrassed she felt guilty of her feelings for him.

It was a further week before allowed in to see him. The Police identification of him no further forward, fingerprints, DNA, Ashford Police station records and countrywide databases, dental records were proving problematical this was not America where they were kept centralised. Although in her mid-thirties Josey felt apprehensive as a teenager she was finally allowed in to see him pushing the door of his hospital room open. He was sitting up in bed looking straight toward her as she entered, his presence filling the small side room of the ward.

"Hello Josey Rainbow it's so nice to see you I gather you've been a frequent visitor to my bedside," his smile bore deep down into her soul she felt her face redden.

"How did you know my name, we haven't met before have we?"

"No I don't think so, the nurses told me about your bedside vigil so I asked them for a description." he lied. "You're a Police Sergeant?"

"Yes I've come to take a statement from you can you tell me what happened to you? I am sorry I don't even know your name," she found it strange talking to the man she spent so long kissing and fantasising over.

"This is going to sound strange to you but I don't know either, the accident, I cannot remember," he looked closely at Sergeant Josey Rainbow he ran his fingers across his lips, something about them he thought.

"Do you mean nothing at all, what's the first thing you do remember?"

"I remember you and your touch Josey," his eyes looked for a reaction in her as he touched his lips.

Her face now permanently reddened with embarrassment. "I… I'm sorry I didn't mean…," she stammered worried waiting for the accusations.

"Please, please Josey I enjoyed it too. As far as everyone else is concerned the first I remember is waking up in this room, I know I can read, write, understand everything, however it's as if I've just been born."

She struggled to compose herself resolving to be professional. "Before I take your statement we need to give you a name, a nickname. I know, I used to watch an old movie about a soldier who became lost outside of an asylum met a woman who cared for him, very, very old black and white."

He was amused at her inner struggle not letting her off the hook quite yet.

"Do you think I'm mad then and should be locked away?" he said softly looking into her ashen grey eyes. "Your eyes are unusually soft to look at."

She laughed feeling comfortable with him. "Your accident has been covered by the local news channels, I've recorded them onto a DVD, and the television has a player combined with it. You should watch it, there are four news bulletins it might help you remember something," she placed the disc on his bedside cabinet.

"I know that one "Random Harvest". I loved it too, Greer Garson and Ronald Coleman starred in the 1930"s movie, regained his memory as a wealthy aristocratic gentleman always missing the time they had together," he never knew how he remembered.

"His nickname was "Smithy" and perhaps you can call me Paula he loved her too you know?" Josey was surprised at his recall considering his memory loss.

"Josey is such a lovely name and it suits you, I'll stick with that if you don't mind?"

She shrugged agreement, loved her too, she wondered why she had said that. "You're not old enough to have seen the film first time around so you would've had to have seen it on the television, you must have a memory of some sort."

"God knows what information I have stored, most is useless without me knowing who I am," he felt a slight emptiness.

"Are we going to fall in love as they did? I would like to get to know you Josey Rainbow, it's such a beautiful name and your eyes sparkle like diamonds they melt my heart."

"Yeh sure," she said dismissively. "How did you say you knew my name?"

"I'm sure the nurses must have said," he lied again. "You haven't answered my question Josey, are we going to fall in love?"

Meeting his eyes, "Maybe, maybe, but first we must get you well and I have to get a statement from you," she emphasised, for her she realised it had happened already.

"Is there anything you remember from before? What of the accident, do you know what happened?

"I don't, in fact I can't remember anything prior to waking from my coma. I'm only just piecing together what happened from Sister Jocelyn and her nurses."

"What about impressions, for example do you feel how old you are? Are you married and have children? Are there any scars, tattoos, aches and pains you could recognise? What about dreams, when you sleep are they telling you something?

Your personal clothing was burnt and left in rags from the blasts exposed to, have you seen them? According to witnesses you'd previously passed it appears trainers, jeans and old hooded sweater were what you were wearing, we can find nothing of your identity at all."

"God you truly are a detective where does all that come from?"

"Come on, Smithy, help me," she pleaded seriously using his nickname for the first time. "So far witnesses, a couple, place you on the foot path running alongside the Great Stour River in Ashford, walking on your own just strolling you said hello to them passed pleasantries, do you remember them."

He shook his head.

"We've traced back along the path several miles and there are no car parks, so we don't believe you drove a car to the path to take the walk, suggesting you may live locally, you had no dog with you so why would you walk down there. It is just a riverside walk going nowhere you appear to be a very fit man for your age so a run rather than a stroll would have appeared more natural."

"My age, what's my age?"

"We put you at about forty so where have you been all your life? What we have so far seems to be a forty year old fit man who likes strolling by the river, probably lives locally and didn't drive to get to the river's edge."

"You couldn't make me 39, I'd much prefer it," he grinned.

"That much we do know about you then, you're as insecure as the rest of us," she grinned right back at him.

"From the charred remains of your clothes the one with a hooded top says 'old navy'," she looked closely at him assessing whether there was any recognition of what she said explaining the likely purchase location, nothing appeared to register.

"Supermarket purchased t-shirt and jeans and Reebok trainers, we didn't find a wallet or keys, all charred beyond repair. Work with me Smithy please because we sure as hell haven't got much at all."

"Sorry Josey, I'll pop to the bathroom and examine myself for any clues, help me up." Holding out his hand to her for help feeling the softness of her hand as they touched, it melted his heart.

His touch sent shivers racing down her spine it had been a week or more since she had been touching him and now he was conscious his touch had become electrifying, she watched him walk towards the door.

While he went to the bathroom she looked through the locker at the side of his bed for any clues, notes he might have made, she found only hospital handouts of underwear and magazines. She sat on his bed remembering the closeness she developed with him. Not sure how she could unravel the mystery of him or whether Inspector Wyndham would allow her the time to.

It was the first real chance he had to discover himself, his head throbbed the more tired he became, his temples tender to touch within the bruising visible on either side of his face. His eyes betrayed his apparent age, two double eye lines and a developing padded under-chin, evidence of his slow march into middle age. He gauged himself as fit although faint beginnings of love handles and a stomach ready for the slide into a paunch if not careful. He looked directly at himself and unaware of how handsome his face is, he just stared at the man in the mirror with two questions, 'who are you?' and 'where have you been?' He fingered a shoulder scar and wondered how he came by it, if he could not recognise himself how could he expect others to. He touched carefully the scaring at the centre of his chest.

"Are you alright in there?"

Josey watched as he shuffled out of the bathroom, securing the robe around his waist he would be a long way from full fitness.

"Ok, I'll try to answer your questions, have no tattoos as far as I can see and certainly do look forty, although right now I feel seventy. These two massive bruises on either side of my head do not help they are so tender to touch, there is a left shoulder scar and in the centre of my chest what appears to be a bullet hole. How I came to have it, I have not a clue. I don't feel married or likely to be a father and you definitely seem far too attractive for me to be gay."

Josey blushed, she was getting used to being around him.

"My right leg muscles hurt, I suggest because of the explosion itself. Just at the top of my spine there's a round burn mark under my neck hair barely noticeable, at night when I wake up it seems to be on fire, probably glows," he joked. "I haven't seen my clothes so I cannot say much about them. As to my dreams, I'm reading mailings, phone books, lists and lists of names, addresses, photo galleries I don't know where from. Faces are constantly flashing at me every moment of the day like emails asking me to read them," he frustratingly sighed. "For the life of me I don't understand why."

"Have you told Sister Jocelyn about the burn mark?"

"No, I forget about it as the day wears on."

Josey left the room and within five seconds returned with Sister.

"Show me please." She spoke sternly to him as if he should have told her. "Mmm, it's an electrical burn a scorch, I'll make sure Mr Broadacre is aware," she disappeared from the room.

"When you were in a coma, you appeared to be screaming inside, tormented, do you remember any of that?
"No, nothing at all, although at times my brain seems to be very full to bursting."
"I don't understand what that means."
"I don't either except I'm being constantly fed information it has no logic and is random in its delivery. I know you, your name and your address for example but your face I knew of when I woke up, I'd been thinking of you without knowing you."
"It could be you saw me as you were arousing from the coma."
"No I don't think so, I seem to react and get mental pictures from a simple touch, have you ever touched me Josey other than when I awoke?"

Again, she felt herself blush deeply. "Obviously I would have straightened your bed clothes or pillows when I visited you it is possible I touched you at some point." She lied guiltily touching and kissing him she recalled had become an obsession with her.

"That'll be it then a picture of you would have come into my mind."

"That's a little far-fetched anyhow, I don't believe

you, here's a pen and paper write my address down," she struggled to remember her touching him for the first time.

Smithy drew a picture of her apartment, penned both her full name and the address including the exact postcode and to her amazement her phone number.

"Your parents live in Yorkshire, you have a brother who is younger than you, you are not married have no children thirty five years of age, I won't go into birthmarks but crucially you have what looks pear shaped and red in the centre of your right buttock!"

"Can you see me naked?"

"No, but that's easily arranged," he flirted with her.

"My god that's spooky, how did you do that? no-one could possibly put all that together, that is so scary," she said ignoring his comment.

"Please don't be afraid I don't know where it comes from either. What I do know is the moment you helped me get up and out from the bed to go to the bathroom the information came to me as fact and I didn't consider questioning it," lately he' been practising his 'skill' on the nurses and had 100% success. He had started to watch TV and although he had no way of checking on the people he watched he felt he knew them and where they lived.

"I have to go Smithy," she was sad at having to.

"Before you do," he held his hand out for hers and pulled her toward him, this time they kissed each other properly.

As Josey left him he felt very alone, his mind full of names, pictures, numbers his whole brain bursting with information waiting to be released, "What the hell has happened to me," he shouted aloud. His ward sister came into the room immediately.

"Sorry Sister Jocelyn, I'm getting so frustrated by not remembering who I am."

"Give it time, give it time," she comforted. "What's this DVD?"

"Josey leave it, apparently it contains some news bulletins of my accident."

"I'll put it on for you, it may help," she left him alone to watch.

He saw the charred remains of the area an amateur video had been taken of the explosion. Highlighting what he presumed was his body on the ground outside the scrap metal yard. The video taker was shouting to some unknown person. "Oh God, get some help here quickly," a level of panic developing in his voice as the video wavered up and down. He kept re-running the picture of himself looking for something that would kick start his memory.

He watched some of the updates that followed including a "News at Six" bulletin with a Police Inspector he guessed it would turn out to be Josey's boss and a Fire chief. It told him nothing more, he still could not remember anything.

Jillie Grantham had gotten her wish.

Inspector Wyndham's office windows overlooked the back of the local shopping precinct in Ashford's Police Station, uninspired he felt the same about the scrapyard explosion case. He turned into what he called his glass bowl of an office he looked out onto his team watching as his Sergeant made her way toward him.

"How is he Josey?"

Josey avoided telling him of her feelings for the man in hospital, she explained to him about the lack of memory, nickname and his peculiar insight.

"You're telling me this 'Smithy' cannot remember anything, has amnesia, but knows where you live, how does that work Josey?"
"I know it is odd, spooky even, he truly doesn't understand it himself."
"And you believe him?"
"Yes I think I do, why would he say so, he could have just enjoyed the attention because of the accident and left it at that, Paul he is as confused as we are."
"I'm thinking honestly, we should wrap this up now Josey, it is wasting our time. Type up what you have for the file, no crime has been committed its clearly been an accident, Insurance company investigators have kicked in at the site now so if he wants to start claiming liability, all we need to do is provide him with a crime number along with any other claimants. If your man "Smithy" ever remembers his real name he should be entitled to a healthy sum of money in compensation, even without it he would be due something. Let it rest Josey," he suggested curling his eyebrow hair. "We have many more important cases needing our attention."
"Please Paul let me have a few more days just to test him a little further, we may learn something more, surely we can't close the case we don't have all the facts yet," she pleaded with him.
"Alright a few days and no more, I've a pile of real crimes you should be working on." Inspector

Wyndham looked seriously at his Sergeant. "Josey quite frankly I don't think we will ever get to know about him, but we do know the cause and there's no foul play involved, so that means case closed we really have to move on."

Josey was thankful to justifiably, spend more time with her 'Smithy'.

She heard her Inspector slam shut his windows with a loud bang hoping to drown out the store drop off noises raised by the delivery lorries beneath, smiling to herself noting he was hardly having a good day.

Deciding to visit Smithy one more time she would tell him of her disappointment at being taken off his case, if he wanted to extend their relationship such as it is she'd be happy, if not it had to be faced.

During the following days Smithy's time was taken up with a voice accent test, clearly an Englishman the task was to find a region he belonged to so he was asked where he lived, he despaired. The results were inconclusive, could be a Southerner more likely a Londoner, but considering the migration of folk to outskirts like Essex and Kent with Ashford being a popular town in particular, it was anyone's guess. He went through mental testing, one of them called GOAT. He recalled what it stood for Galveston Orientation and Amnesia Test, and the first question they asked what is his name? He despaired, they even tried hypnosis, and nothing worked.

When she arrived back into his room she grew jealous, a couple of the nurses were sitting on his bed giggling and teasing him. The television was playing an old re-run of an episode of "As time goes by" Smithy turned the volume down on the remote control as she entered.

"You seem sad Josey what's wrong?" The nurses excitedly disappeared as he spoke to her.

"The case is closed Smithy, this is my last visit to you."

"Why? Does it have to be? You've been coming to see me for weeks, we're friends aren't we?"

"Well yes, I suppose we are, but this is not quite normal, my visits were, are official Police business I've got a real job to do."

"Surely you can visit me as a friend? Why don't you take some time out to help me set my life up," he was genuinely worried about his future despite having no past, all he knew was now and it was not much. It scared the hell out of him. "I've nowhere to go, to live that is nor a job, money or even clothes, I don't have a clue what I'm going to do when I leave here, it can only be weeks if not days away before I do," his voice developed a trace of panic. He was lost and she knew it.

"You will need help because without proof of existence or any record of you, it will be hard. I'll get in touch with Social Services they must help you."

"I want you Josey, just you," he blurted, feeling scared he would lose the one person he can relate to.

"Let's not worry about it now, I'll come and visit you as often as I can," she felt strangely warm and comforted by his need of her.

Josey took the television remote from his bedside cabinet and changed channels to find some news turning up the volume on the set. She was interested in the latest regarding a missing boy, a five year old. The pictured face of the bright-eyed small blond looking boy peered out of the screen at them both.

"What's that you're interested in Josey?"

"A five year old boy has been missing for four days, the parents have pleaded for his return, no-one knows where he's gone and there is concern about abduction or harm." He watched a tearful mother's plea alongside her a Policeman in front of the media cameras flashing, with a desk full of microphones the reporters attempting to extract the last drop of information they could.

"Is that your boss?" Watching the man pulling at his eyebrow hair.

"Yes, that's Inspector Paul Wyndham," he looked at the man in front of the Ashford Constabulary banner.

"Are you dealing with the case as well Josey?"

"No, but I should be," she said unfairly. "I'm sorry Smithy, I'm a Police Sergeant it's what I do, right now my Inspector, Inspector Wyndham expects me to be out there looking for him," she emphasised gesturing at the screen. "As a team we are having no luck in tracing the boy."

She looked at him carefully his eyes tightly shut he appeared to be in pain.

Smithy's head began pounding hard he shook his head from side to side his head hurt feeling pressure bear down on his eyes like a lead weight needing to be lifted. He lent back on the pillows pushing his head back hard onto them.

"Smithy, what is wrong, what's happened I'll get the Sister," she worried for him.

He waved shaking his head indicating it wasn't necessary the pain subsided he had what he needed, he looked closer at the boy's picture on the television, reams of information literally being generated pouring into his mind without him understanding how it had gotten there.

"I think I know where he is Josey," his pressure pain subsiding, mental bombardment forcing itself to be recognised.

Hit like a thunderbolt between her eyes.

"What, how, for god's sake tell me if you know anything, anything at all," she looked at him suspiciously. "Have you done something wrong, is this why you've blanked out your memory? Please, please tell me for god's sake, tell me now," she barked sternly. "We must get to the boy, do you understand?"

Taken aback not liking her Police persona one bit.

"Josey, Josey, I felt we had a connection, do you really think I could harm someone let alone a child? Besides how long have I been in hospital?" Not expecting an answer but was hurt at her lack of trust in him. "The boy has only been missing four days you said so yourself, how on earth could I be involved?"

"Quite frankly we know very little about you or what you're capable of and nobody keeps you in chains around here," she said coldly doubts rushing through her. "What do you know Smithy," her voice like stone adopting fully the authority inbred in her. "Tell me and let us be the judge, tell me now!" She demanded.

Ok, ok there's a young woman aged 23 her name is Laura Davenport, light brown shoulder length hair wispy, five foot two inches in height slight of build almost anorexic she is wearing blue jeans, pink blouse I think. She's with a man called Ben Sandham stocky, muscled person works out short cropped hair greying, black trousers, black t-shirt plain," he continued slowly feeling his minds pressure release as he let the information flow out from him. "He is older than Laura at 43, they're both in a small way part of a criminal ring who are targeting children for resale to childless couples in Europe and beyond, I don't have a handle on who they are." he paused she was writing this down as he spoke, he noticed her hands were shaking. "The boy is with them in their red car he wears a child's dark blue duffel coat, hood up, can't see his face," he wrote down the number for her," It may be a Renault."

She was astounded her emotions moving from one extreme to another. He has been here in this hospital. It is just not possible for a person to know this unless he is in some way involved.

"Where is he, tell me if you know?" She said sharply her body language rejecting him as a person. "And what else?"

"Please understand I would do better if I had something of theirs to hold then I would receive clearer information."

'Receive information' it was a strange remark of his she thought. She let it go. "Go on quickly," the coldness of her voice cutting through the air as a knife, five minutes previously she had been showing her love for him, she realised she doesn't know what to do and certainly didn't know him at all.

"They are currently queuing to board the Channel Tunnel bound for France at Folkestone, they operate with several car lanes then one by one they feed onto the side of the tunnel train from the platform. Once on they will drive along the carriages on the inside until parked within a carriage then each section sealed to keep the cars locked in. The passengers can walk around, I say this because once in you may have difficulty catching them.

They have the boy registered as Laura's real son Charlie who apparently died six months ago," he looked closely at Josey her attitude toward him had changed, hoping it was repairable, he continued unsure how he was getting this information, he also gauged it was running out without touch or something to hold of the people involved. All he knew he was learning to trust what he received. "Laura has been disturbed ever since she lost her own son to illness. I get that she's been duped into helping to do this, not sure why, I'm sorry Josey it's all I'm getting," he closed his eyes in rest it had taken a lot from him, his mind seeming to rebel as he poured out the information registering in his brain.

"No wait! It was tuberculosis I believe!"

"What?"

"Her son Charlie, it's what he died of," his mind felt raw as if the information previously burned onto his mind had been extracted forcibly.

He recognised this represented a diversion for him, he had pictured the man and woman without 'seeing' them because of their proximity to the boy he had already began making assumptions. Gradually learning about his 'gift', he believed he had to see a picture of a person before being able to tell where they were. This time he knew them by association after seeing the boy. Usually he would have seen the boy and know of his activities. He realised within his mind he was doing some detective work piecing together fragments of information to provide the whole picture and in this case without any property of the person sought. He was learning all of the time, he knew he had to work out the scope and the extent of his skills it was as surprising to him as it would be to anyone else.

Noting Josey's reaction toward him it was time to be careful about telling people just how much he could do including her.

She was already speaking to Inspector Wyndham who told her to guard Smithy with her life until he can get some uniforms down there. She looked at him with rising contempt an emotion not known was within her, it hurt so much to believe he was involved, but there seemed no other logical explanation. Unless what he is actually saying was true, impossible.

"It's not what you think Josey, I promise you I have absolutely nothing to do with it," he needed her to believe him.

"How can you not, no-one could have that much detail about three people in a car, suggest where they're going and how they're travelling and not be involved," she looked into his eyes directly. "Or worse still make the whole thing up."

"I promise you it is true, all of what I say is right please believe me," he begged, her attack leading him to doubt himself.

Interrupted by her mobile 'bloom' ring tone. Josey listened and agreed she should stay where she was.

She went across to the window and looked out down towards one of the hospital car parks beneath the ward room windows for a moment watching as a car pulled into an open space without thought. A male stepped from his car searching his pockets for change for the parking ticket meter. She carelessly watched him walking back to his car brandishing a ticket, which he placed on its dashboard emerging with a bouquet of flowers from inside the car. She began to cry.

"Josey, what is it please tell me?"

She wiped her tears. "That was my Inspector, the Channel Tunnel train had departed by the time we arrived, however they caught the couple with the boy by stalling the train at the central or middle entrance section to the service tunnel just before it crosses the border to France, they boarded the train on mass to avoid them possibly escaping. The boy is now safe, he has not been harmed and as we speak is being returned to his parents, I've been asked to wait here with you."

"You've been told to guard me haven't you?" he was disappointed at her reason for staying with him.

"Yes, I suppose I should thank you for making sure the boy was safe," she said coldly, angry at the feeling of contempt she felt for him.

For the first time since he had come out from his coma, there was complete silence between them. He realised Josey was struggling to even look at him. He hoped it had not turned into hate before she understood how he had known right now as a Policewoman unsure if he could convince her of his innocence, only the evidence could do that.

Josey's thoughts were racing, hating the way she now felt about him she certainly would not believe him, but also knew she loved, but realised all the bullshit surrounding such love as trust and loyalty can be questioned at a moment's notice and hating herself for feeling this way. She felt lost unsure of what to do next.

Inspector Paul Wyndham made his way from the hospital front car park puzzled and unsure of his next step toward a man who had just solved a very tricky high profile case. If they had not stopped the couple abducting the boy on the Channel Tunnel train the boy would more than likely have been lost in Europe forever. As the Police head of the missing persons operations within the Kent districts for the last 3 years he had never known anything like it. Others were asking him how he'd managed to solve the case, he huffed and bluffed about being lucky wanting to keep this guy under wraps at least for the time being until he knew more of the man.

Walking through the maze of William Harvey Hospital corridors were a nightmare to him seeming to stretch for miles, at one point, he found the Kings Ward but told he was at the wrong entrance and would have to go right around the block of corridors. He arrived, taking a deep breath walking through the hospitals Kings Ward intensive care unit and was immediately corralled by a group of protective nurses questioning his purpose for being there. Satisfied with his explanation they hurried off in differing directions leaving Sister Martin to direct him to room 11.

He looked through the small-wired glass window of the door his Sergeant was standing at the base of the patient's bed obscuring his view of the patient. He threw open the door sharply as if making a calculated forced entry. It worked and made both occupants of the room jump.

"Oh, Inspector Wyndham, this is "Smithy" our accident victim and our informant," she turned greeting him her voice cool towards him, the patient recognised him from the news broadcasts on the DVD.

The two most important men in her life shook hands warmly she was bemused at her Inspector's attitude toward him, positively genial.

"Now young man, you and I need to talk," he said, despite being at least ten years younger," looking at Josey he gestured at the television. "Turn that thing off and take some notes," it puzzled him her body language was offensively cutting, looking around the room it seemed clinically grim and cold he shuddered glad not to be the one in the bed.

"Checking your photograph with our computers didn't incur a match. I also checked it with the boy's parents and the boy himself, as well as the couple who had taken the kid and no-one, unless they're all bloody good liars, could link you in any way to the abduction crime or knew you at all, in short," he paused for effect looking straight at Josey. "I'm convinced you've had nothing whatsoever to do with the boy's disappearance, the abductors have provided what little they knew of the criminal ring trafficking children, the fact we even knew about it caused them to open up to us. Therefore what I want, need to know right now is how the hell you knew where to find him?"

Josey gasped stifling her cry with her hand to her mouth, moving to the window to compose herself.

"Where did you get my photograph from?" he sidestepped the question.

"I took some when you were in your coma," she offered turning toward him sitting on the window ledge, her ashen grey eyes filled with tears of total relief, she suddenly felt very tired, weary and afraid her mistrust of him would ruin any relationship they might have had.

"I must have looked dead," he said amusedly, attempting to get a smile from her, it didn't work, at that moment he knew he loved her, she was struggling to come to terms with his innocence the evidence had kicked in, he could wait.

"Yeh, a lot of people remarked on that when I showed them, don't look much different awake I must say," he joked tugging at his eyebrow, his eyes twinkling instantly liking the man's sense of humour. "All that's beside the point of course, come on tell me how on earth did you know?"

Josey was desperate to talk to Smithy alone, their banter made it worse.

"They were on the Channel Tunnel train bound for Calais in their red Renault Megane just as you said, the girl broke down almost immediately she needs help to get over the loss of her own child and this just makes the loss even worse for her, we have care workers involved for her and the boy."

"And the man?"

The man is singing his heart out Josey, he's known to us as a petty thief but he realised he'd overstepped the mark with this one," he said hoping she would be impressed. "Giving us names of everyone involved that he knew, although it is pretty much operating on a one to one basis handing down of the tasks to do, however the kid should now be back with his parents, all in all a great afternoons work." He looked at Smithy crooking his neck waiting for his response he was not accustomed to people ignoring his questions. "And all thanks to our mysterious patient here, so come on out with it how's it done telepathy, psychic what?"

"I really truly don't know how Inspector, let me give you an example," Smithy nodded to Josey. "Would you pass me the pen and paper please?"

Josey placed them gently into his open hand and cupped his other hand around hers in affection. Somehow, she must tell him she was sorry, his smile and wink told her they would be OK, although she did feel guilty at not trusting or believing in him. Paul Wyndham noted the tenderness between them and knew her well enough to see she had been struggling with her feelings for this man.

"Here Inspector, I've written some information you should recognise," giving him the paper he had scribbled on.

"How in hell?" Smithy had written the Inspector's address, telephone number, his wife's and his two children's names and what school's they attended.

"Sadly your parents are dead, your mother died five years ago and your father six. Both are buried together within the same plot in a London cemetery, in Lewisham actually, you and your two brothers decided against cremation at the time."

"Stop right there, just where are you getting this from," he looked across to Josey with suspicion and noted her shrug in ignorance. "You'll be telling me their names next!"

"Parent's or brothers?"

All three laughed aloud easing the tension built up in the room between them.

He still had not answered the question because he was unsure how he knew maybe in time he would find out why. Explaining as best he could, he told them how pictures presented themselves to him automatically and along with touching the person or having an item, belonging to them helped him. Notes came to him in the form of a printout that he read in his mind allowing him to piece together all the information. He had no way of knowing whether his condition was a result of the accident or whether he could always do this. They suspected it had to be a by-product of the explosion.

Chapter 5

It was almost four months since his accident and finally discharged from the hospital, no one could fathom out why the monitors had been so erratic, why he had lost his memory or whether it would ever return. The monitors gradually calmed down the longer he was awake but still stayed unusually active during his sleeping hours. He said his goodbye's to his beloved Sister Jocelyn with kisses and a hug, her nurses playfully planting their own kisses on his cheek in fondness. He was sad to leave them they were the only family he knew, like every patient discharged he promised to return and see them, even then he wondered if he ever would.

During the past three weeks, Anna his allotted Social Worker visited three times. She had only just qualified and he was her first case. It was her intention to see how far she could push the system to get the maximum amount of help for him.

Anna had given him a set of keys with an address to go to with an appointment at a job centre in nearby Ashford for the following week.

They had provided him with the sum total of thirtysix pounds to spend on groceries with a "how to budget" booklet. Although ill-fitting the second hand clothes two sizes too big were gratefully appreciated, they were provided by the 'League of Friends' charity within the hospital, apart from the tweed jacket and corduroy trousers he suspected were someone's who recently died. The rest seemed to fit well he managed to retrieve his own worn size eleven blue Reebok trainers. Whatever happened from now on, he would make sure he always kept these they were the only link to his past.

After going through the charred remains of his own clothes noting the "Old Navy" and "Varsity" motifs which was about all that was once a hooded sweatshirt, nothing could be usefully saved but for the Reebok trainers. Nothing jogged his memory either. By the hospital clock it was 11:00am, slowly he walked the corridors towards the main entrance nervously coming to terms with a sense of freedom, within minute's he knew what it meant to be alone.

He found himself in the cold under the canopied entrance of the hospital opposite the car park in the shelter across the road several sick patients were furtively smoking themselves to a premature death. He realised he didn't know the place at all or how he was even supposed to get out of the hospital complex, he watched the cars moving around jostling for spaces he felt he would be able to drive looking at them but he had no evidence of it. He had no car in the car park he was facing. He decided to follow the path they were taking presumably towards the exit of the grounds.

He was in the cool fresh air and staggered at the intake, his guess at the season would be autumn the surrounding brownish tinge to the trees confirmed his impression. He felt comfortable being outside of room 11 and the hospital itself where he had spent the past three months. He walked past the diabetic eye clinic called Paula Carr's turning back he decided to pay the clinic a visit. He needed to rest and take time to look at the papers from Social Services that Anna had given to him he assumed they would have a waiting room.

Quickly he spotted an armchair amongst the waiting patients seated in line in the clinic. The receptionist looked at him expecting him to register his arrival with her automatically looking for a man's name on her patient list. He noted she consciously dismissed any thoughts she had for questioning him as he sat down and smiled next to a woman patient about his age subconsciously believing him to be a patient's husband. The woman was the next to be called to see a doctor giving him enough time to read the papers from Anna, for the benefit of the receptionist he mouthed the words 'good luck' to the woman's back, suspicion of him erased he opened up the envelope he held.

His name for identification purposes would be Michael Smith and he had a national insurance number. He preferred the nickname "Smithy" Josey had come up with perhaps it would do for just the two of them. Anna had put a note in the envelope listing the items supplied.

She obtained a student card for identification purposes although, what he was supposed to be studying at his age he was not sure and because he needed a national insurance number she had to register him as a new born. He noted the temporary Birth Letter for Newborn's no parents listed, despite him being forty. he did wish he had been made thirty nine, too easy to round up he supposed, he continued reading her note this was the only way she could get a number and for him to be able to get a job although what work he could do escaped him. Bureaucracy she complained, she would sort it out later. She found him a place to live, not great admittedly she told him in her note, but it should do for now, he fished into the padded envelope for the keys, the address was on the tag. He looked on the Singleton address with no idea where that is. She hoped he was ok and gave him her mobile number if he needed anything. He knew it already of course, and everything else about her, twenty eight year old single mother of one living at home with parents, daughter called Jenny aged six. Anna had been great he thought, he never told her about his skill.

The woman patient, the receptionist had linked to him had finished her retinal examination with the consultant and was now leaving he smiled in her direction hoping she would not find him strange. His smile for the benefit of the girl behind the desk and followed the woman out of the automated clinics doors.

Walking outside toward the hospital grounds exit he was startled by a cars horn a familiar voice called behind him. "Smithy, Smithy, get in quickly, don't stand out in the cold, I thought I' missed you," Josey opened her car door for him to get in.

"I'm so glad to see you, I wasn't sure of where or which way to go," he kissed her tenderly feeling safe once more.
"What address have you been given, show me and I'll take you there." The car was warm and comforting they hardly spoke he watched her driving nothing on their path appeared familiar to

him.

They arrived at a five-storey building, a small tower block his place according to the key ring label number 27 on the third floor. A grey hospital carry bag was the sum of his luggage he could move in now. They took the lift aluminium inside painted in graffiti art, the urine smell touching both their nostrils unpleasantly the floor held wet cigarette butts.

The apartment freshly painted magnolia was pleasant enough, at least he had somewhere to sit, eat and sleep, he thought. Clean and cold, it sent a feeling of despair surging through him. He knew no better it was true, spending so long in his hospital bed unfortunately reading the glossy magazines had given him a rosy view of what his life could be like on the "outside". Somehow he felt cheated he looked out fingering the Venetian blinds apart he opened the window looking down onto a schools playground beneath break time it seemed, a sea of children in blue uniforms were raising noise levels to competition standards playing with each other in groups, he closed the window wondering where the local shops were. Realising this would be life from now on, he shuddered resigning himself to the situation and wondered whether he had been better or worse before the accident. It felt worse without knowing. Despairing it made him wonder about his previous life.

Josey read his thoughts and quickly made a decision she grabbed his hand. "Come on, let us go to mine, we can come back here later if you need to, but I doubt you should be on your own quite yet," In a split second she made up her mind, no matter what became of it this was the man she wanted to spend the rest of her life with. It made sense he lived with her at least for a while, she knew instinctively he hated the place.

During the following week's he felt rested, he loved and enjoyed the warmth of her apartment and her lifestyle, he found he played with his "gift" bumping into people when they went shopping, he would call them or their children by name. Most just answered without realising what he did others thought him strange and moved away from him. He was starting to get restless, he had not kept Anna's appointment made for him at the Job Centre and wondered whether he should have done. He was a kept man and felt it he had no money to contribute.

Josey, I feel like a spare part, I have been living here, loved being with you now for three weeks."
"But?"
"You have your life and I should begin to create mine," he dreaded the thought of going back to his own apartment.
"Are you sure you're ready for the world out there?"

"I need to try and stand on my own I'm not relishing returning to my own apartment though."

"Smithy, you needed to convalesce, however I love you and you're right, I had hoped your memory might have returned by now so you could have resumed whatever life you previously had, with me included of course."
"And if it didn't include you?"
"I'd be happy as long as you were," she lied.
"Without a history, a point of reference, background, anything I've no idea what I should,

could be good at frankly, it's unnerving and frightening at the same time."

"I've been thinking about that quite a bit lately, will you come with me today to my Police station, I'm sure Inspector Wyndham would like to see you again, we both have a proposition to put to you."

"Mmm, sounds intriguing, lead on, anything is better than the nothing I'm doing now."

A sea of faces greeted them as Smithy and Josey walked into the Missing Persons unit of the Police station. The grapevine had told them the one who had solved the missing boy case was coming in, each wanted to see him for themselves and Josey was leading him through the open plan area of the department populated by detectives and uniformed officers towards one of the four glassed partitioned offices to the rear of the floor. Nervously, unconvinced walking past the rows of desks this was a good idea.

The hospital, shopping, her apartment were the only places he had been since he woke up and they had not prepared him for real life yet. Each desk occupant "nudging" the person next to them so they noticed his presence as he passed them by. He spotted the Inspector through the glass of one of the offices standing hands on hips waiting for him to arrive.

"Hello again," Paul Wyndham said awkwardly shaking his hand and directing them to the round table and chairs away from his desk. "How are you any progress?"

"Sadly none at all, I have what is termed traumatic amnesia apparently I will either recover or it will be permanently lost or as the doctors tell me the condition is of either anterograde, retrograde, or both. The length of time it will take is according to how severe the degree of injury was in the first place."

"Meaning no-one has a bloody clue right! I'm truly sorry for you," he tweaked his eyebrow nervously.

"Please, luckily I know of nothing else, I cannot be sad about a memory I do not recall ever having had," he suggested not very convincingly, grinning. "After all I was only born about four months ago."

"Yeh right!"

"Stop right there the both of you, you're starting to joke around again," she pleased they were together again as friends. "We have some serious work to think about."
"Still 40 years is a long memory to lose, whatever life you may have had," enjoying the moment he went on. "Mine would not be as long as yours anyway, but it must be tough?"

"Inspector! Stop it, you'll make him depressed," she scolded smiling. "He'd prefer to be 39."

"Josey said you had a proposition for me?" He was amused enjoying both their company.

"Yes we do Michael," it was the first time he used his new name and both were surprised. "I'm sorry, I cannot and will not call you Smithy, it's ridiculously girly," he said still tugging at his eyebrow.

The three laughed.

"We want to use your gift to find people just as you did with the boy."

"Missing people?"

"It is what Josey and I do, the team do," he gestured out of his windowed office to his team outside. "We're part of what is now called NPIA."

"What does that mean?"

"National Policing Improvement Agency, were the Missing Persons Bureau in Ashford for Kent as a county."

"Look Michael we have hundreds of missing people throughout the county and the country, will you look at six case files we've picked out for you as a start?" he looked at Josey. "I guess it's for us to gauge the extent of the help you can give us if you're willing. Anyhow we need you to read each file carefully and tell us what you make of them."

"Inspector, I don't work for you yet, but we are becoming friendly so I will also refuse to call you something so impersonal, could these be tests you're presenting me with?"

"It's Paul to you, both of you," he offered looking across to Josey she would still have to follow protocol when in the company of their other officers. "And yes it is a test," relaxing he continued. "You appear to have a gift if you're agreeable we may have found the perfect vehicle, something useful for you to do. What do you say?"

"Come on Smithy, it will save you going to the job centre."

"Ok Paul let just see how I get on," he said agreeing. "Do I just pick one from the pile?"

He took the first green foolscap folder. Both Paul and Josey watched his reaction carefully.

The woman pictured in her early 50's dressed in a grey checked full-length coat rounded red hat a slight feather coming out of the peek, he guessed the man arm in arm with her in the photograph was her husband. She apparently has been missing for fifteen years. She would be 68 now he calculated. He read of a frantic husband and family keen to know why she never came back from her normal weekly visit to the local shops one day. Something felt odd about this.

"What you have is typical, no grounds for foul play just a woman unhappy with her lot who apparently decides to walk away, at least that's the way it appears." Josey offered she was dismissive of the case, he wondered why.

"Have you anything of hers Paul?" He felt his mind starting to react inside his head pulsing rapidly, outwardly no-one would've known or realised, pages of scripts images pouring in front of his mind's eye, he felt himself reading all he could quickly as if the information might disappear.
We have a watch she always liked to wear it but left it off that day. The husband gave it to us, if we found her and she did not want to return to him. It has an inscription on the back from him."

Michael fingered the thin gold watch with its brown leather strap. He read the inscription aloud. "Our love will span life and beyond," a dizziness, nausea almost overwhelmed him. Still something was odd.

Touching the watch carefully looking at the brown haired woman posing in the photograph a shiver swept right through him, he closed his eyes, his mind for a second, blanked out, black no thoughts or feelings came. Darkness was in his mind this had happened before, he recognised the signs, and he was becoming used to how his mind dealt with different circumstances. He needed to be patient information would come, he waited for his brain to catch up it seemed an age it was only a split second.

A rush of pictures followed, he sped on a path, he embraced another's life, watched their journey in which he played no part. The folder told him the point, where the woman last seen with a date and time. He recognised the journey starting immediately from that point, he was watching her progress literally reading notes with snapshots presented to him in his mind, and he followed the script wondering where she would go next. Years past in flashes of high and low points in her life, the words beat out in his head like a ticker tape machine tapping the messages. He sped through her journey as if she was constantly drawing him toward her, powerless to stop.

When he arrived at the journey's end the information flow suddenly stopped, he was confused checking the date and time to be now, today. Yes, the signs were right something was wrong, he trusted his instincts and opened his eyes, frustrated he knew why.

"This is the first and last time you will test me like this, this takes a lot of effort and drains me completely, and I just don't appreciate this!"

"Smithy, what's wrong I don't understand," Josey pleaded with him to explain.

"Ask your Inspector," he said pointedly using his position title he stood up and walked to the window overlooking the shopping precinct. "This woman is no more missing than I am, she is one of the canteen ladies working for you downstairs, am I right Paul?"

Paul sheepishly nodded to Josey's shaking head. "I apologise, Michael, I had to see for myself, to check if it wasn't a fluke, that you still had a gift, please take a look at the next folder, I do assure you it's very real."

"Don't do this again, otherwise I walk do you understand?" He was annoyed and showed it.

They both nodded apologetically, raising their eyebrows at one another accepting his gift.

"I'm sorry Josey genuinely didn't know," he playing with his eyebrow hair. "Look Michael your involvement with us is vitally important I can assure you," Paul now felt he needed to convince him to help him.

"Let me sell it to you Michael, let me say missing persons is the most ill-considered amongst both the public and the Police Force not only in the UK but across the globe. I feel it's the most important, where murders, rapes, abuse and paedophilia all result from a capture or kidnap of someone or a lost soul may get lured into goodness knows what. These are the real missing persons add to these an old person who forgets medication or suffers mentally or anyone who is challenged in this way. They are all in danger of non-survival the public perception on missing persons is about the little old woman in her carpet slippers or the drunken lad, unfortunately, the real danger for the kidnapped is when the sheer magnitude hits the abductor. They have taken someone and need to decide what to do with them, this changes the person completely and it scares the hell out of them, for what started out as an attempt to frighten in most cases. They quickly realise they don't want to get caught so to cover their tracks or the mistake they need to get rid of the problem."

Michael listened in awe of the man, the sheer passion evident in every word.

"They haven't stolen sweets from a candy store they've actually stolen a human being literally, this is very real pressure especially if it's gone public. The media does so well in alerting people, but unfortunately, it places a good deal of pressure on the abductor. How to stop the person telling on them, they don't want prison, somehow the victim needs to be kept quiet, it doesn't work when the abducted promises not to tell, they're never believed," gauging Michael's interest he continued.

"The other stuff comes while they're planning on how to put it right. What kicks in is, they become annoyed and blame the mess on the victim, their own fault. The abuse and beatings begin, the torture starts and suddenly they realise they have power, control over another person. Again, they turn in to a different human being, another edge, the abductor becomes unrecognisable because their victim is begging them to stop and will do anything for them if they would just let them go, but now they've become a possession to be played with. What happens if the victim tries to be their friend and sees things from their point of view a whole different psychology then comes into play."

"The abductor is frightened scared, but enjoying themselves at the same time. Phase one, what do I do to avoid getting caught I must get rid of the victim. Phase two playing and controlling. The final Phase is perhaps the most dangerous and it is the need to return to a normal life. The pressure, internal and from external media is huge, justifications, reasons why kick in, they see themselves getting caught, time to kill. Dispose of body, no body no crime, no DNA, life becomes a calculation.

The kill no longer matters, shoot, stab, drug or creation of an accident whatever it is, once decided, it escalates to a different problem the disappearance of the body. How will they do it, drop into a river, cut it up messy that, create a fire take your pick, it's a task no more than that, no guilt just work to do. I'll let you picture just what people are capable of."

"Wow, you're world is the pits Paul."

"Michael these people have to be stopped before they even consider the second phase, we need you, more than you know," he suggested sincerely. "It's truly an uphill struggle."

Peace restored Josey got some coffees for them and by the time she returned Smithy had laid all the papers from the next folder across the round table.

Michael shrugged and began looking through the papers, an old grey bearded man stared up at him from the photograph he placed in the centre of the table, and Catweazle came to mind. Missing for more than a year, he walked out of an old folk's retirement home. Family frantic, hospitals checked, his bank account closed, suspected foul play. At the time the media joined the hunt, gradually life has moved on, it becomes another unsolved missing person and the media moves on to another more lucrative headline.

"When was this picture taken?" He looked closer at the man wearing a blue stripe dressing gown, plain grey pyjamas and multi-patterned slippers adorning his feet. Behind him, the double doors of the home to his left the retirement home sign is displayed "Bridges for Life, Quality for the Elder Citizens".

"Two days before he went missing a year ago, is it important Michael?"

"Look at his face, he's grinning, happy, normal and certainly not ill."

"Well it is a home, not a hospital or institution Smithy."

"True, but look at his eyes closely there's a purpose behind them, they're scheming, he knows what he's doing mentally I suspect he asked for this photograph to be taken, what do you know of the family members?"

"You can see that Michael?"

He nodded.

"Why ask for the picture to be taken?"

"To create a record so no blame can be levied against the home," he offered.

"I believe you're right Paul."

"I don't like any of them, it seems they've only contacted us because they are not getting any value out of him staying at the home they're paying for," Josey had seen too many cases where the family were waiting for the elder to die, an inconvenience gone. "If we pronounce him missing presumed dead, they won't have to continue paying and they can collect more money in due course from the insurers as well as closing down the trust fund, which will automatically revert back to the family. They could suggest foul play by the home workers and get money that way if not in court, outside of it where reputations have to be preserved."

"Mercenary bastards," Paul hated the victim's families.

"What have you got of his," Michael at first thought this was another test, but decided against it, because he wasn't getting the same feeling about this old man as he did the woman, this time the feeling was strange but for a different reason. His mind played with the pictures and notes registering, one by one supplying information he knew instinctively where the man was and what he'd done, he smiled to himself.

Paul handed him a grey cotton scarf. When Michael touched it, his head automatically filled with information about the man and his life. His temples throbbed with the influx. He realised even though the last case was a test, he had found by accident some structure he could work to information mentally would flow enabling him to understand the person. What he was interested in was the journey the person had made once they disappeared and he found if he picked up on the date and tie of departure he could follow, putting the pieces together like a jigsaw. It seem to work better that way, he decided to keep this to himself, he'd no wish to raise expectations higher than they already were. He looked through the papers and found what he was looking for, his eyes searching his mind for information. With it pouring into his mind at random, he had to decipher and put it in some order.

He placed the man at the home that last day and noted he was not sick, frail or mentally unstable in his judgement, no reason for him to be there. He watched the journey notes passively, what takes months to unfold sped through his mind within seconds he started to understand as the journey unfolded and finally come up to date. He decided to try to go back further into the man's life accessing why he was in the home in the first place. After ten minute's he was ready to speak.

Josey and Paul had watched Michael closely he had shut himself down literally. Twice they stopped themselves touching him, forcing themselves to be patient. His eyes closed with not a single twitch or movement perfectly still. They gauged this was him 'receiving' information. Not having seen this in him before made them feel awkward looking at him waiting in the silence. They looked at each other and smiled raising eyebrows high to the ceiling. They were fine with it if this was what it took to produce results.

Michael opened his eyes and rapidly reeled off information fast, urgency in his voice as if he would lose it in the translation. Josey scribed as fast as she could attempting to keep up not daring to interrupt.

"The man is 68 years old and had been put into the retirement home by his two stepsons and two stepdaughters. His wife had died some five years ago amid much acrimony; her family had been part of an ancient aristocratic family where old money made out of the land and vineyards long gone.

Unknown to his wife's children their stepfather had financially rescued the family from ruin following an investment downturn in the money markets, he married their mother lovingly and at the same time maintained their old ways of living, so her will automatically left everything she had to him. The children would not accept their legacy was really his by right, the history of his help never shared with them. They believed even now he had gained his own empire on the back of the old family inheritance they should have had plus more instead of the other way around. They set about discrediting their own stepfather believing they'd been robbed by him."

"Bloody hell, I'd hate to have his family Michael."

"There's more, Joseph Brennan was declared unfit to manage his affairs within a year of his wife and their mother's passing, so the four siblings were, through the courts made executors of his estate. Despite his lawyers pleading with him he never contested the case against his beloved wife's family nor tell them it was only his money helping them survive this long, despite a paper trail to prove it. For them it was a bonus to take his money as well."

Michael looked at both Paul and Josey and spoke seriously. "Great harm has been done to this man by his children. You do know that don't you?"

"Have they actually harmed him then?"

"No Paul spoken like a true Policeman, not in the way you mean, they've taken his dignity and legally stolen his money."

"Not our remit if there isn't anything illegal or criminal to answer for."

"That's cold hearted Paul."

"We have to be realistic there's only so much we can do and family feuds we try to avoid."

"So he's alive Smithy?"

"Let him finish Josey," Paul needed more to determine whether a likely crime had been committed.

"He was, is a very wealthy man, once they put him in the home the four family executors proceeded to sell off all his assets including his engineering business and both his English and French homes, his net worth has been estimated at over forty million pounds, and yes he's alive"

"Bloody hell, he was that rich?" Paul was astounded.

"Thank God Smithy, where are you getting this information from, I don't understand it's not in his file?"

"Shut up Josey, let us hear more," suddenly Paul was not very proud of his job.

"She's right Paul it is strange, I gained a fair amount by just looking at his photograph together with the thorough notes in the folder. What I gained was more of the background, the journey he'd taken."

"What the significance of the scarf, something happened to you when we gave you it?"

"It helps me gain a fuller picture of events, something close to the individual, but like a dog reacts to smell, a scent to trace what you're looking for. I'm trying to get used to my "quirk of fate" if you like, I don't know how or why I have all this information about a person, any person, but even that information is somehow magnified tenfold if I have something of the person's to touch," he looked into Josey eyes. "For example although I knew of you, who you were, until I actually touched you only then did a whole raft of other information come to me about you."

"Is nothing sacred, like what?"

"So I get it, you liken yourself to an old dog with a bone!"

"Paul please don't be so rude!"

"Can we get on?" Paul smiled impatiently. "Let's stay focused on the case before us."

"Don't be a prick Sir!" She emphasised.

They laughed they were getting too heavy in their

attitudes toward each other.

"Sorry both of you, I'm truly amazed at your gift Michael and want you to solve everything fast but I'm realising you mentally have a way, no a need to take time to put together all the information first, but is nothing sacred as Josey says?"

"Not much, anyhow the scarf gave me so much more on Joseph Brennan. His children set up a small trust which was effectively enough to pay for his nursing home, once done they helped themselves to roughly ten million pounds each of his money."

"Should he have come to harm Michael, it gives us a motive if we ever find him dead."

"OK Paul, as I said he really is alive, well and living in Spain on funds he salted away a year prior to him being placed in the home. Ironically, he actually brought the situation on himself. Together with his wife their mother they decided to create for him a new life and identity, instead of putting his business profits back into the company, he began moving money around setting up bank accounts to place the funds out of reach, his beloved wife a victim of pancreas cancer had suggested the idea to him. Both knew her own children would not allow him to live properly without her, this way he would at least gain as much as them without a fight, the aristocracy background would see they get their way.

It appeared to his accountants and family that he was losing the company profits ruining the cash cow, they and her sons and daughters couldn't allow that to continually happen.

"The accountants were in it too?" Paul sensed fraud, a crime at last.

"Did they ever know of their mother's illness?"

"Yes Josey but only a month before she died?"

"They must have been scheming from that moment."

"I believe they were waiting for their mother's death not in a sinister way of course but watching him and the finance. They suggested he was spending alarming amounts of company money, which wasn't true however, Joseph Brennan did the suggesting subtly or course, the odd comment, a paper just happened to be left on the study desk. It was the children' inheritance as far as the siblings were concerned so they set out to make him appear to be senile, enough to take the company reins away from him. They worked together to ruin his credibility in business and each became members of the company board something Joseph would never have allowed, fortunately for him with his wife he saw it coming, as being inevitable, he'd joined a family of materialistic people, linked as they were with the bean counters. By the time they gained control, over half his fortune had gone, disappeared."

"So he was put away because he spent all of his own money, surely they couldn't do that?"

"That's right," agreed Michael. "However he ran the risk of being declared mentally incapable and be locked up."

"You mean sent into an asylum."

"Yes Paul, the plan was for her children to push him into a home from which he could walk out from. An asylum locked up meant no escape so he willingly agreed to go into "Bridges for Life" retirement home.

"But it wasn't his was it, the money it was their inheritance." Josey offered cynically.

"As he wouldn't tell anyone what he'd done with the money, although he did leave a trail of casino cards purposely and on checking they believed he did gamble the money away. This led to the grounds the family needed to fight for control of his estate and in court where they exercised every connection possible, they won."

"Smithy how much are we talking about him taking, if their share was forty million?"

"Probably around twenty to thirty million if you read the before and after statements produced by the accountants for the court hearing."

"And you've read these?" Paul was confused. "How on earth could you have?"

"Mentally it's been possible to piece it together," Michael confirmed.

And you know exactly where he is right now?"
"Yes Paul."

"Is he happy?"
"Don't be soft Josey wouldn't you be happy with that amount of money?"

"We're not all like you Paul, where is he now?"

"Yes Josey he is happy and I do know exactly where he is," he wrote down his location for the file. "Whether you have to inform his family is your call, personally as he's untouchable and happy, I would leave him alone. Can you not just close the file and ignore the findings Paul?"

"Sadly Michael it's not that simple to close the file, I have to tell the so called executors of our findings as they raised the case as a missing persons, but I'm sure they'd try it again even if he is in another country." Paul sighed at the hopelessness of it. "Because they cannot close the trust fund or gain the insurance if he's not dead."

"I didn't look at it like that, will he be safe Paul?"

"As I said earlier it would be a motive if something ever happened to him."

"Then at the very least Paul tell the old man first, allow him to get opposing doctors to certify he's fit or enable him to do a deal with his family to leave him alone." Michael decided not to tell them of the woman in the man's life believing they needed time together, they appeared to be planning a wedding very soon. He smiled and knew the family's inheritance he salted away would be well and truly gone once that happened in favour of his new wife's family. He would try to give the man that chance. "Please take your time closing the file it's important to the old man." Paul nodded in agreement.

Josey felt her "Smithy" knew more. She kept quiet.

"Good idea Michael, will you take a look at the other files for us."

"Of course."

"Smithy, would it help if I pinned the papers up on the walls so they could be discussed as you looked at them, it might be quicker."

"Yes it would and as my "gift" seems to function far better if I have an article of belongings, clothing or watch, something they would have at least touched please hang those up too."

"Michael, here's what we have, a twenty three year old girl went missing four years ago apparently went home alone from a nightclub not seen again. We have her handbag, again full media coverage, regularly re-enacting on television nothing, family fully investigated, with zero result."

Michael looked closer at the young girl, the picture showed her at a party, her brown shoulder length hair pushed back behind her ears hooped earrings dangling from them, with a bottle drink in her hand surrounded by other girls and young men behind her in the picture she looked happy to be there enjoying herself.

"When was this picture taken?"

"The night she went missing,"

"Were they the clothes she would have left the nightclub in Paul?" The girl was wearing a flared almost ballerina black skirt, with an unusual multi coloured t-shirt, her neck adorned by Mardi Gras beads. "So it's likely the people in the picture were the last to see her?"

"It seems so it's been confirmed in some of the statements from those at the nightclub."

"The Z7 club's CCTV is inconclusive," offered Josey. "It's old with black and white footage.

Michael went through the notes and looked at her handbag hanging, clipped to the side of the wallboard. He would not touch it just yet.

"Smithy, the second is a 10 year old boy seemingly ran away from home, we have his schoolbooks."

The picture part of a school group photograph blown up to get more of him it showed a black boy wearing a grey school uniform. The school's crest emblazoned on the breast pocket of his blazer, short trousers and blue satchel with the same crest and school motto he was unable to read, he ran away it seems four days ago. A known runaway from all of his fostered homes, his parents were dead. The media avalanche descending fast wanting answers.

"The third person takes the form of a thirty one year old male construction worker only a week ago, we have his donkey jacket."

Michael looked closely at the man in the picture with a stubble rugged face a young woman and two young children with him, a family man, an imperceptible shadow around him, a trick of the light in the room perhaps, he knew better now.

"Finally Michael, a lady of 96 hasn't been seen in or near her home for three weeks or more, her family obviously fear the worse, we are told she's still compos mentis so has all her faculties, here is her pink woollen cardigan."

"Is this normal?" Michael looked at them both.

"Quite a number of the elderly walk out of their own or care homes, perhaps they've seen someone they knew or recognised walking by and followed them then they get lost, others have to get out believing their home is some sort of prison. Many just wander it is very sad."

"No I meant are these typical of your cases?"

Both Paul and Josey nodded.

"Michael we get upwards to a hundred missing persons a year in this area alone we are losing the battle."

Like the old man's photograph, he looked closer at the picture, there were three women smiling for the camera behind them a cruise ship, he could not quite make out the name.

"Which one is it?"

The one on the right Smithy in the light blue blouse black trousers and white cats emblazoned t-shirt."

He should have seen the pink cardigan carried across her arm, she and her friends looked happy.

"And the ship?"

"Oriana, Mediterranean bound. P & O cruise I believe."

Michael touched each photograph Josey had hung up on the wall and then each of the garments or items. As he had done before, touching each garment understanding the dates and times they each went missing he closed his eyes and went on their respectful journeys. He took a deep breath before he told them of his findings.

"I'm sorry there are two dead, first the construction worker he was moving some debris at his new office site as he did so scaffolding collapsed on top of him hitting him soundly on his head. He spent several hours in a daze before he actually managed to free himself and staggered to get help, unfortunately in so doing he fell down the drainage shaft on site and is now lying one hundred feet below ground in the sewer, he died immediately he hit the bottom. He's half covered in water."

"Oh my God!" Josey squealed, the enormity of an automatic answer stunned them both. Most Police work took time painstakingly putting the individual pieces together, enabling them to unconsciously come to terms with who, where and why a person had died. They had learnt from Michael everything within two minutes, both Paul and Josey had not been prepared and could not have known the impact it would have, visibly they both shuddered. If they looked in a mirror at this moment their faces as deep a grey as could be.

Michael was strangely untouched, he cared but it was just information he was passing on. Emotionally he was just dealing with facts.

"Are you OK?" he asked them both their faces telling him they were not.

Grimly both nodded feeling sick. "It is time we took a break, Michael I'll get someone to the construction site immediately."

Michael drew a layout of the site and pinpointed his location as near as he could on Paul's wall map of the area.

Paul waved to one of his team through the glass of his office, updated the junior officer giving him instructions to complete the case.

Michael was conscious of Paul's team just staring at him through his office window unsure of what had just happened.

Josey phoned the local delicatessen for some sandwiches and arranged for more coffee, leaving Michael pouring over the details of the folders on the table and the wallboard.

Idly, Michael looked out of Paul's office windows towards his team and began to put names to the faces. He watched Josey walking towards him with the tray of drinks and food. She stopped to speak to a good-looking young man, Darren he noted, they flirted he felt a pang of jealousy rise. Paul was talking to a uniformed sergeant, Steven thirty six about to be married to Somaini Ariane a Swiss Italian girl, her family pronouncing their surnames first they met two years ago on a skiing trip in Salzburg Austria.

They ate in silence awkwardly.

"Please continue Michael," Paul himself struggling to prepare himself for the next case, and what shock that may bring.

"You said two Smithy, who's the second," Josey braced herself expectantly.

"The boy I'm afraid, he passed a sub-post office in Kingsnorth at the wrong time, a robbery was taking place inside by two men, they wore masks they tied up the postmistress and the three customers, one of the men stamped hard on a man's leg who yelled in pain. Ironic,It was meant to keep the others quiet, they escaped with only three thousand pounds. Coming out of the Post office the boy sitting on his bicycle saw them take off their masks they grabbed him and drove off in their van. Innocently he was yelling because they'd left his bike behind, thinking it must be a game."

"What happened to him Smithy?" Her mind destroyed at the thought of it.

"He was thrown over a railway bridge to his death." He said coldly writing the details in the file. "The boy did put up quite a fight, shouting and screaming to be let out of the van. The two men stopped on a railway bridge and I would suggest this was not planned he was to them an annoyance they needed to be rid of. They strapped his arms and legs together with grey builders tape and covered his mouth with it." He paused gauging the feeling for the detail, noting Josey's head buried in her hands he continued. "He had no chance, no chance at all, one took his arms, one his legs and began swinging no one passed by this bridge as one side was to an open field the other entrance was at the end of a small housing estate.

The bridge sits across the local railway line running from Hastings to Ashford. They swung him wriggling over the railings onto the train they would not have realised was coming. His body literally bounced several times on top the speed of the train threw him into the surrounding trees and hedges, a tree branch pierced right through his heart the force propelling his body downwards he died instantly. His dead body is in the weeded growth out of sight beneath that tree waiting for someone to claim him before some animal starts pulling pieces from him." Angrily shaking his head not understanding how anyone could do such a thing, he pushed over the notes he made within the file.

"Oh shit, I can't take any more of this, I just can't do it," she was crying openly now this was worse than the first.

"I'm sorry Josey we have to continue for their sakes if nothing else, do you know who did it Michael?"

"Yes Paul," he was scribbling again furiously. "You should find all you need on that," passing a further sheet of paper toward him, on it describing the men in detail, the van's number plate and likely addresses.

Paul noted the names Joey Sawton and Reece Evans.

"I'll fucking get those bastards you mark my words, they'll pay for what they've done I know them," Paul angrily stormed from his office, calling for everyone in his team to pay attention. Immediately to a person all stood up to listen, once told they all knew what they had to do. Within seconds the floor was empty but for them inside

Paul's office.

"What's happened to the other two Smithy," drying the tears from her eyes.

"Right now the young girl needs your help, she's living under a false name in Batley, Leeds, she lives in a quaint old back to back house set up as a bed and breakfast she has a small room there and works for a local insurance company dealing with administration. The night of the party she was raped brutally by a gang two of them in particular, I see them in the picture," He used a marker to pinpoint above both men's heads they were drinking in the background watching her.

"They followed her as she went outside for a cigarette, her friends expecting her return didn't smoke. Four men, boys really including the two I have highlighted were involved. One of them smoking, walking up and down past her in the street outside the club. He chatting to her in the end it became simple for them, she began walking and talking with him up and down sharing cigarettes and walked one way longer each time until there became a point when the other three dragged her into an alleyway, they beat her then raped her and left her for dead." They were listening intently shocked at his level of insight of the events.

"Hours later she managed to leave," he pondered. "When she crawled out from the alleyway the club already closed, after finding her handbag she managed to get a taxi to her home. It took her an hour to pack her bags. Quietly she left her parent's home before they woke up, they haven't seen her since. The embarrassment, fear, whatever made her disappear," Again he passed across details not only where she now lived, her new name and gave them the names of the gang members as well. "At least she's alive, Josey we have to be thankful for that."

"Poor girl must be scarred for life, I'll warn her parents."

"Josey, this does make it worthwhile, you know that don't you?" she nodded to her Inspector as he walked back into the office she had to agree with him.

Catching the tail end of their conversation Paul acted decisively and called to a nearby uniformed officer who missed the others leaving the floor passing her instructions to help the girl and set up a small team to get those responsible.

Michael watched as Paul spoke to Constable Sophie Mason, only it wasn't her only name either, something bothered him about her, nothing to do with the cases but she was involved with others who were not on the Police side, it would keep for another day.

"And finally?" she was beginning to come to terms with the impact of his gift on her.

She brought Michael back from where his thoughts were, dismissing them for now his mind playing tricks with him.

"And finally Josey, the ninety six year old woman is alive and well. If her family meet her at Victoria coach station in London tomorrow afternoon at 3 pm., they will learn she does this often. She goes travelling for weeks on end."

"Surely the family would have reported her missing well before now Michael."

"The simple fact is the family only contacts her on the rarest of occasions and mostly because they want something from her, normally to borrow money. She goes on holiday mostly on cruises around the world with friends she has known for many years. In short she has built a life away from her family, they would know this if they saw her more or bothered to listen."

"Good for her is what I say," she managed a smile at the thought of someone who is quite safe.

"Thanks Michael, I'm sure you'll agree we've been most successful this morning, now we have this idea," Paul said enjoying seeing him for once uncomfortable. "Clearly you passed every test we could throw at you and feel we could use you more, trouble is I'm bloody standing up and down like a yo-yo with every case you solve so far, you have done well," he went out to find a member of his team once again as Josey explained.

"Initially Paul and I felt you could come and work for us, but the fact is the Commissioner didn't agree, given we have no idea on your background."

"You mean I could be a criminal possibly a serial killer."

"Stop it Smithy be serious."

"It is true Michael, employing you has its risks," Paul agreed standing in his office doorway.

"Better yet I might even be his brother."

"Be quiet and listen what we came up with is to set you up as a Private Missing Persons Bureau almost mirroring ours except you'd probably have more cases and get quicker results."

"How's that different to what I've just done for you?"

"We would pass to you families where we just don't have the resources to deal with or can't detect any foul play you will then be able to charge them for your services. This means you get an income, a business to run and be self-sufficient all in one go."

"And frankly Michael we get greater results, which after all is what it's about," Paul stepped back into his office.

"In return Paul?" He was waiting for the catch.

"In return for the "leads" so to speak, you help us with our worst cases for free. That way we both get what we want and if your ones turn out to be of criminal intent you have a readymade Police force to tap into, what do say Michael?"

"Actually I think it's a splendid idea, When do I start?"

"You already have Michael."

Chapter 6

Within three weeks, Josey had found him a small business suite complete with a small apartment attached. The suite consisted of two main offices, reception with washroom facilities and furniture in the form of desks, chairs, filing cabinets and sofas together with the all-important coffee percolator everything seemed to arrive without question. Michael quickly appreciated the apartment attached being far better than the one allocated to him by Social Services.

For the first time since leaving hospital he called Anna his social worker to let go of the flat in Singleton, she was grateful for his call pleased that he had an opportunity to have a good life. His new place had the plus of being close and at the same time independent from the business. Even though he loved living with Josey, her place was too small for them. They both needed space to grow together in their relationship rather than live together immediately.

For the business, she had devised a cost per session and worked out the finders fees. Both Josey and Paul were already giving his newly created business cards to potential clients. Customers or missing person relatives were already calling for his help. Josey found him his new receptionist Penny a blond Australian girl who is stunningly pretty, it gave him a message that Josey, having given her the job was totally secure in their relationship. Penny Whitmore was a whirlwind, already busy arranging appointments and deliveries into both the offices and his apartment.

The gold plaque went on the outside of the entrance doors. Finding Missing People Consultancy – FMPC had been born. The modern offices and apartment, grey in colour externally glassed with a silver tubular structured appearance, overlooked the Medway River in Maidstone twenty-three miles from where he was "born" in Ashford. Purposely she created the distance between the two of them and the working relationship with Ashford's Police Station.

Penny had created a very comfortable office for him complete with rubber plants and cactus, the modern desk functional, with a separate table and chairs in one area, sofa and coffee table in another. It crossed his mind, his very own waiting room, he felt like a doctor. He would have no time to enjoy the solace. Penny literally wheeled in his first customer.

He greeted the young man in his self-propelled wheel chair it squeaked, his mouth wide open ever since he'd set eyes on the beautiful Penny.

"This is David Forrester he has been recommended to us by Detective Sergeant Rainbow of Ashford Police Station," she handed him the new customer form she had designed already filled out giving some of his details.

"This is Michael Smith our Chief Consultant who will be working with you on your own special case," her eyes flashed at David Forrester, making him feel very special to her.

Michael was in awe of Penny's professionalism. He thanked her and shook the man's hand in greeting.

"What brings you to us," he briefly eyed the form. "David if I may call you by your first name?" he was not used to his business approach just yet.

"Well, as your receptionist err…."

"Penny."

"Yes, Penny," he stopped himself daydreaming realising he gained her name at least. "She said I'd been recommended to you, but I'm not missing anybody."

"So what can we help you with David?"

"I've been robbed."

"You should be talking to the Police about that not me, Sergeant Rainbow surely would have advised you?"

"I've done that but they can do nothing, please I'm desperate, I'm stuck in this wheel chair 24 hours a day, my computers in my workshop have all been stolen."

"Again this really is a Police matter."

"I know, I know but…."

Michael noticed a degree of desperation, a panic over his loss of equipment.

David wheeled his chair around and started for the doorway in disgust.

"Wait! Wait! At least let me try to understand, why you are so desperate?" Michael stalled him hoping he would explain.

"Since my illness which is getting progressively

worse, I have been confined to this damn thing," he banged the arms of the chair in frustration. "My only life has been my network of computers, my contacts, my friends on-line it's all I have."

"Equipment can be replaced David," get a life came to mind.

"I want the people who could do such a thing to someone like me caught. I know it's a bloody Police thing, but they have a mountain of cases just like mine and will do nothing about it," he despaired.

"Very true, let me start by giving my understanding of you, obviously you're wheelchair bound and the reason is you have spinal degeneration, it's an advanced stage of disc disease degeneration."

"That's not on my form," David became suspicious. "You've already spoken to Sergeant Rainbow!"

"I can assure you I haven't, what's on your form is you're 24 years old, have a computing degree and apparently before the onset of your disease held a high ranking position working for NATO in Belgium," he thought carefully. "Do you have some of their data you shouldn't have?"

"For Christ sake yes, how did you know?"

"A guess and that's what's been stolen? I'm sorry to have to ask but was it your data to begin with?"

David shook his head. "I don't know how important what I have is or what any of it could be used for, I've never actually looked at it, I only downloaded it because I could, does that make sense?"

"No not to me, but I hadn't been employed as the resident systems hacker, do you believe the people who stole your kit of computers were looking for NATO data?"

"I don't see how, I was very discreet and covered all my tracks."

"Someone could have been monitoring what you were doing."

"Impossible I ran checks."

"Ok so it's a random theft, tell you what take off your watch and tell me the date and time you left NATO?"

"Whatever for?"

"Please humour me and I need a couple of minutes alone," he buzzed the intercom for Penny, she opened the door to his office.

David gave him the information he needed as well as his watch although he was confused as to why.

"Penny would you look after David for a few minutes while I consider what he's told me," she whisked him away, he was not about to object.

David thought she was gorgeous and while making him coffee she made small talk chatting to him about everything possible. She genuinely appeared interested in him. He told himself it was the job, never mind he adored her already.

Penny wondered about David, business and pleasure do not mix, but she found herself attracted to him. Pity he would leave soon she would have loved to get to know him better.

Michael held the watch and looked at the dates on his note pad, he chose a few weeks beforehand as he felt he might get some answers about David rather than about the robbery itself. The journey he unveiled was uneventful he could not actually 'see' what had happened only notes of the events were mentally displayed to him. Piecing the information together it appeared David had imbedded himself so much in the workings of NATO he'd become indispensable, being given so much responsibility one day he collapsed, he was already working under pressure trying to compete as a paraplegic in an upright world. Due to his superior computing skills he could pretty much do everything, he became overloaded and had a breakdown.

NATO coldly retired him claiming he fell into a risk scenario, leaving him with his home backup systems he created and no one to use them for, during his rehabilitation he found other areas to enjoy, Facebook friendships, YouTube, EBay even twittering. He played with the Internet taking supporting server's offline without warning at banks, ministry of defence sites, multi-conglomerates no one was safe from his interrogation.

Damn right his servers were taken he became a menace throughout the normal business world as well as NATO. The robbery had been to order, the question was who asked for it?

Mentally Michael walked through the information and found what he was looking for, he needed to be stopped not for the data he taken, no one knew about that, but it was his own NATO offices, his ex-boss in particular who had ordered the theft on behalf of the ministry of defence. David was becoming too dangerous his computer equipment was been destroyed within hours of the theft. Michael believed he had a lucky escape.

"Penny, would you ask David to come back in please."

He explained to David what had happened and explained that he had a warning he had better move on and do something else.

"How do you know all this, what contacts have you?"

"I do my own research David."

"Oh Yeh! What the fucking hell am I supposed to do now, look at me will you, I don't have a queue of prospective employers knocking on my door, with no money to replace the systems I'm lost," he was embarrassed at his angry reaction.

"Knock, knock."
"What you talking about?" David reddened.
"Come and work for me David."
"I'm not a fucking charity case, piss off."

Michael warmed to him despite his belligerence.
"David, this is a fledgling organisation and what we are about is finding people and that means we will need to access computer records across the world if necessary, we need you."

"Surely you haven't been waiting for me to turn up you don't even know me, despite the fact you somehow guessed what could've happened to me, you never had time to do your so called research."

"You're welcome to check to see if I'm right David, although I doubt they'll admit it."

"Will you have that much business?" Dismissing his offer as small beer.

"It's growing daily with backlogs building, join us please, I'll supply you with any computer kit you need, whatever it takes."

At that point, Penny brought in the coffees for them, her perfume filling his nostrils as she placed the cups on Michael's desk. "Maybe that wouldn't be such a bad thing," he said accepting his offer at least he would get back on line any more than that he would have to see how it developed.

As he wheeled out of his office and seeing he was besotted with his receptionist, Michael called out to him to stop.

"What's the matter, changed your mind don't want to employ a cripple?"

"No apart from that oversized chip on your shoulder I was just going to mention it was a good interview David," he looked fondly at the young man full of misdirected passion.

"I'm really sorry Michael," he felt humbled they smiled at each other David knew he could work for this man.

Penny could not believe it she was so excited at David coming to work for them she danced around the offices for the rest of the day. The following day his arrival allowed her to fuss over him like a mother hen. She ordered the equipment he needed and insured she was indispensable to him, her feelings catapulting each time he spoke had taken enjoying the work at FMPC to a whole new level she found herself skipping around the place and David felt he'd arrived in heaven.

The offices of FMPC were looking very good, a smart executive style feel as soon as he walked through the door, it smelled of likely success, key in the business of finding people. Inspector Wyndham was hearing of the many success stories since he and Josey came up with the idea for Michael, these days they had the luxury almost God like deciding who they should try to find next. Very soon, the Ashford Police Station would have to call on other stations in the area for missing person work. He was reluctant to do this as then the use of Michael's time would be limited for him and he was quite jealous of their arrangement. Today though, he had a different agenda.

Hi Paul, what brings you here to my humble offices, my friend?"

"Michael, anything, but humble from what I see, you've already a thriving business, your second office is filled with staff and pretty soon you'll need to move out and find something bigger."

"Yes I'm grateful to you, it's working out very well thanks to the leads you pass onto us, and we've helped many, many people."

"We have to be careful, all these people found gives us very little to do."

"That's not true is it I thought you had lists going back years and years."

"You're right of course and we are being more selective who we decide to work on rather than the next on the pile."

"Come on Paul out with it, it's a month since I've seen you, what do you want?" Michael believed he was here for a reason.

"Is this enough for you, I know it keeps you busy but is it enough?

"I'm more than happy, fulfilled and it's all worthwhile," he meant it.

"Have you regained any memories of your past yet?" he knew the answer already.

"Unfortunately, none at all, not even, the merest of flashes. The doctors tell me I should have had images, thoughts or feelings, deja vue, by now, perhaps if I did, I wouldn't be able to see into those missing souls past lives, who knows, I have to be grateful for what I have, honestly," he emphasised.

"You don't see much of Josey at the moment do you?"

"No Paul, I believe she's letting me establish my life as it will be, I love her I know that much but right now all I can offer her is a man with no name, no past and no memory, at least this way I have an opportunity to create a future for us. Until a month ago I didn't have a home or even a function in life."

"Love conquers all, my friend."

"What if I wake up from this dream Paul and find all manner of demons, I could be blotting out so many truths."

"What truths? We cannot trace you, never existed. You could be an alien plant for all we know special gift and all," he laughed aloud. "When and if you get your memory back were friends now so we'll deal with the fall out together rest assured. Besides your personality or behaviour patterns cannot be that different fundamentally, stop worrying."

"I may be married, a father, a criminal, a murderer even all of it, who the bloody hell knows?"

"Well I got news for you old fella, you're the bloody expert Michael, if you don't know, I can't help you."

They both laughed their friendship growing with each meeting.

"Michael I've a problem, I'm not sure if you can help, you find lost people and know where they are, how they got there but the help you gave David Forrester gave me any idea," he tugged nervously at his eyebrow hair.

"How did you know about that?" He realised he had called Josey and mentioned it to her. "Sounds ominous what is it?"

"You know where people are right?"

"Right," he answered with some scepticism.

"So if we know where they are how much of a leap is it to either find out what they've done or what they're doing at any moment in time."

"That would mean I'd have to focus on that individual all the time, I cannot see like a movie you know," he had to attempt to get him to appreciate his limitations. "I see just pictures flashing that's all, the rest is words displayed to me in my mind. I have to align the picture with the notes and make a deduction I may not get it right."

Paul took a deep breath. "Here goes, four men are committing a series of armed robberies and the general criminal community is tight lipped so no-one is talking."

"You say robberies just what have they done?"

"There are five robberies, no that's not true there's far more but let's stick to those we know more about, they range from a security van, works payroll, bank, bookmakers to a post office."

"You say post office, they're not the ones who………..?

"You mean killed the boy, no, no, we've dealt with them," although Paul knew the two men were stirring up trouble inside Maidstone prison where they were currently residing, desperate to find out who told the Police causing them to be caught, they would make sure whoever it was they would be made to pay, they never let it rest.

"Oh I hadn't heard."

"You aren't meant to," he gave him a man of the world look.

Michael realised it was best left alone.

"These other robbers they haven't left a single

clue? How do you know it's them?"

"They tell us, well laugh at us more like. They provide us with enough clues or calling cards on several of their likely raids. We have even tried to infiltrate the gang on occasions, supplying an explosives expert, locksmith and drivers. All have been used to a point and then kicked off the jobs at the vital moment. The four are a closed unit, they are as tight as a drum and they like to give us the run-around suggesting several targets. By the time we realise which one they're actually going to rob it is too late, so far they haven't killed or harmed anyone which works in their favour, but a small clue left behind or a mistake would change all that."

"They're good criminals, is there such a thing?"

"Good God no, however no-one's prepared to talk about them, family, friends even so called enemies everyone is tight lipped which can only mean people are more afraid of repercussions from them rather than us as Police."

"You're telling me I'm at risk if I find something and they know it is me?"
"Yes Michael I am, these are real villains and not the cosy gone missing old man or woman with slippers on, I'm afraid it's the nature of the game we're in criminals always look for revenge make no mistake," he wanted his new friend to fully understand the risks involved.

"Now what am I supposed to say to that? Oh yes I know, bollocks Paul, I must be wasting my time," Michael felt in one sentence he minimised the work he did. "Wasn't it you that persuaded me to do this with the talk on how important finding missing people was and how others downgrade it, you're doing it to make a point."

"I'm sorry Michael, really," he offered grinning from ear to ear.

"Yeh right! So what are you expecting from me?"

"Anything you can give us, ideally we catch them in the act."

"Will you send Josey to help me and if you can get me items belonging to each it may help," he appreciated the friendship they shared life was too short to stay angry.

"I'll see what I can do, she may not want to come, of course and I cannot force her." They both knew she would jump at the opportunity.

"Do you mean to me or the bum who finds the carpet slippers?"

"Shut up, here's the file full of the robberies we've attributed to them, I'll try and send Josey over with the rest, thanks Michael let me know how you get on and please be careful," Paul wasted no time in going in case he changed his mind.

Tom from the other office working opposite David came in with a pen and pad and shocked him back to his bread and butter reality. Tom was proving a God send, sent from the job centre a week ago he was starting to be very valuable to the team a young man well educated who worked hard to fit in, they'd hit it off immediately and Tom loved the "success" of finding people. Michael's team was building slowly. What Tom had not realised Michael was aware of the secret he had kept from him, he did not mind so long as it had no effect on the business.

"Client rang said we found her grandmother last week, would you know where her cat is?" He asked smirking.

"Three doors down, they've been feeding it for the month she's been missing and it's stayed there," that will wipe the grin off Tom's face.

"You're bloody joking, no one is that good."

"True but you never know do you Tom?" He winked at him, in his naivety Tom generally believed all he said as a faithful servant does, in this case, he never had a clue about the cat, but it was worth a shot.

He pulled the buff robbery file toward him and began spreading the contents out onto his desk. Mainly summarising the robberies and sketchy information on the robbers themselves without pictures he decided to wait for Josey to come before he tackled this one.

"Come on Josey, why are you angry with me, I've only asked him to look at the files and see what he can come up with."

"You're getting him involved in Police work that he's not trained for Sir!" she emphasised his positional title.

"You'll be there to help him, hold his hand, together you could crack these cases," he realised he had not asked her yet and she never considered his comment.

"What if we do, he'll have to testify in open court, great witness, Mr Nobody suddenly becomes an expert. The defence will crucify him even if the gang doesn't find out and they will won't they?"

"Bit harsh about someone you love don't you think?" he realised he touched a nerve.

"So he's agreed to this has he?"

"Yes will you?"

"Of course I'll help him and I also want to solve the cases."

"Besides if they admit to the charges, he won't have to testify, anyhow he knows the risks, he wants a new challenge and this gives it to him."

"He doesn't need a new challenge, I need him safe."

"That's just it Josey, it's not about you."

"That's unfair and you know it."

"Look I like Michael, 'Smithy'," he offered pandering to her nickname for him. "But he's become too successful for his own good, he's rapidly becoming a one man Police force, people are starting to question our success rate for finding people. We have to slow him down or divert his attention to bigger things, if not we will lose him to more politically powerful people. Wolves are already at the door."

"Who Sir?"

"It doesn't matter who, just keep him busy."

"What's that mean, lose him? Is he in danger now?"

Do not be naive Josey he could be 'persuaded' to join a different team and yes we would lose him, Murder and drug squads would kill for him let alone the political use he could be. With his talent, we have set him up to get results and that is exactly what he is doing. The commissioner is not going to be content with just using him for missing persons, he's better than that."

"And he'll get killed won't he?"

"You're being far too dramatic, there's a wider picture he can get involved with."

"What if he doesn't want to get involved with those other people?"

"It may not come to that, some people won't give him a choice. Right now we need to keep him focused on our work, God knows he's making us all look good the MP solving figures are going through the roof."

"Is that all you're worried about, statistics I thought you were becoming his friend Paul, you should be protecting him better."

"I am doing the best I can Josey and I am his friend, but you and I have to be realistic, who knows how long his talent will last, another few days, months, years, we have to make the best of him while we possibly can. All we can do is our job and right now we have a great tool in Michael to help us."

"At what cost, his life?"

"If that's what it takes to make a difference then it has to be."

"Cold hearted bastard," she scolded.

"Sergeant Rainbow," he became frustrated with her. "Stop belly aching, you are assigned to Michael Smith forthwith, you're to look after his requirements in respect of this one case and see where it leads," he softened towards her. "Josey look after him as best you can, he's our prize asset and despite no background he is a rather good bloke," he knew she was right, they as Police lived with the threat of harm every day, information is trade to criminals so there is a risk to Michael it was up to them to minimise it.

She realised it was the nearest she was going to get from Inspector Wyndham for an apology and accepted he too cared about her 'Smithy', maybe she could at least stop him from making mistakes and help him survive in the world of criminals and politics. She was pleased to be working with him she hoped he would be, at least she could look after him.

Chapter 7

Penny gave her a hug the moment she walked back through the door into the offices, she introduced her to Tom and David squeaked wheeling into the corridor to say hi. Michael heard her and then watched her kiss David, it was good to have her back, sensing he was there she turned and leapt toward him like a schoolgirl to the surprise of the others as she openly kissed and held him tightly feeling she had her family back.

"Smithy help me with these two boxes I've brought with me, they've the case notes in them, we've raided each of the gangs homes and 'obtained' items in the pretence of collecting forensic evidence from them."

"Bit American that isn't it?"

"That's what they said and laughed in our faces, they really do believe they're untouchable."

"Tom," he called out loudly. "Come in and join us it's time you became more involved, God these boxes are heavy Josey, you come in too David," it was time he involved the team more. He lifted both removal style cardboard boxes onto his rectangular shaped meeting table.

Inside the boxes were files, pictures, investigative

Police notes and diaries, statements from the individuals interviewed at the time and maps relating to each robbed site, profile of the suspected robbers themselves and individual possessions of theirs to help him.

Michael suggested Tom took one box David the other and sorted the items ready for them.

"Are there only the four suspects, I mean we're convinced it is this gang," he considered. "No other suspects?

"No its impossible, we've checked and double checked it has to be them, they have told us when it could happen within a range of dates where within a certain radius and what type of place they would rob. Naturally when one happens within those boundaries we believe it's them"

"Aren't you assuming too much, surely they don't commit all robberies?"

"No Tom they don't however they email or phone us to say it might happen and then it does, we have to believe it."

"But you've no proof?"

"True David," fed up with the interrogation, they had done the legwork and come up with nothing. "That's why these boxes are here for us together to try and solve that very problem."

"Ok so we know our boundaries and we're not looking for anyone else as suspects," noting her impatience with Tom and David.

"Definitely not Michael."

"How many robberies do we believe they've committed?" Tom asked only finding details of five robberies in the boxes.

"Roughly fifteen including these five."

David whistled in amazement. "Why have you

only given us the records for five of them?"

"They're the most recent and the start of when we began realising it was the work of this one gang, still no proof on the other ten anyway." Josey went on. "When a pattern began emerging we applied the criteria to these five to that which is how we tie the five robberies to them specifically."

"Surely they must make mistakes?"

"Unfortunately Smithy they never do, perfect crimes it seems," she linked her arm in his fondly to be close.

Tom and David noted her term of affection for their boss. Tom lifted one of the boxes off the table and placed it in the lap of David who wheeled himself from the room closely followed by Tom carrying the other one. Once at their desks they set about analysing the contents of each box.

"Those two are good," she judged. "David and Penny what do you think?"

"What do you mean?"

"Smithy for someone who has so much insight can't you see they're in love with each other?"

"Haven't noticed a thing."

"That's because they need a nudge in the right direction," her eyes glinting at the thought of her doing some matchmaking.

Three hours later Tom and David returned and placed the boxes back on to the table.

"Ok who wants to begin?" They were ready he thought. "Let's start with what type the five robberies were."

"First the Security Van, this was quite ingenious,

the van had a daily supermarket route for takings pick up. It travelled across the town each day visiting Sainsbury's, Tesco, Lidl and Asda and only went to these four every day. Every fourth day they changed the pattern, visiting the first last the second fourth and so on," Tom saw in the schedule what he was looking for. "The schedule itself seems to change every four weeks only to revert back to its start point," he laughed, if you watched it for three months that's three times it would at least travel the same route with some certainty."

"What happened?" Michael was intrigued.

"A recovery trailer van or two I suspected waited at one or two of the supermarkets, those where the car parks are obscured from the relevant offices, while the guards are collecting cash the trailer stopped a short distance in front of the security van unlikely anyone would take any notice," Tom read from the notes and paraphrased. "It looks like the men climbed back in the security van having placed the money through the hatch in the back of the vehicle, locking themselves in."

"Is that normal? I always thought another guard was inside."

"I'm not sure myself David, I've personally always believed it too but there's no reference of a man in the back so I've assumed not."

"What happened next Tom?"

"Once the guards were in effectively trapping themselves inside the recovery trailer van backed up toward the security van placing them in alert mode as they couldn't move forward."

"What stopped them from reversing?"

"While they were gauging what was to happen, a thick metal bespoke strap with a winch for fast tightening was placed around it length ways like a wrap. Within seconds this strap was winched tight onto the van sealing the guards inside while they were still watching the pick-up slowing to a stop in front of them." Tom looked at the others assessing their interest and continued. "Two hooded men operating the gas strut which simultaneously opens out a drawbar. The winch used to pull the two front wheels of the security van onto the drawbar, once locked in position the security van was going nowhere backwards or forwards without assistance. The whole operation took two minutes to achieve. It took that long for the guards to think clearly and set off the alarms both on the vehicle, through the mobile unit and make sure the tracking device was working as well as calling their base."

"Very clever."

"You're right Michael, their procedures told them they would be better protected providing they stayed inside the vehicle so they didn't try to escape, little knowing because of the metal strap winched tight around them they wouldn't be able to anyway. Meanwhile a security guard was assuring the passing public the fault with the vehicle had caused its fail safe mechanism to be activated raising the alarm which they were hearing, they were then told them this actually meant the other guards would automatically be sealed inside."

"Plausible," offered Josey.

"According to witness statements, the guard pointed to the two men with an audience watching who were waving at the passers-by frantically as it turned out trying to attract help. He suggested for security the straps were there to seal in the contents, thus protecting the money and of course, the men themselves, he added it was good to know the system works. Witnesses statements describe the comments as plausible at the time."

"So the spare guard was a gang member, bloody smart what happened next?" David was fascinated.

"With the tow truck in place and with alarms flashing people in the car park assumed without looking too closely the van had broken down and the alarm system was telling other motorists they were moving toward them." He looked to Josey who picked up the story.

"With the guards assurance seemingly organising the recovery everything appeared fine, the robbery took place in front of everyone. With so much happening the recovery, the alarms, men setting straps, the guard directing and the fact people were coming and going doing shopping, no one person could actually say what anyone looked like, it was a busy time and people have better things on their minds rather than a broken down security van."

"It's right that is the way people think."

"No it isn't Tom it's their attitude."

"It appears they drove no more than a few hundred yards into an open backed articulated lorry encased in metal, it's suspected it contained some sort of electronic warfare jammer to negate the frequency location the vehicle was emitting."

"Sounds like Trevor Cole's handiwork," Josey suggested recognised as the technology buff within the gang.

"With no one tracking them they moved off to a lorry park near Kingsnorth. Inside the gang separated the recovery trailer from the security van to create space around it and then warned the guards at gunpoint to release the lock's, give up the money or die by this time they were terrified."

"Dangerous that it involved guns, where would they have come from?"

"Difficult to say Tom, they have to be old there is a mention of them in previous robberies," Josey frowned realising this was an avenue not previously followed up on. "We suspect they were for show as a threat."

"How did they know when to do it for maximum return?"

"How much did they get away with as a haul Josey?"

"Half a million pounds Smithy."

"How did they know that amount of money would be in the security van?"

"That's the research bit they had to have done. One, the raid happens on the evening of the third Sunday of the month, maximum shopping figures because of monthly paid shoppers and two, it has to happen on the right cycle on the fourth supermarket pickup."

"Something like this would have to have taken months to follow and plan."

"You're right David that's why we lose each time, there's not enough manpower for the long haul. They can choose when they act whereas we wait and see what they do."

"I'm surprised they carry on why not retire?"

"I agree with Tom, why carry on?

"I guess," she said looking at both Tom and David. "Because they can we never find any trace of the money."

"What's next David?"

"I've got the Works Payroll, sawn off shotguns smash and grab with masks."

"What type of business was it?"

"Furniture makers in Canterbury, Kent."

"That's surprising do people take their wages in cash these days David?"

"Seems so Josey, it was goods delivery day so they had a lot of labourers and hired lorry drivers to pay they also got away with the monies collected at the delivery point from the customers."

"How much did they get away with?"

"By comparison to Tom's around thirty three thousand pounds," David felt cheated and said his was lower than Tom's.

"This is the point, I'm trying to make to you all," suggested Josey seriously. "The levels of results accepted by the gang breaks any pattern, we cannot rely on for example that it's a certain type of business or above a certain amount, it is more about whether they can and it's a challenge for them."

"Ok let's move on to number three a high street bank, Tom it's your turn again."

"If it's that low they could be teaching someone a lesson."

"It's a good point David God knows why they would choose a raid with so little reward against the size of risk otherwise."

Tom explained, each day the banks on closing did a computer audit against actual balances held in the locked drawers and main safe. Two people are responsible as counter checkers for verifying the computer total's, it appeared once the branch closes. The majority of frontend staff are more intent on making sure the reporting and computer spreadsheets are balanced. With no protection, the two check the actual balance of cash left in the three ATS machines, tills and safe.

A cursory check by security before they close the bank is done but once the doors and the building is secure everyone tends to relax even the guards go for their break. By hiding in an empty office of the bank after closing, it was a simple process of making those two middle age woman and the young boy trainee experience their fears at the end of a shotgun. Surprisingly they weren't caught on camera and they'd only gotten away with seventy four thousand pounds, while staff still worked upstairs the gang walked out the back of the building into a waiting car with the cash, simple."

Penny arranged for a buffet lunch to arrive courtesy of the local delicatessen.

"Let's move on what's the next one it's a bookmakers isn't it?"

It was David's turn to explain a very simple robbery. The boss and owner of five John Mackays Turf Accountant offices collected the takings from each and normally took the proceeds to the bank. Most of the business operated in cash and despite his own family constantly complaining about his old fashion ways of collecting being dangerous, he ignored them, unfortunately for him, one day he was stopped on his way to pay in an amount of eighty nine thousand pounds to the bank, he refused to part company with the wrist chained holdall. He gained a broken wrist and chain for his trouble. He had a lucky escape at least he left with his wrist.

The final robbery was a post office it was in the main town of Folkestone an old building with the actual safe full ready for Tuesday's pension day, what was surprising on this one it was a wonder it hadn't been robbed before. The previous Monday evening a JCB opened up the back of the building and removed the brick embedded safe and lifted it onto an open backed Mitsubishi L200 truck, never to be seen again, twenty eight thousand pounds this time.

"Been done before that one hasn't it?"

"Yes Tom, couple of years back probably where they got the idea from, that time it was an ATS machine, this time they knew exactly where in the buildings back wall the safe was positioned."

"So what's next they're obviously taking the piss, we've established they certainly don't need the cash anymore."

"David, please!" Josey scolded him for his coloured language. "We have a choice of three, a DIY superstore, a gaming casino and the ticket office of an upcoming music festival.

Josey and Tom put up the details of each likely robbery on the wallboards.

Watching them pin up the details David was puzzled he stretched yawning in his chair. "How on earth do we know they're going to rob these places?"

"They leave messages on our Police answer phone suggesting these are the types of places we should be protecting during the coming two weeks in case of robbery," she described how they would give a code number to make sure the Police knew who it was, sheer arrogance.

"So if they didn't call they could quite as easily commit a robbery and you would likely assume it wasn't them?"

"Your quick David and we suspect that's exactly what they've done luring us into a false sense of security so to speak."

"What do we know about each of the men?" Michael was getting impatient.

In the centre, an A3 sheet of paper listing the names of the four men allegedly involved.

"Brothers Ron and Gerry Fielder, Ron the hard man, Gerry the brains, the other two make up the numbers, drivers, bag carrier's, extra muscle, Trevor Cole and Lawrie Berger, he's credited with being Gerry's number two."

"We've got some items belonging to each, trainers and gloves, Ron's baseball cap and a watch of Gerry's. Trevor's glass case and key ring, Lawrie's is a crowbar found in his garage and cigarette lighter, pretty pissed off one and all I can tell you," she gleefully added raising her eyebrows to David who noted the swear word, she almost saw the thought "one rule" cross his mind.

"A crowbar, you're not serious, hardly a fashion statement is it?"

Josey said pointedly looking at David. "It's all we could get?"

"Thanks Josey and you Tom for displaying the papers on the wall."

Michael turned to listen to Josey discuss the

suspects as did David and Tom.

"These men are classed as true old honest villains of long ago where they have decided success is dependant only on them alone, never relying on anyone, learn from everyone but the jobs are decided by the four of them and could only be carried out by them, no-one is allowed to come between them." She expected questions they just listened.

"If caught no-one would break down, certain in their solidarity. They have been in and out of numerous Police Stations during the past ten years they have never been charged or been in prison, the cases never getting to court, because in their early days they literally got away with all their crimes. Becoming resigned we wondered whether we ever would catch them. Meanwhile they have become cleverer and more experienced in the art of robbery."

"Do you class robbery as a skill Josey?"

"Oh yes Smithy, over 15 robberies that we know of, probably more. Around twenty million in cash they gained along the way. Never any clues, never caught, I'd call that a very definite skill."

"They must have come close to getting caught surely?"

"Just the once we managed to be on the real inside track and infiltrated them, we were able to build a good case against them, only for suddenly the family member of Berger we used ended up dead, "accident" of course and the job was cancelled. We had to start all over again, but we learnt our lesson more importantly so did all family members of the gang, it served as a warning to them."

"So they could be killers?"

"Yes they could we had no proof the family and friends wouldn't need any."

"So much for them being true old type honest villains," observed Tom. "I read the accident can be explained."

Michael wondered why Paul warned him to be careful, now he knew why.

"Tom talk us through the robberies similarities you've identified."

"I hope this is right, I divided them into the locations, the type of robbery and the actions of each of the robbers."

"First the locations, each of the five are within a radius of 25 miles from each of their homes, if they stayed within that range soon enough they'd run out of places to rob, of any worth that is."

"Hang on Tom I've a list of the previous robberies, as I've said we suspect they've probably been involved in, at least ten before these according to our records."

"Thanks Josey, have we a map to pin up?"

"Yes here's one Tom."

"David, what have we got?" Michael was pleased at the way the team was working together.

"Not including the one's we think they're going to do, I make it two within the first five miles. Four more within the next five, three the next and four the next and finally two in the last five miles. Suggesting there are more in the last five miles radius to come or they're going to spread out to thirty miles."

"If they do that it will make it more difficult to determine where they would strike next, their choices are increasing with each expanding radius point.

"That's true Josey but they are moving to more rural locations and so while their local knowledge might diminish and therefore give them a greater chance of making mistakes, people will still fear them locally with less protection from the Police on offer so will keep quiet about them. I'm not sure if they would initially go outside of their immediate circle of influence anyway."

"You're not telling me they'll really run out of robberies to do?"

"No Michael it's just that they could revert back inwards, within the radius."

"Quite feasible Tom."

"So rather than solving the existing crimes looking for clues we're already looking at their next robbery."

"I thought that was the way it works don't we need to catch them in the act Josey?"

"Yes definitely and we will only do that by analysing their previous robberies for likely errors they would take forward."

"As to location for now we need to concentrate on targets within the range of twenty to twenty five miles they would consider."

"Again that's manpower we just don't have in the Police force Tom!"

"Tom let's move on to the robberies themselves, analyse them as Josey says."

"Ok apart from the locations each of the recent five involved safe breaking except for the security van which can be classed as a safe for this purpose."

"Just a thought Tom," interrupted David. "Josey what if we created a target with enough rich pickings without a safe, they might make some mistakes?"

"Certainly, they seem well versed in safe breaking, one of them must be regarded as the locksmith," Tom continued. "The similarities are obvious, but it is worth stating, there's only ever four people carrying out the raids. It will be the size of the raid, not too big for the gang, not too small, never enough to attract full media coverage, which translates into less pressure for the Police to solve the cases over and above all else, without the use of the hard pressed resources trying to solve the cases they get away easily. Which must be how evidence gets missed, I have to say its ingenious they must have considered this would be how the Police would react."

"Don't get carried away with your admiration Tom, these are hardened criminals, they take shotguns on each job, one day they'll end up using them so far they've been lucky," she scolded. "And David there are enough robberies they're committing without creating one as a trap, we'd get laughed out of court literally."

"I'm sorry, I only meant…," both Tom and David spoke simultaneously.

"Let's move on," she suggested coolly, fed up with the gangs seeming elevation to hero status.

Tom shrugged. "Anyhow they only ever take or go for cash notes, no coins, stamps, papers or jewellery etc." he looked at Josey for confirmation.

"You're right untraceable proceeds, no-one bothers about getting cash back, it is normally the keepsakes that put on the pressure to find like jewellery, picture and letters. It means no need for any fencing of goods no one else need get involved."

"Cannot money be marked?"

"Yes but we have to be specific about what and

where to target Smithy, a retail shop impossible, a Post Office half possible if it was all outgoing, we'd have to mark every note received over the counter impossible."

"I get the picture."

"What about getaways, cars, bag sizes, weight of haul, clothes and face masks have to be purchased?" David asked. "And guns, shotguns you said, they'd have to buy those."

All of them laughed at his naivety and Josey explained they would not purchase those from a high street shop.

Michael came to his rescue. "David's got a point though, the size of the haul has to relate to the size of the vehicle if they steal them, the bags, masks and clothes they must use the same each time so any trace would be long gone."

"It's either a small van or an estate car which are the easiest to obtain, unfortunately a needle in a haystack, we haven't yet been able to find the vehicles they use," she said regretfully.

"But that only means they either clean them thoroughly, put them back without the owners realising they're gone or dare I say it, the Police don't relate the theft of someone's van or estate car to any robberies," he waited for the backlash from Josey in defence of the Police.

"David, that's brilliant truly, that's the problem we have to try and relate the haul size to the vehicle that could've been taken and see what had been stolen prior to the robbery probably up to a month before." David started to impress her at last, he was thinking, as she would have done. "Not having a vehicle to check for forensics has lost an element in these cases we truly needed."

"What about the other vehicles they used like

pickup trucks, articulated lorry, JCB in one case surely these could be tested for evidence?"

"Tom, you're absolutely right if we could find them, none were reported missing, therefore they were just 'borrowed' stolen, or hired either way how do you link a muddy old working JCB on the many sites within the county let alone the country to a robbery when you don't know which one," Josey paused for effect. "The problem with this gang is they are experts in clearing up after themselves, no smash and grab raids for them, they have what the army like to call an exit strategy."

"Tom, talk to us more about the four men themselves, what else do we know about them?" Michael asked.

"From what I've read out of these boxes, while they are clearly armed robbers in the true threatening sense, they have never certainly on these five cases harmed anyone. Sure they may have shouted tied people up, locked them in rooms waving their shotguns around and, in the statements from the people they were robbing, apparently they treated them with utmost respect, in fact, three people actually talked of the respect shown to them, even making sure the elders amongst them were sitting down and not stressed." Josey dismissively shrugged at their considerate behaviour suggesting if they were not carrying out the robbery in the first place, they would have no need to show respect. "The other ten cases were any people harmed?"

"No none at all, I believe," she raised her eyes to the air. "Shit, we're looking at model robbers the public just loves that spin. You'll be telling me next they're Robin Hood types rich to poor stuff with the proceeds."

"Well funny you should say that."

The group groaned.

"No seriously, the Police investigations show the money which over only the five robberies accounts for almost three quarters of a million pounds, with no trace anywhere after ransacking their homes checking on travel arrangements out of the country any large spending both amongst the gang or their immediate family suggests they must give the money away.

"What makes you so sure they don't hide the money for reclaiming later on?"

"I can answer this Tom suggested it to me," David looked at Tom for confirmation. "So I ran a credit check on each gang member and not surprisingly they have no debt at all, houses all paid for and a small balance of cash in the bank and savings accounts at the local building societies. Each are well insured should anything happen to them, their families would become legitimately quite wealthy, all policies fully paid up presumably in cash as there is no trace of any banking transactions."

"How did you come by this information David," she asked, ever the Policewoman.

"Don't ask Josey," Tom suggested.

She let it go, assessing David with suspicion.

"What is amazing is the known family and associates of which there are quite a few, certainly about sixty odd, not one of them has any hint of debt at all, suggesting …"

"Oh God, suggesting," Josey interrupted. "Is that they really are some later day Robin Hoods giving away the proceeds of the robberies to all that would protect them, which is exactly what people will do."

"And protecting them for retirement. High insurance payments mean later high pension returns, bricks and mortar and above all no debt ever," Tom offered cynically.

"Surely we can check on how people have been able to afford their houses, cars, holidays without loans." Michael commented.

Frustrated she replied looking around at all three. "Do you know just how much man power that would take and how many legal hoops we have to go through to find out that sort of information, despite David here illegally hacking for all he's worth," her despair evident for all to see.

"Tom let us get back to the men themselves." Michael suggested.

He went to one of the spare wall whiteboards and wrote each of the men's names as headings.

"I'll start with Gerry Fielder 38 year old and as mentioned earlier is the brains, nothing I've read suggests otherwise. The younger brother of Ron, from the Police investigation notes it is pointed out whenever the group are questioned together they follow Gerry's lead every time. The others are more sceptical about being "stitched up", he caught Josey's disapproving look. "Just been listening to a couple of tape re-runs of interviews."

He continued. "This goes for both Gerry and Ron, their father and grandfather who is no longer alive have been in and out of prison most of their lives the grandfather died in prison. Their father is currently serving two more years of a sentence of eight for armed robbery. He's different he shoots the guards, that's why the long sentence and his previous form of course."

"So he just followed in the father and grandfather's footsteps?"

"Unusually no Michael, he actually joined the army when he was 18 and rose to Sergeant he served eight years of the nine years he signed up for. Bought himself out, interestingly if he had have stayed he would have been put forward as officer material. The reports show above average intelligence and guess what I have just read he is a trained locksmith and explosives expert. That's about all I have for him except about a year before he left the army he was investigated in respect of a bank raid in Genoa, Italy where he was stationed, records show an army vehicle he was responsible for was seen in the area, around half a million euros were stolen."

"Nice pension fund then," David suggested.

"More like business start-up funds," Tom closed the file on Gerry Fielder. "One other point no-one could prove he was involved in the bank raid, but they later wondered how he could afford to buy himself out of the army, however, what is interesting he paid the money out of an Italian bank account which is still current today."

"Do we know how much money is in it?"

Tom shook his head. "I did ask the bank but they wouldn't tell me."

"Give me the details let me see what I can find," David offered.

"Money gains friends then," added Josey sarcastically not happy that David was about to bend another rule.

"Tut, tut, what are you suggesting about our armed forces?" David raised his eyebrows to her.

"Interesting shows a pattern, isn't that what you'd say Josey?"

She smiled at her Smithy.

"There is one other thing before I leave Gerry who has never been caught by the way," Tom offered. "His corporal at the time was Lawrie Berger, suggesting that's how they met and also investigated at the time."

"Let's all have a break," Michael suggested.

Tom and David left the room to Michael and Josey.

"Are you alright Josey, what's wrong?"

"I'm afraid we're taking you down a route that's, well…"

"Dangerous, yes I know Paul told me as much, you mustn't worry, I may have only been born yesterday, almost literally, I am a grown up and can think for myself, I love you for looking after my welfare," he pulled her close to him and held her tightly in his arms.

"Now I've found you Michael, I never want to lose you,"

"Don't worry Josey, I'm going nowhere," he gently kissed her forehead, her hair catching in his lips as she nestled her head between his shoulder and breast bone, he put an arm around her shoulders and they sat together without a word just enjoying being with each other.

An hour later, they reconvened with Tom talking through Ron Berger's life a 45-year-old supposed hard man, followed more closely to their father's style of hit out first approach. Been in prison many times but not since Gerry came out of the army and they hung out together.

"Ron seems to take the role of reinforcing his younger brother's status within the gang as leader essentially he's the gofer of the group."

"David, what about the other two?"

"Michael as Tom has said Lawrie Berger was a Corporal in the army and where he met Gerry. He has never been in prison, if the suspicions noted in the files are true it had to cement him and Gerry's friendship with the Genoa success. He's slightly younger at 36," he paused to consider. "What is interesting there has been no suspicion that he's anything but honest and law abiding, until he met Gerry that is, meant to be very intelligent though!"

"And Trevor?" Josey asked.

"It's unclear how he joined them he almost mirrors Ron, he's 44 has got some previous," he looked towards Josey. "Is that what you say?"

She nodded thinking everyone wants to be smart, too much TV.

"A brief link same cell once at Brixton with Gerry's and Ron's father in prison."

"Tom have we established each of their alibi's?"

"I can help with that one Smithy, Ron Fielder and Berger supply one for each of the others as do Gerry Fielder and Cole."

"And where do their families think they are when the robberies occurred, any discrepancies?"

"Again according to their statements given to the Police none, each member of their family say that each two are out together and as Josey says, each two are backing one another so they are still untouchable."

"Surely suspected criminals especially on the same job can't cover for each other can they Josey, it makes a nonsense of the whole process surely?"

"No that's true, nonetheless they did give us those as alibi's and we have to check them out, unfortunately it is likely these are also confirmed by others, trouble is if we had something else like evidence for example we would tackle the alibi's more seriously."

"What else Tom?"

"To summarise as far as I can see the types of robberies are small enough for four, normally safe's, cash only, likely stolen cars they clean up and leave well behind, very easy alibi's, all have local knowledge, and are Robin Hoods into the bargain so we're never going to get informants."

"Ok Tom, what about their individual actions?"

Apart from what we have already covered one maybe two of them have to target and steal the cars, this itself could get them noticed. I suggest this is either Trevor or Ron. I note from Trevor's record, he has been on remand for hot-wiring a car, in his younger days. Clearly Gerry is the locksmith and the explosive expert but I would expect Lawrie to share that with him," Tom looked to David for help.

"They would all need to study the layout, I gather Trevor has a dark room and is an amateur photographer doing the families weddings and christenings so it is likely he would be the one to take the pictures. I'm guessing but he learnt his photography in his younger days while working for an architect's office, I would suggest there's not much of a leap from there for him to draw diagrams one of them needs to be good at that why not Trevor. There has to be a 'boss' who makes the decisions when, where, which and how, they wouldn't discuss or analyse a likely raid in their own homes, so where do they work on the planning, we've already agreed Gerry fits that one."

"Good work David and you Tom, you're suggesting they must have a lock up or some place on a permanent basis. If we could find that it would lead to many, many clues," they both had impressed Josey. "Don't forget Smithy they'd need a place even to distribute the proceeds."

"Then all their gear, uniforms, masks, bags and tools would need to be stored between jobs," Michael considered. "We need to determine what sort of place has to be big enough to store cars and equipment and test the plans themselves."

"What type of place should we be looking for Josey?"

"I'm not sure but as Tom says they need to steal cars, which suggest their place has to be big enough, possibly to respray the cars with no-one able to see them. It's likely to be somewhere quite remote, but used as a showroom or a garage for repairs something like that."

"Look folks, I'm up for calling it a day, I'm a little tired now, what do you think?" Michael suggested to the group."

"Fine by me Michael, I'm sure you and Josey want to spend some time with each other," Tom winked at Josey who blushed.

"I'm pretty whacked myself, so it's fine by me," David had enjoyed the day, he liked working at FMPC.

"Thank you Tom, David, for your kind consideration," she offered sarcastically.

"Where ever did you get Tom, Michael he's a real gem, very, very good as is David old and wise for his young years."

He laughed. "I confess to being lucky," he watched the back of Tom as he retreated through the office doorway. "Well you know how David came here he was sent by you as a prospective client who'd had his equipment stolen if you remember and Tom came from the Job Centre, but his father is a Police Superintendent somewhere in London so I understand." He knew there was more to him than he was letting on and his father was closer involved than he had admitted yet, Michael had decided he could wait for it to play out until the information came from one or the other of them.

"Name?" Josey said coldly smelling a rat.

"Miles Broughton, It must be where Tom gets his investigative powers from."

"I'll check on him, he may be able to help us," she did not believe what she said to him for one minute, they were being infiltrated, surely Michael appreciated that she thought. Tom was too experienced to be someone directly out of the Job Centre time will tell she thought needing to find out why.

David asked Tom if he fancied a drink before he rushed off, his offer rejected in favour of the imminent train, which would take Tom back to his home in London. David wheeled himself toward Penny's desk and watched her typing furiously on her computer.

She became aware of him and it was putting her off, she tried to concentrate ignoring him.

"Penny er, I don't suppose you'd, no ok," he stammered.

"Yes David, come on lets go for a drink although I'm hurt at being second best," he was crestfallen.

"I'm kidding, let's go," she teased.

For an hour or two Michael and Josey both enjoyed each other's company albeit one sided, he was becoming frustrated at having no past, no point of reference, nothing he did jogged an ounce of his memory. It made him much more interested in Josey's background, her life generally, her schools, friends, parents and career even her loves and losses. He absorbed, claimed them as his own family history.

Strange he knew of the world's historical events, countries, recognised world faces and locations. He just could not place himself in his own history as it was affected during the past forty years, where was he during wars assassinations, Olympics, sporting moment's World cups, World Series, elections and what were his life's achievements. What of space travel, technology, how had it affected him? He had not a clue. Questions circled around and around his head, what had he been good at, what level had he been educated to, who were his parents, did he have brothers and sisters or family in general.

At times, he felt lost inside of himself today and tomorrow's man never yesterdays. He had no definition he shrugged and told himself to stop feeling sorry for himself. He was alive and he'd found Josey, he'd developed a 'skill' which he needed to make the most of while he could, he was doing OK and yet he would always wonder what he might have been.

They both took the short walk to his apartment he had a surprise for her, following a shared spiced pizza the television beckoned as they clutched their glasses of red wine.

"Is this a date David?" They were sitting in a

newly brick sandblasted beamed public house in Maidstone.

"I suppose."

"Oh very romantic."

"Sorry I'm not used to…."

"How long have you been in a wheelchair?" Her voice unconsciously softened toward him.

"At University in Coventry I was always regarded as the resident nerd, advanced for my years they used to say, top of the class stuff especially technology," not answering the question.

"So you weren't in a wheelchair then?"

"No stupidly I got it into my head I had to prove myself as normal as the other "fellows" and started doing sports football, rugby and athletics in general."

"You were injured right?"

"At rugby I scored a try and the whole team celebrated and dived on top of me, I couldn't move."

"Oh God that's what caused it!"

"No but unfortunately the hospital found my spine was crumbling, it was only a matter of time before I wouldn't be able to walk at all."

"Are you able to now?"

"No not anymore properly anyhow I try the odd step or two, normally I can only force myself to stand up if I need to," he looked into her eyes. "Does it make a difference to you Penny?"

She answered him by tenderly leaning across kissing his lip's gently.

"What about you how did you happen to arrive in my life sitting here drinking with me?"

"Well I'm Australian."

"I'd got that, your accent somehow gave it away."

"I'm a Brisbane girl which is the capital of Queensland and I left the St. Lucia campus at the University there and worked as a trainee accountant."

"Why did you come here?"

"Oh that's easy everyone is encouraged to take a sabbatical to broaden the individuals horizon supposedly to come back after a year worldly wise and be able to contribute to the country. It's common with us and the Kiwi's."

"Kiwi's?"

"It's the recognised nickname for people from New Zealand."

"Will you go back?"

"Of course it's my home, how soon depends on what keeps me here David," she emphasised his name.

"And FMPC?"

"Well I'd gotten to know Josey professionally, a person at the company I worked at went missing reported by her family, so I helped the Police, well Josey anyhow, to find the people who she was close to at work and looked up files and stuff. So when FMPC was set up she thought of me and offered me a job."

"Was she found?"

"Oh yes boyfriend had taken her off on holiday."

"Will you stay?"

"Of course, it got much better when Mr Squeaky arrived," she smiled at him.

"Who?"

She held in front of him the wheelchair arms and started pushing him backwards and forwards. At first he did not understand then, he found himself listening to his wheelchairs squeak, he grinned sheepishly, on one of the forward movements, he pulled himself up out of the chair and stood his full height and she stood up with him. He kissed and held her tightly steadying himself not wanting to let her go or fall down, he knew he would never leave her or FMPC.

"What are we watching," Josey made herself comfortable on his sofa she was starting to appreciate their time alone together.
"Just you watch," he touched the remote as the picture came to life.
Josey gasped and cried at the film opening credits,

which read "Random Harvest" she embedded herself in his arms, she never felt better than right now.

They were both tearful until the end, when the storyline brought the couple back together at a beautiful white cottage. They could not love each other more than they did this night.

In the morning Josey left early for the Police station, he walked the few yards to his office, sitting at his desk, morning coffee in hand he studied the wallboards, it was the weekend he liked the quiet it helped get his head together, pondering the robberies placed on the walls. Realising he had not touched any of the four men's effects yet, he nervously approached the table with them. He knew the moment he did touch and feel them the case for him would no longer be the same again. He was trying to solve them without gimmicks, tricks and his skill he would not be able to avoid them he felt compelled to touch.

Looking closely at Gerry Fielder's baseball cap and watch, this was the supposed mastermind of the group he would begin with him.

He tried the Skagen titanium watch on his own wrist, it was working the hands read 8:23 it fitted comfortably, strange only then for the first time did he actually realise he was right handed as he placed it around his left wrist, he realised he never had a watch of his own. He rubbed his hands around the rim of the cap, the tick of Nike on the front above the peak, he placed it carefully upon his head, it too fitted comfortably, he walked to the window and looked at his reflection the cap suited his face. He became dizzy and had to sit down quickly.

He started to realise he was reading and receiving picture flashes of Gerry Fielder's past as his own, perhaps why he has no memory this detail coming to him needed space like a computer needs disk, storage of information cannot be downloaded without space. He was unable to stop the process once started. He progressed through Gerry Fielder's lifetime journey and for a moment, he was in his own mind looking at the papers on the desk and from these he realised no one event caused Gerry to become a criminal, but his father and grandfather before him had all set the path for him. They had been in and out of prison throughout Gerry's life.

Right now, he knew Gerry was having an early breakfast in a café, his father and two uncles were currently serving time in a Kent Prison at Maidstone. Grandfather was buried grandly in a paid for family vault in London. An idea came to him he needed Josey's help to test whether he was right and could be able to see all of the gang together, to do that he would have to wear the differing items the Police had taken from each of the four.

With Gerry's watch and cap on, Ron Fielder's trainers didn't fit him they were a size nine one size too small, swearing he forced his feet into them, he wore the one sized black gloves. As Gerry's, Ron's life flashed rapidly through his brain, he felt the pressure of the information seemingly filling his brain space and replacing Gerry's. Ron was out early morning shopping with his wife pushing a trolley up an aisle, bread he read the thought, in Morrisons the supermarket. He touched the cap, Gerry again like a Computer Windows program his brain seemed to flip notes to where Gerry was still in the café at Singleton.

He placed Trevor Cole's empty glass case in his trouser pocket, the Florida sun pictured key ring he attached to a belt loop on his trouser waistband. As before information poured into his brain like a hammer Trevor was currently in the Bookmakers Corals in Ashford High Street. He checked he could automatically flip to the other two they were still in focus.

Now he tried the same with Lawrie Berger and his cigarette lighter, he placed it into his shirts breast pocket the crowbar made him laugh out loud he couldn't wear it or store on himself, he decided he would just hold it for this purpose. Lawrie was standing right beside Trevor in the bookmakers, strange he could not see him when he looked for Trevor. He realised he now could not see Trevor either, but was aware of him being there at this angle. He thought about this for a while and touched each separately.

This was going to be easy while the pictures were updating rapidly they still were snapshots of a single person and not moving images, which are why he would never see them together. He realised this as a limitation to his skill.

Cap and watch Gerry's, Ron's gloves and small sized trainers, Trevor's pocketed glass case and belt strapped key ring together with Lawrie's cigarette lighter in the other trouser pocket with a hand held crowbar in his left hand. Even though, he knew the others were near including the closeness of Trevor and Lawrie all he was getting was snapshots in his mind, each of the four in their own bubble.

Feeling foolish and conscious of holding the crowbar, the cap and too small trainers he looked at himself in the office glass divider. His image reminded him of someone out of the old music hall acts, Max Wall the information in his mind playing tricks, he began discarding the items from his waist, hands, feet and pockets his mental views shut down. Images no longer flashing, notes no longer reeling like ticker tape, He got what he was looking for, simultaneously pinpointing all of them.

  He would get Josey to test his theory by wearing or having any items on him and get her to check on the individuals,   All he needed to do was to be wearing the items on the day when a crime was being committed, very easy he thought dryly which day would that be then? He asked himself sarcastically. Meanwhile he would retrace his steps down the river Stour in his own bid to find his memory.

Chapter 8

Thomas Broughton had an early Monday morning appointment with his father in the MI6 offices situated on the south side of London's Thames River next to Vauxhall Bridge. He walked out from the underground railway tube station with the distinctive art deco designed building imposing itself on the surrounding area. His father always took great pains to stress the difference between 'his' MI6 with its service remit working outside of the UK.

The other MI5 is more confined to local issues, he always laughed when making the comments, more than once he likened the difference as the USA"s CIA versus FBI, he was the CIA"s counterpart. Waiting for Miles Broughton, he watched a Police patrol boat speed under Vauxhall Bridge below pulling alongside a cargo barge preparing to board the vessel.

His father came into the office with an entourage in tow.

"My son Tom," he said to the three people and politely introduced them, their names not registering with him at all.

"What have you got for us Tom, who is Michael Smith and where does he come from?"

"Nice to see you too Father, been a while, how've you been?" he sneered sarcastically reminding his father of the family connection. He sensed the entourage squirm waiting for the famous Miles Broughton explosive rage. It did not come, instead they got the patronising that's my boy look and he got his glare.

"I'm sorry son it's the job you get into the groove you know?" Tom did not, but he had heard it so many times before he just smiled for the entourage.

"Look Father, I don't like this honestly thought I would but," his voice trailed off in the guilt of spying on Michael.

"Don't be so bloody squeamish Tom, quirks of fate just don't happen there's always a reason and what we need to know is who he works for and how did he obtain this so called talent of his."

"Father as I understand it this quirk of fate as you call it happened because of a gas explosion his injuries included a loss of memory. Apparently as a result of the explosion he seems able to know where every person is dead or alive."

Miles entourage laughed at the suggestion, he forgot they were there and did not want them overhearing, he promptly dismissed them from his office.

"He's obviously helping the Police because they set him up to operate as a Missing Persons bureau, but they're beginning to use his talents for more complex criminal cases."

"Tom, don't be so naive," he waited until the door

to his office closed and they were alone. "Don't you think we want to use him if he's straight we'd grab him immediately, but before we do we need leverage, something that would make him need to work with us."

"What leverage?" Noting his father's American speak. "If he won't play ball what then?"

"Just leave that to us Tom," his voice portraying a sinister edge to his approach."

"I happen to like them Father, they're all straight people," he said sincerely, it caused his father to consider his approach more carefully he had never seen his son so committed before.

"Look Thomas, you were given a task and remember you do work for us not him? You asked for some responsibility to get you out of my shadow in the department, well this was it, you knew that, you surely wouldn't want this Michael and Josey to find out what you're doing there, would you?" He realised he was applying leverage to his own son.

"No Father, I'll do what I can," admitting defeat reluctantly. "At some point we're going to discuss this further, you do know that father?"

Miles nodded to his son as he left, feeling proud his son had gained some balls of late.

Now that Josey had her suspicions about Tom she was unable to let it go, every time she sought information about his father Miles Broughton she hit a blank wall. The term they were so frequently using about the robbers came to mind about him being 'untouchable'. All information checks for both father and son were mysteriously unavailable, even Paul told her to let it go. She was worried

Smithy, he was still too fragile to get involved in terrorist activities, MI5, MI6 or whatever she wasn't sure, but knew Michael could be in danger, were very, very valuable but it depended in whose hands they would be used by, at that level once his usefulness had been served he would become expendable.

Somehow, she had to find protection for him. She worried that she was just a lowly detective sergeant however, there were some favours she could pull in unfortunately Inspector Wyndham was not one of them. At least she could rely on him to do what is right for his own career. She regretted her thoughts about him, a reaction not a fair assessment.

They got together around noon that day and Michael was agitated. "Where the hell have you two been? I'm onto something," not bothering to listen to their responses. He went on to explain about him wearing the robber's items and had wanted Josey to prove his theory by pinpointing each robber's location as a test. Both Tom and Josey felt this could be useful.

"There's more, we said a DIY store, casino or a music festival but I know where each of them are and what they've been staking out, if that's the term, an art gallery on the high street in Tunbridge Wells, within I might add their twenty five mile radius. This gallery had an exhibition yesterday and David checked the Internet for me and confirmed it by telephone with the gallery staff. It leads me to believe they would be ready now to bank cash."

"It's exactly what would appeal to this gang. But surely most who can afford exhibition art prices would pay through bank drafts, credit cards or cheques and not cash which is all this lot are interested in?"

"Don't you believe it Tom hard currency is untraceable to the buyer as well as the seller, non-taxable and rarely loses its value if placing the investment in a picture or two, let me look at their website David," Josey was impressed at the amateur detection. "Good work."

After she studied Praetown Art galleries website it was clear yesterday's exhibits would have attracted a good few purchasers it held some sought after masterpieces and with luck, if the majority paid cash the gang if successful stood to gain several million pounds. Not bad for a local gallery Josey was willing to bet they wouldn't have proper security in place and more to the point if she realised this so would the gang.

"Smithy I think you could be right, rich pickings for them I'm sure."

"Josey I don't want to alarm you but my senses tell me the robbery is probably happening right now," he touched Gerry Fielder's Skagen watch, pictures rolled around in his head like an old fairground slot machine.

All three Michael, David and Tom watched Josey turn into a completely different person in that split second, Michael shivered he'd seen her in action before laying in his hospital bed, it was best to keep out of her way. Both her own mobile and the office telephone was used to bark orders to those on the receiving ends, within minutes Police were racing down the high street of Tunbridge Wells towards the Praetown Art Gallery.

"Come on lets be at the scene hopefully to see them caught red handed," she'd arranged for them to be picked up and taken directly there.

"Don't worry about me I'll see you later when

you get back."

"We're having none of that David you're not missing the fun. You helped more than anyone."

"Tom please help me with David's wheelchair at the car."

"Will do boss."

Josey noted David was grinning from ear to ear.

They and the Police arrived too late and although they quickly rounded up the gang within the hour, again no evidence, one plus the gang was clearly agitated it had been close.

Tom and Michael watched the Police interrogations through the two-way mirrors at the Police station in their interview room. Josey attending with Paul Wyndham in a cold bare room, brickwork painted cream with a table and four chairs the only furniture.

The confidence visibly draining from each as they were being interviewed Michael interested in seeing his picture images come to life, Gerry Fielder denying the charges in particular and wanted to understand, why the Police picked on them and who had suggested it. All of the gang rattled by being picked up within the hour of the robbery.

Not a great haul by their standards, it turned out Tom's prediction had been right banker's drafts, cheques and credit cards were used and very little cash amounting to a reported two million pounds, with the overall takings being around sixteen million pounds. Gerry realised he'd been lucky if the load had been more it would have taken them longer to pack up the haul, it could have made the difference between getting caught and not. It was too close a call, they all knew it, and someone else was involved the Police must have had help they had to find out who.

Michael watched Gerry Fielder's face who occasionally looked directly at him searching the two-way mirror for any clues.

Mainly, he refused to admit anything, repeatedly asking how they came to pick on them, where did the information come from. Michael was conscious of the anger behind the façade in the man's eyes burning like a furnace.

David in his wheelchair sat by a row of seats adjacent to the custody Sergeant's station watching, listening to the four as each was officially released from custody. Gerry and Lawrie shook their heads at the other two gesturing silence, paying little attention to Michael and Tom who joined him as they had finished watching the interviews.

Barely audible Gerry commented. "We need to talk urgently because someone has, that was too close for comfort." He looked around to see if anyone had listened and noted the man sitting on the blue row of seats, vaguely familiar, their eyes briefly met and Gerry's eyes dropped away to the man's hands his left wrist catching his eye, the man was wearing a similar watch as his, the one he had given to the Police. The implication did not register they were released without charge.

It confirmed to Michael he had been right to continue to wear the items and place the items on himself, it was strange being so close to Gerry Fielder and wearing his watch no picture formed in his mind as if watching the man was enough unifying the images. It occurred to him if the person was near enough to touch he was unable to gain any information about them, unless he actually shook their hand or in some way managed to touch them.

What puzzled him where did the money go? He was concerned they had not been caught properly and were now being released despite his efforts, Michael hoped next time they would be caught red handed, judging the gang would wait a while for their next job, but he turned out to be wrong they were already working to another plan. This was a normal ploy by the gang to further use up Police resource by splitting them up and dividing their energies on more than one case to solve which included them.

Deciding once out of sight of them he would retrace the gang's steps in his mind. Later that evening alone he watched the pictures playing in his mind concentrating on what Gerry was doing throughout the raid. He wore his cap and watch and followed the journey, apart from helping to load the bag with the stolen cash, he never left the building with it.

Key ring, lighter, crowbar, gloves, trainers and the glass case, it was useless he couldn't in his mind drill down the pictures to that level of detail pinpointing who had carried the bag out one way or another. Frustrated the only pictures within his mind showed them climbing into the getaway vehicles. None of them had left with the trolley bag full of the cash. Where was it, he asked himself the Police had not found it.

He was sweating and would not believe the conclusion he came to, it was still there either in or near the gallery. The dark of the night now falling, the men had been released from the Police Station late afternoon he would have to hurry. He literally ran from his building and flagged down a passing cab, on arrival at the gallery he noticed an alleyway running down the side of the gallery premises, dark but for the street lamp reflections at the entrance. He suggested to the taxi driver to wait outside in front of the gallery for him, taking him out of sight from the alleyway's entrance he intend to go down it on the pretext of collecting a package that had been left there for him, he told the taxi driver.

Slowly he walked towards the side entrance checking the door, locked. Just beyond the doorway further down the alleyway under his torch light, he noticed fresh brickwork surrounding an iron grid. If he had not been looking for something out of the ordinary, he would have missed it, to others it would appear natural and in keeping with its surroundings.

Looking around, no one had seen him enter the alleyway, but opposite the back door of the gallery, there were similar doors to other businesses. He checked for lights or activity anywhere, nothing, he guessed tomorrow it would be bustling, tonight the cardboard boxes surrounding blue trash bins took on a sinister edge to them, tricks of the light, populating the darkness making him uneasy the only evidence the alley is used. Bending down in front of the metal grid holding the bars he pulled hard. It moved slightly, a fraction, he pulled harder conscious of the need to hurry, another pull it gave way he wrenched the grid out of the wall revealing a square deep hole in the brickwork.

He knelt down on the ground and stretched his right arm fully to his shoulder blade he felt nothing he reached down harder the side of his head pressed against the brick wall of the building, it was painful reminding him of how tender his temples still were. Forcing himself further in, he felt a leather strap on which he tugged. Carefully he pulled the bag toward the holes entrance, lifting it onto the alley's tarmac. He opened the bag by the top horseshoe zipper, checking the cash was there, he had been right.

They never intended to leave with it, which is why they are never caught the proceeds are never found because they plan to hide it nearby for later collection. He breathed hard excited at his find he opened and stared at the money zipping the bag closed. He ran up the alleyway and jumped with the bag into the waiting cab. As it drove away, he turned around to look out of the rear window only to spot Gerry Fielder and Lawrie Berger's black Mercedes pull in by the alleyway to collect the proceeds of their raid. Michael's driver turned a corner and he was out of sight.

Michael bet that each robbery was planned this way to include some sort of storage area for later collection, never any evidence if caught, it was clever, he guessed they would not be happy to lose the haul, he laughed they would hardly complain.

Now what to do he asked himself, something told him to keep the cash and not give it up to the Police, who would know, what if his memory came back how useful would he be to anyone then, what would he do with his life, he started to think of it as a sort of retirement fund. That night on his return to his office and apartment building, he was sweating he'd carried out the robbery and gotten away with it, in a small way he appreciated how the gang must feel. He opened up his office and placed the bag in a locked filing cabinet drawer. He had no need to decide what to do with the money until later much later.

Chapter 9

David sat in his apartment in front of his new array of routers, terminals, satellite antennas, servers, modems and a couple of laptops. He was in heaven back to his old self when he worked for NATO. He loved Michael and was as close to him more than he'd been to anyone before, he loved the man as a brother, father and definitely a friend and he intended to help him all he ever could, he, Josey, Tom and Penny had become family.

His visit to the Police Station proved fruitful, while Michael and Tom went to the interview viewing room and Josey joined Inspector Wyndham, given free rein to explore the station. He found himself in the detective area and made for the missing persons unit in particular. When challenged he told them he had come with the Inspector who had asked him to wait in his office.

To his joy he found himself in Paul Wyndham's office where he was supplied him with a drink biscuits and left alone. He moved aside the desk chair and wheeled his own up close to the desk, best of all Paul's laptop computer was in the "Computer Locked" mode for the windows entry to whatever system the Inspector had access to. By keying Ctrl-Alt & Del, it presented him with the next screen

"Unlock Computer" and told him that it was in use by Paul only him or the administrator could gain access he needed to fill in the username and a password to gain entry.

The screen already gave him the username by virtue of suggesting only Paul or an administrator had rights to log in, he keyed in the username as WYNDHP01, the hard part was his password. He looked around the Inspector's office in search of what is personal to him, family photo, cat and dog displayed prominently, he looked around the room at the pictures on the wall, clearly a sailing boat fan several reflected different types. He looked in his unlocked desk drawers for a slip of paper or the telltale sign of a password.

Most wrote theirs down to remember, nothing under the laptop on the desk either. Paul's office proved pretty soulless, he wheeled his chair around full circle and studied each picture, only one had Paul in its picture, he tried to look at the boat's name. He was too far down from the wall to reach it for a closer look he struggled to stand up out of his chair and slipped back ungainly into his wheelchair, not today.

The door opened.

"Hi you're David right? I'm Sophie anything I can help you with?" She was always interested in the Inspectors office use and his visitors.

David looked at the Policewoman in the doorway, he immediately felt guilty deciding it must be the uniform she wore he forced the wheels of his chair away from the desk toward her so she could not see what was on the screen.

"Are you alright?" she asked noting his reddened

face having watched him try to get up out of the chair. "You appeared to be struggling."

"I was just trying to look at the sailing boat with Paul on board up there," he said pointing at the picture. "I couldn't see it properly."

"No problem," she picked it off the wall and placed it on his lap, as she did so she looked beyond him and saw Inspector Wyndham's screen at the login prompt, and knew why he'd seemed guilty his face flushed with colour, he obviously tried to use the laptop while waiting. She dismissed it as someone bored and pressing a few keys on the keyboard rather that anything malicious, after all, he would need a password.

Thanking her asking. "How recent is this photograph?"

"Oh only a couple of weeks I guess, he recently went sailing in Southampton and never stops talking of his hired sailing boat."

The description at the bottom of the picture stated the fifty-foot motor schooner built in the early part of this century was made of steel construction and had a fuel capacity of three thousand miles. Paul stood proud on the desk with his cap parading as captain of his ship, more importantly it bore the name of Gemini7, turning his wheelchair around to go back toward the desk and laptop ready to key in the boats name as a password, forgetting she was still there. He prayed she did not suspect what he was trying to do.

"Shall I put it back on the wall?"

"What?" Jolted he agreed.

"By the way, I nearly forgot why I came in, Sergeant Rainbow said, they'd probably be another hour and suggested if I saw you would I ask you to meet them at the Sergeant's booking in station. It's on the ground floor near the entrance where you'd previously been dropped off by car," she placed the picture back on the wall and left the office closing the door behind her.

David did feel guilty, in the right place for it he thought. He put the password of GEMINI7 in the empty password space on the screen, immediately it responded with "Password incorrect". Fretting he knew this type of system had three attempts to get it right, if he didn't the user name would be locked at the central computer department and questions would be immediately asked. Even if the service desk did not, Inspector Wyndham would want to know why his screen locked he knew he could lose his own job. He considered the type of password convention he needed still convinced it was about the sailing boat. Second strike he entered GEMINI07 the system came to life he was in, relieved but sweating he had to work fast, he found a paper and pen and wrote down the many systems Paul logged into regularly.

Paul was able to connect to the PNC Police national computer, but also INTERPOL the world's largest international Police organisation. DHS the US Department of Homeland Security, FBI the federal bureau of investigations for domestic security and crime investigations, the CIA international intelligence both of these linked into the system related to NSA the national security agency, together with AFIS, which is the US fingerprint system. Our own DVLA the licensing and vehicle register, NAFIS for our fingerprint records everywhere it seems including BOP The US federal bureau of prisons and NCIC their National Crime Information Center.

He noticed a small icon not within the main body of Paul's screen, but on the task bar running along the bottom he selected it, opening up the UK"s social services child protection network. David was flabbergasted how many areas it opened up never imagining Paul was so well connected literally, it would normally take weeks if not months to gain access through authorisation to all his systems. David gauged he would expect to grant himself world wide access to every system in the world within 24 hours and all starting from Paul's login. The potential was enormous with his own back door entry still available to him for the NATO systems he would literally have it all.

He brought up onto the screen the Police intranet and located the IT Services pages, and searched for procedures for authorising access to these systems. Noting access granted upon receipt of an authorised 'appropriately' graded senior officer, and after applying, they would return a confirmation of receipt email, which also required a response thus double-checking the right information and authority. By understanding the levels of Paul's access to so many systems, David was in no doubt Paul would have the necessary powers for authorising.

David wrote down the many URL's the uniform resource locators identifying the pointers to Paul's range of systems on his laptop so he had the correct web addresses to access them at home. He sent an email to the IT Service Desk authorising access to a Gerald Robbins a new member of the team and typed all of the systems required with emphasis on remote working for covert activities. Now he would have to wait wondering what the expected response time would be, he had already begun to sweat, if they were busy, it could take time he did not have.

Three times, he thought someone would come into the office a message flagged a confirmation email at the bottom right area of the screen. He opened it as per the procedure it gave remote login instructions and suggested a code for entry which could be changed on access with all likely to be granted within the next four hours at which point another email would be sent to both Gerald Robbins and Paul Wyndham that it is actually completed and ready for access.

He returned the email then granted rights to Paul's email as ROBBIG01 praying it would be the only user name of this type. He sent via email all details of access to his home systems.

In the second drawer down of Paul's desk, he spotted a diary now placed in front of him on the desk and thumbed through it. He found the network access login details needed to gain entry out of normal hours, for Gerald Robbins this would be on the final email from the IT Service Desk within four hours he needed access sooner to keep the email away from the eyes of the Inspector. The access codes were jumbled letters and numbers, no one would remember and would have to be written down these would be needed if ever the desk computer changed. David laughed at the non-existent security. He wrote the details down carefully noting the order with uppercase and lowercase notations.

It was time he left Paul's office having deleted the sent email to himself and any records of communication with the IT Service Desk his one worry being their response. He shut down and restarted the laptop so it would be as he found it leaving it switched on at the login prompt.

Once in remotely he would automatically by getting into the network itself be able to log in locally as if he were connected to Paul's laptop instead he would pick up his profile and gain his access he wouldn't need his laptop to be logged on at all. Unconsciously he winked at Paul in the sailing boat photograph. He wheeled himself out of the office and down the corridor waving as he went to the Policewoman who had not realised how much she had helped him, he took the lift down to the Sergeant's station and sat innocently waiting for Michael and Tom to join him.

One by one, he recognised from Josey's case boxes the men involved in the robberies, he was excited to be so close to actual criminals especially those the team were investigating, each gang member seemed desperate to speak to each other with Gerry Fielder stopping them.

He was confident by experience no-one ever noticed someone in a wheelchair he was just not in people's eye line, effectively invisible. He studied each man carefully, they were obviously rattled, annoyed at being caught, the fat man Ron was trying to bully the desk sergeant to hurry up making him take even longer, David covered his grin. While each was signing to reclaim their belongings, Michael and Tom sat down beside him. He noticed Gerry Fielder looking at Michael as if a dawning of recognition occurred, the gang were dismissed by the custody sergeant on duty and shown the door, which led out to the car park. Seeing them go Michael and Tom updated him on what they had seen in the interview room. David did not intend updating them on his activities.

David lived in a warehouse apartment in Allington, a few miles from Maidstone. Now at home, he sat at his desk connecting through his array of communication devices using the remote access codes of Paul's, logging into the Police network then logged in as Paul a message he wasn't expecting, immediately appeared on the screen it read SECURITY ALERT "User already logged in" the screen asked him to contact the Service Desk for assistance. This was a new feature he'd not come across before and it threw him completely, his hands were sweaty, he was visibly shaking, he calmed himself quickly logging out of the network assuming Paul must be currently logged in at his desk or he could have a blackberry for emails accessed from anywhere, he'd not taken that into account.

Stupid of him a Policeman works twenty-four hours a day always on call. He would likely to be noting his messages he hoped all he had was an ordinary mobile. David still shaking wondered whether the Inspector could be reading them at his desk particularly the one from the service department, alarm bells would start to ring, he expected his door to be smashed open with Policemen populating his space, nothing happened and eventually he calmed down, he decided to try and log in again in an hour.

It seemed forever as he waited for the time to pass, finally, he tried and gained his entry to the Police systems. Paul must have gone home or at least shut down his laptop or this message automatically came up when systems were being backed up or having support maintenance carried out on them, he logged in as WYNDHP01 and checked his email, full access was granted to his alias with the remote code given. He deleted the email sent by the service desk which had arrived ten minutes before he'd logged in he was convinced Paul would never have seen it, he relaxed and logged out removing all trace of his entry completely.

He began again this time logging in as Gerald Robbins he had found it amusing to use his old lecturers name at university he'd always been so pompous. Once in suddenly heightened his edge this was always his high adrenaline fix, he soon hacked in to each of the systems to grant himself higher privileges that in turn would continue as a hierarchy to give him more rights in other not yet accessed systems throughout the world. He placed himself in many groups so he could authorise further access to anywhere, this would keep him busy for quite a while. He would in time hack back into Ashford's Police network anonymously and remove all trace of the Inspector authorising a Gerald Robbins full access from the service desk files.

By the morning he'd logged into almost every Police network in the world including restoring his old access to NATO"s systems. He was back in control, as a check he searched all the systems for two people himself and Michael. Amusingly he read about the account of his own accident, bright career at NATO destroyed 'blah, blah' as gradually his old sporting injury impacted on his daily work he was retired on health grounds from service. Michael was on record linked to an explosion by a riverbank, David skipped through the story listed with no background details, interestingly the MI6 records told him he was under investigation, he wondered why. At last, he found something to help Michael to begin repaying him for his support and for his faith in him. He would keep a check on MI6 and watch his back.

Chapter 10

"What the hell happened here, I know we're in the frame for every bloody robbery in the country but we were whiskers away from being caught this time," the gang met in a back room out of site above a working garage. They had masterminded several raids from this sound proofed room, designed to keep out even the most avid investigator. It also stored most of the equipment they used.

"It wasn't one of us Gerry you know that, it's our way."

"I know Ron I know, but someone did, if not us, if not the family, who?"

"Lawrie get that woman Sergeant followed, she seemed to be right on us and knew everything we'd been doing, her name is Rainbow, Inspector Wyndham was just following her lead, she's the one who had the information."

Gerry went over in his mind the planning for robbing the art gallery, it was airtight and they had staked out the place for weeks. They had told no-one, lost the constant Police tails, it was Trevor who supposedly represented the landlord to the local business disguised as an official workman to create a much needed air vent to link with the supposed ventilation shaft running inside each building. In truth, Trevor never had a clue about ventilation; he was there to make a hole in the brickwork so it created for them a storage area outside in the adjacent alleyway, which proved as it turned out to be invaluable. The Police were only seconds behind them, how he kept asking himself who else knew but us four.

He went over the Police interviews and the account the others gave him, Inspector Wyndham and Sergeant Rainbow were not just fishing or believed they committed the robbery this time they were 100% certain of it. They even suggested how and walked them through their own process for doing it all it would have taken is for them to be caught with the money. They behaved as if someone was sitting on their shoulders watching, uncanny. He needed to make a call to Sophie she would know what was going on.

"Lawrie, it is time we claimed the money out of the gallery wall, the tails should be relaxed now I doubt they think were planning another raid so soon."

"Gerry we'll have to ditch this place won't we?"

"Yes Ron but not quite yet, we'll use this a supposed base and let the Police still be comfortable and make their own mistakes by getting lazy watching meanwhile we'll operate from somewhere else, I have a place in mind already."

Late into the evening, they drove in their black Mercedes frustratingly at varying points changing directions to lose any Police tail they may have.

Driving Lawrie commented. "You know just once I would like to drive somewhere directly, just once,"

"My friend, I'm afraid that suggests a change of career," they both laughed.

On arriving at the Praetown Art gallery they parked by the entrance to its alleyway, Gerry looked straight ahead at the black taxi cab moving away in front of them, briefly he noted the man peering out from its back window barely registering the significance, he seemed familiar, the vehicle disappeared.

It was unusual to see another vehicle this late at night, they had staked out this gallery for several weeks for the best hit times around the upcoming exhibition and early on the Sunday morning directly after the exhibition. On the Saturday having learnt when the gallery would certainly bank the takings on the Monday, extra staff are kept on overnight until early Sunday to package orders and remove any trace of an exhibition, working to return the gallery to its normal business state for the Monday morning. This gave the gang a window of opportunity to rob the gallery.

The staff had been rushing as this gave them a full day to get over the exhibition, Sunday the local businesses were closed, with no residential homes in the area no-one was ever around this late, as he and Lawrie walked down the alleyway he dismissed the cab as paranoia.

It soon returned when Lawrie removed the grill to the wall hole making the comment about it being loose noticing the mortar from the wall on the ground beneath, stretching his arm fully down inside he could not locate the bag put there by himself only sixteen hours before.

"For fucks sake Gerry I think we've been robbed."

Gerry shone the torchlight on the hole in the wall also spotting the misplaced brickwork and dust below. The irony was not lost on him.

"You're right and we've just missed that person by seconds going off in that bloody cab," his head was pounding, for once in his life, he had been outwitted he needed to think and this was not the place to do it. He was angry and it confirmed once again that someone else was on the case. After so many robberies, he was beginning to realise that their time was up. He would not share that with the others just yet. Someone better, than the local plod was wise to them he never wanted prison, but it beckoned if they continued much longer.

"Come on Gerry let's get away from here quickly," Lawrie tugged at his arm and steered him towards the car. "I suppose we could always complain to the Police."

They both nervously laughed realising the implications.

"It's over you do know that Lawrie don't you?"

"Yes I'm afraid I do, we are well and truly marked now, but we'll have a tough time convincing the others."

"I know, I know," his mind filled with the image of the face peering from the back of the cab as it drove away. "Pretty shit day all round."

Chapter 11

The next couple of weeks passed without incident, Michael helped a woman find her husband, sadly, placed in a cemetery deep in the ground, but not before medical science had evaluated his worth to them. With the loss of identification on a decomposed body, the keen 'right of way' activist had not made it home one day from his regular walking jaunts testing the access throughout the area of countryside he had chosen at the time. The coroner after reclaiming released the body to his client for a proper burial. It had taken her two years to find him she would not have without Michael.

Sisters looking for the whereabouts of their maternal mother, having previously been put up for adoption together had come to FMPC in a final attempt to find her, forty year old records were not very helpful to them. Michael gave them their mothers address leading to them walking away because when they met her she did not want to know them.

It was the Chief Executive Officer of a major insurance company who came to see him, which had the biggest effect on FMPC highlighting the seriousness, value and criminal nature of what he could tackle and giving a sense of stability to their business. They offered FMPC a permanent contract to determine whether missing persons were fraudulently claimed for or not and to provide the checks when large policy sums were involved running into several millions. Josey negotiated the deal, it would keep them in business for several years to come he was pleased FMPC had just become respectable and stable, not bad in such a short time.

It was not long before Josey spotted her tail, she thought they were clearly amateurish, in fact, it was the brother of Lawrie Berger, who denied doing anything and claimed it was a coincidence. It told Josey two things, one they were worried and two they were getting closer to Michael.

His walks along the riverbank proved fruitless how quickly his accident forgotten, still only months ago and all trace of the scrap metal yard had disappeared replaced by builders laying housing foundations in its place. With newly erected wooden fencing and wallboard's circling the compound the local council had approved both the purchase and the planning application for residential homes and because of the accident agreed with the local parish council the clearance of the scrap metal site as well. The Roddrick brothers had a result.

Aptly named 'River Bank View' development, it saddened him the only connection to his past was being ripped away, At least the old river barge still existed it was moored opposite in the same place. Repaired following its sale by the man who at the time of the explosion was in the local public house, where apparently he now resides. His old barge now infamous was having its own facelift in order to gain another layer on top, with the intention for it to become a riverside bistro.

Sometimes his mind went to a strange place hoping, wishing for a past and yet he was unable to mourn for something he did not know of. It frustrated the hell out of him, but he had a true purpose in life. Michael had spent some time considering his gift, his quirk of fate as Paul and Josey were inclined to call it.

Even the memory of the riverbank was not a true one it existed after the accident not before.

By looking at photographs and papers, he could generally work out where the person was, dead or alive. His mind was getting used to the rushes that seemed to emerge as if calling the record from the database of his brain. How the information got there he wasn't sure, everyone's theory while he was in the coma, remembering how the monitor was so erratic, there had to be some major electrical download to his brain, quite how and why no-one knew, he found himself rubbing the back of his neck, the burn mark fading gradually over time. No longer hooked up to the monitor, it might have caused the anomaly of initially downloading information there's no way of knowing, but how or why it keeps refreshing minute by minute when following someone's path he couldn't fathom.

Michael felt he was using his gift to help people, how he knew of everyone else and not himself he never understood why, he'd obtained his charred clothing from the Police investigation laboratories and decided to take a picture of himself as well and nothing at all happened. Whenever he did have something of the individual it always helped him not only to determine where the person lives or where they are, but what they are doing at the time and who with. He judged this was his limit he could not read minds or tell if they did commit a crime. Where they had been or what they had previously done he would only get if he had something of theirs to touch. He was as now today, appropriate when he thinking of what he knew of himself in only the past three months since he'd been 'born' and learning to live with who he is.

Opening the letter, he had received from the hospital, in some vain hope of a cure. It stated it was time to re-evaluate his condition he hoped it would help the appointment was scheduled for a week's time.

David had been putting all their successes on file in their computers and Michael was himself impressed with the results, but he wasn't sure what to do about Tom or his father, he knew Tom was a 'plant' the moment he employed him and this was substantiated by how good he was, is. Even David had somehow found out he was being investigated, Josey was also beginning to suspect him now, so she will find out more and supposed she will confront him at some point. Until then Michael would keep his own counsel until Tom decided it was time he knew.

In the corner of the office seemingly forgotten the robbery details and their items lying on the table he did not understand why today, he felt drawn towards the items. It could not harm him if he put them all on and carried the items around with him for a short time in the hope an insight may come to him.

Instantly as if by his own will he had a mental picture, feelings no more than that, of all four of the robbers together in a closed room, touching each item he flipped fast between each, he knew they were together, forcibly slowing his mind down in its thought process he discovered them one at a time. They seemed to be within a car repairs works garage, the pictures as stills in his mind quite strong and focused suggesting the group were preparing themselves, maybe for another raid. This was the first time he had seen people collectively, by flipping it blurred into one picture. Looking at the filing cabinet not daring to open it, he wondered what their reaction had been not finding the money. Guessing about a new robbery being planned he called Josey anyway.

Josey on receiving Smithy's call mobilised everyone possible she was not about to make mistakes. The address he had given her proved a surprise right in the centre of a high street and it was working garage. At last, here was a start the next few days they watched and waited monitoring the comings and goings. Cars regularly went in for servicing or repairs. Each car gauged as to the likely service length or type of repair needed, the license plate numbers were recorded and the staff followed to and from the garage. It showed up as a normal working repair garage with no sign of the group of robbers.

As the process went on, they monitored each cars turnaround and on average, each took no longer than two to three days at most. At first, the Police officers watching were keen wanting instant results, but when they didn't come they became edgy a pattern began emerging where they were able to gauge that two of the entering vehicles after two weeks did not show back out of the garage. Unfortunately, they were not showing as stolen either when they went in the garage. Left with two vehicle numbers recorded these two had to be robbery vehicles they decided to recheck against the car registers highlighting the two vehicles being reported stolen after they had seen them enter the garage it was a breakthrough buoying the team. A light white commercial Ford Transit decorators van and a dark blue Volvo estate, while the gang may change the colours and numbers of the vehicles they could not conceal the type or make.

Michael continued to keep check on the gang member's locations plus when the vehicles moved outside of the garage. The Volvo now silver in colour and the Ford Transit in bright red. A Police vehicle check confirmed the registrations belonged to completely different vehicle types with legitimate number plates.

The moving of the vehicles from the forecourt of the garage took place just after midnight and caught the stake out officers napping literally. After a frantic search of the surrounding area, they admitted they had lost sight of them.

Unknown to Josey who was furious with the officers involved Michael was having trouble sleeping, too much was going on in his mind, he stayed up to chart where each member of the gang were. Soon realising they were always on the move. He looked at the whiteboard on one of the office walls split into four with each section relating to a gang member, each were coming from differing locations.

He could not tell for sure but one of the gang he thought was Gerry Fielder drove a car and stopped a mile from the garage left it there and started walking back toward the garage. Lawrie Berger drove from his home left his car a mile from the garage and walked. Trevor Cole had been at the garage and driven the Volvo, Ron Fielder had taken the Transit. Ron picked up Gerry and Trevor picked up Lawrie, the gang were on the move, his brain bursting with the complexities splitting his mind into four different ways his temples throbbed.

Wearing their items, Michael was frantically working out their route tracing them to an obscure industrial warehousing estate on the outskirts of Ashford to a specific unit 22 and they stayed there. It was two days before Josey got in touch, ringing his mobile and admitted, they had completely lost the gang two of them had quietly entered the garage premises late at night picked up keys and drove the vehicles off the forecourt. It caught the surveillance team napping.

After realising, they had lost them Josey and her team entered the garage premises that night and found the hidden back room, it was empty.

"But you do know where they are now don't you Josey?" he started to get uneasy. "I knew you were busy so I didn't get in touch, I thought you had them covered."

"Frankly no, we were hoping you might know."

"Forgive me for saying this Josey, but I thought this was top priority and you had to catch them in the act, they could've by now carried out whatever raid they wanted and been long gone, no wonder they've been so successful, " he was astonished.

"Smithy, get off that high horse of yours, for God's sake if you know where they are tell me please I'm aware we messed up big time," angry he was right, she just didn't want to be told.

He gave her unit 22"s address. She hung up obviously upset.

During the following three day's, Josey's team of officers now on high alert monitored the gang's movements, every now and then they would lose a member of the gang only for him to return to the unit. What the three days proved to the Police is that each one of the gang members could lose their tail easily. They were being monitored and although Gerry Fielder couldn't understand how, they were found again, once more he realised the Police were being helped, never the less, he intended to use it to their advantage feeling he held the cards the gang knew when the robbery would take place and most importantly they knew which one they would go for.

Once again, Michael realised when each were missing according to Josey's team, he tracked them to four places of interest they were alternating their individual time at each location. This cleverly meant they could keep all four options open until the very end and still have information on the other three for a later raid. There was also the attraction of having in place three decoy locations, which inevitably splits the resources the Police, have. A twenty-five percent chance of success not deemed the greatest of odds and they knew the Police would know this. Michael started to respect the man's intelligence and planning skills, something nagged him in his brain, related but unrelated, someone else was involved, he shrugged letting the thought go.

His arrival that morning at the William Harvey hospital felt like he was coming home, the appointment with Mr Geoffrey Broadacre his consultant would be routine nothing more. He followed the signs to the Neurological department and sat in its waiting room having purchased a number from a ticket machine.

Number 33 was called and he followed the waiting nurse towards a small room housing Mr Broadacre to his surprise and his favourite nurse Sister Jocelyn, he hugged her like a long lost friend and shook the stout man's hand standing up to greet him, family he thought feeling at home.

The consultant coughed loudly masking his embarrassment at the familiarity between them all.

"How are you Michael, you're looking very well?"

He grinned fondly at Sister Jocelyn. "I am very well, fit and pursuing an active life."

"What about your memory?" he was familiarising himself with Michael's medical case notes.

"No luck there I'm afraid still the same, blank as ever."

"Any recall at all, images, dreams, thoughts, deja'vue that sort of thing?

"Unfortunately nothing at all."

"Ok, what I've arranged if you have the time is to have another Magnetic Resonance Imaging or MRI scan it is a technique to have a look at the internal parts of your brain. I have arranged for you to talk to one of our laboratory technicians who looked at the monitoring machine we had you linked to when you were last with us, he'd like to carry out further tests with you if you don't mind?"

"Not at all anything if you think it will help," his expectations low.

"Yes it may, there is one other process we could try," the consultant looked closer at him for reaction. "So far we have been looking at you in a physical sense, harm to the brain, lost brain cells but if you were mentally shutting up shop so to speak, I might be recommending you see a psychotherapist."

"Do you mean you think I'm imagining the state I'm in," his hair bristled at the back of his neck.

"No, no, let me explain. The mind is a complex tool for the human being, as a self-preservation mechanism when there is danger or trauma it could shut down. Remembering becomes difficult, places become harder to find, people get lost off the radar, mental blocks stand in the way of someone being who a person really is."

"Are you saying I could be blocking out something from my past?"

"It's a possibility Michael," Jocelyn touched his arm in comfort. "We have to consider it."

"So you're saying I'm avoiding thinking about problems, blanking them out?" He recalled the moment he recognised the boy on TV when in his hospital room and Josey's accusations.

"No what I'm saying is because of the accident your mental state has become locked, induced a form of mental self-preservation, something to hide from, shutting out reality, it is only a theory."

"It is treatable in most cases if it's what we think it could be we've no way of knowing until we test you further."

"What do you want me to do," he was resigned to anything Geoffrey Broadacre could throw at him he gave him his trust.

After the MRI scan and you've seen Darren our technician in the laboratory, I'd like you to see our own psychotherapist her name is Doctor Annabelle Churchill and she'll run some tests on you," he looked at Michael closely it was a puzzling case. "Mmm good, for now I'll leave you in Sister Jocelyn's capable hands."

He and Sister Jocelyn held onto to each other's arms as she took him to have his scan assuring him she would wait. He loved her as family, he felt she also loved him in the same way and suspected she had never gotten this close to a patient before, traumatic in her line of work, vowing he would keep her friendship forever.

The scanner is a tunnel one to two metres in length surrounded by a large circular magnet. Laying on the couch that slides into the scanner. He understood it is supposed to pick up radio signals from the body. Keeping very still for about 30 minutes made it become uncomfortable, the whole process a very noisy experience despite the music played through the headphones supplied.

"Come on then Michael," she grabbed his hand as he came out and steered him towards the laboratory technicians department.

She introduced him to both Darren and Kelly recalling for Michael how the Neurodiagnostic machine had been behaving and that Darren wanted to talk to him now he had woken up.

"Michael it really, really bugs me about not being able to work out how this happened to you," Darren suggested. "So can I hook you back up to the machine again, but with an initial test on Kelly here?"

Placing the electrodes of the machine on Kelly's forehead, even Michael could see the patterns were normal.

Darren then placed them on Michael with the immediate effect even now some three months later the monitor was struggling with the peaks and troughs of the output almost bursting to get out.

"Still impressive isn't it Sister?" offered Darren. "Michael I don't have a cure, but having looked at your notes thanks to Sister Jocelyn, I have a couple of theories you may like to ponder on. The first is before your accident you could've been involved in some program, maybe even a Government one that was trying out drugs or diseases on you to assess response, medical science that type of thing."

He looked at them believing they were crazy.

"Look before you object there's a drug Midazolam which can induce amnesia, a few other drugs on the market can have a similar effect, but this is the proven one."

"Amnesia means patients would have difficulty recalling the past, but have conscious access to the present it's a form of encoding the brain to not remember anything personal and seemingly remembering a general level of education, influences without any relationship towards events or historical times."

"How does that suggest the Government being involved," it puzzled Michael.

"I only offer this as no-one in their right mind, would do it freely to themselves, there are numerous projects worldwide malicious or not which could go wrong and you may be a part of it, your release could be intentional or an accident and you could be being monitored."

"Bit cloak and dagger stuff isn't it?"

"It could just as easily be used as a cure, for say a deep rooted depression," Jocelyn considered. "The only cure requiring the elimination of memories."

"I did offer it as a theory only, no more," he went

on noting Michael's pained expression. "The other one I have is electroconvulsive therapy or ECT, having looked at your notes Michael are you aware you could have suffered an electric shock during your accident."

He shook his head no-one had mentioned this to him although he had wondered about the burn mark on his neck.

"Well it's in your notes as a possibility the key issue is they had to shut down the local electrical substation when they found you as it had become activated to a live state, presumably 'on impact'."

"What impact?"

"You my friend, my theory is, it became live when you hit it with such force during the explosion bouncing off the river barge and into the substation gates."

"You've done your homework," Sister Jocelyn noted.

"Is that to do with the burn mark on my back at the top of my spine?"

"Yes does it hurt?"

"No Jocelyn only when my brain is overworked," he avoided talking about his skill in front of the technicians.

"Look there's no suggestion you have suffered because of contact with electricity but we cannot rule out some sort of electric current directly or indirectly running through your body at some point as a result of impact to culminate in the burn mark left behind," Kelly suggested.

"Again, picking up the point made by Sister about drugs being a cure for deep rooted depression, so is an ECT or an electric shock. My theory is while your brain suffered such trauma during the explosion with the "bounce" losing you those vital memory brain cells, ECT"s have shown that while they don't cause brain damage, certain types of shock, electric shock has been known to cause persistent memory loss. Unfortunately the degree is individual."

"What you're saying is don't bother trying to regain my memory, because the varying combinations involved in my accident would have undoubtedly erased brain cells and consequently my memory for ever."

Darren grimaced leaning his head to one side raising his eyebrows acknowledging the point and agreeing.

This was a new way of looking at his condition and Michael was grateful to him for showing it to him.

"Bear in mind Michael, it is just a theory, either drugs or the ECT variation," Kelly sympathetically offered.

"None the less it's a bloody good one," he felt saddened at a loss he would never know and did not expect when he turned up at the hospital earlier. It obviously made sense not to keep chasing a memory, which would never reappear.

Looking at both Darren and Kelly, he thanked them both for their efforts and walked with Jocelyn slowly taking in the comments. "Now where to Jocelyn?"

"Second floor at the other end of the building,"

she held him tightly he was downbeat they walked together silently.

Inside Doctor Annabelle Churchill's wide office, everything placed neatly matter of fact reflecting its owner's personality. She observed him from behind her silver round rimmed glasses stroking her grey hair flattening an already plain stretched back style culminating into a small bun inches above her neckline.
"Leave us please Sister," Michael nodded to Jocelyn he would be ok.

"Please sit down Mr Smith, has Mr Broadacre told you what we will be doing here today?"
He shook his head, no doubt he did not want to scare him off, and she was scary he thought.
"What we are going to do is to treat you as if you have a trauma related disorder, this means as if you have had exposure to a traumatic or distressing event," she paused for effect. "I note that you were involved in an explosion of some sort several months ago, good, let us get started.
Michael thought she would be just as happy running the test on her own.
"The test or treatment is called EMDR which stands for Eye Movement Desensitisation and Reprocessing," she offered.
"Is this where you reprocess me? So what will I become a dog or a cat?" He joked.
"Please Mr Smith sit in front of this panel of lights, I want you to think of a pleasant place you have been in your mind," she ignored his stab at humour coldly. "We may need more sessions, but this quick test will determine whether we could get results by working together."

"So let me get this straight you want me to get to a pleasant place in my mind where I have no memory but for the past few months, where I've been hurled through the air whacked my head bounced back and hit my head again. At the same time probably electrocuting myself in the process and for these months I've been a mental cripple and you want me to find a good place in my mind, I don't believe this," he did of course, but fed up with her attitude, he thought of Josey and relaxed.

"Please work with me on this, you've surely got something pleasant to consider?"

The bar in front of him showed a row of lights. Suddenly he felt her soften towards him speaking gently.

"There are not many advances in psychotherapy, as a rule, however I gather you've had numerous tests without success so we felt at least we owed you a shot at a new advance."

"Tell me what I have to do Doctor," he said placating her. "We are going to activate these lights so you can follow them with your eyes the idea is any unprocessed parts of your memory particularly of a traumatic event. We are hoping you retain high levels of sensory and emotional intensity even though several months have passed since your accident, I can assure you we have had some quite good sustainable results in other patients," she stated proudly doing her best to pacify him as far as her own temperament would allow.

He did not really understand, but he listened intently. "It's what we call a bilateral stimulation of the brain so where have previously shut out a trauma it will bring it into the present day, to the fore so to speak without harm, enabling you, the patient to deal with it on today's terms."

Once the lights started moving she directed him to watch the lateral movements of the lights, she made hand-tapping sounds and asked him a series of questions to do with what he could remember of the present, past and the future. She quickly appreciated he had no past for her to even begin to work with, his present and future appeared to satisfy him, she realised she couldn't help him.

"I'm afraid unusually I cannot help you, there is no demonstration that you mentally have suffered from the accident, but neither do you have any recall of such events before and immediately after, truly remarkable although our test was very brief and extremely crude, through experience I can tell whether I can help and I can't. I'm sorry," her manner, although kindly was blunt, refreshingly so he thought, at that point he felt dismissed no longer useful to her, escaping he found himself back out in the corridor and searching for Sister Jocelyn he explained to her what had happened. Doctor Annabelle Churchill was already speaking to Geoffrey Broadacre on the telephone.

After a very brief catch up with his consultant and the promise of future appointments the results of the day except for the MRI scan ones proved to be negative in terms of him ever regaining a memory or any old life he might have had, they solemnly together walked back towards the entrance of the hospital.

He looked at his dear, dear friend in Sister Jocelyn. "I doubt the results of the MRI scan will show up anything different will it?"

She shook her head sadly holding him tight. "You

must keep hoping Michael and believe nature will find a way."

"Time to get on with my life isn't?" He kissed her gently goodbye holding her two hands in his, letting go slowly he walked sombrely towards the car park, turning once to wave, she had disappeared back inside the hospital, unknown to him, full of tears, she walked hurriedly back to her ward, attempting to shrug off her sadness for him.

Before returning to the office Michael decided rather than mentally picture the four place's he knew the gang were considering to rob and why, he would go and see them for himself and hopefully see one of the gang members there.

The first place appeared initially to be a jeweller's, he had read they would not want the hassle of getting rid of the goods. A closer look he realised it was actually a pawnbroker's and money-lender they should have a fair supply of cash with people either taking items back or placing them in for cash.

Sitting in the taxicab outside the small shop he dismissed this location as not being 'Rich Pickings' enough for the gang. He also thought that a pawnbroker himself would be a type of help to the poor, the gang might not want to take from him, who knows what connections the pawnbroker had he decided it wasn't the one.

The second was an amusement arcade and again plenty of cash floating around but mostly in machines, they'd never go for coins so that would be a no too, he wondered if the Police thought this way. He walked around the arcade as the taxicab waited for him, change machines and the glass box of an office with its serving change window would be the only places to retrieve cash notes confirming his thoughts that this was a no-go, he gave the driver a new address. The third was a fair possibility, this was a shopping mall outside of the previous radius at 28 miles, security guards periodically, would be entering each shop at varying intervals. Their role it appeared was to remove cash takings from each of the stores and securely protect it until the end of each day, each collection in its own small metal box. He later learnt, this reduced the losses that could be incurred by a 'chancer' a robber who would just make a grab at a till for the cash and run.

He also found out robbing from the shopping complexes offices was far easier than at the individual store itself with the 'have a go' public around to interfere with them, all they had to do was to pick up the readily boxed cash takings. Simple if you had the nerve and this gang certainly had that.

The final location was definitely a favourite, a London football club just on the edge of the 25-mile radius his taxicab drove around the stadium and back again it had easy access to the ground itself on match days. With an average attendance of forty thousand at an average of fifty pounds entrance together with bar, snacks and restaurant takings combined with the retail outlet side for team strips, scarves and varying sporting memorabilia, programmes and souvenirs. The likely take on a good home match day was likely to be above the one to two million-pound mark and although the money was kept secure in the safe it would likely be kept on the premises until Mondays banking day or collected by a security service.

When Michael discussed his findings with Paul,

Josey, Tom and David, he learnt the football club does use a security service the takings picked up directly by security van during the second half of the match. Any further monies made on the day would be left to bank until the following business banking day, which in the case of a Saturday or Sunday match would be Monday.

The shopping mall's cash boxes picked-up in exactly the same way during the late afternoons trading where there would likely be less public around to affect the process. Both offered good security and both, would be a good haul for the robbers as a better challenge they all agreed the football club represented by far for the gang a bigger return of the two with the greater risk. If they had not been following them, they would have a far better chance of success. The only thing now left to do was wait and see which one they would choose.

Paul and Josey had agreed with the two locations nearby Police stations they would jointly cover the sites along with Ashford Police as they were already tracking the robbers.

Chapter 12

Gerry Fielder was worried, he was normally so confident when planning for a raid, but this time the gang had been pulled in several times by the Police recently. They had almost gotten caught last time out and they were approaching their next job angry, always dangerous and angry at losing the money. If they as group had not been so tight and trusted each other completely that anger could have turned within. He did not understand why his Police contact had not turned up anything. Sophie, his and Ron's cousin by marriage, had helped them on several occasions but this time she couldn't get near to finding out what was being planned by either Josey Rainbow or Inspector Wyndham. All she knew they were spending a lot of time in Maidstone and in London, she would try to find out why and who they were with, they were being followed, somehow they knew of the four locations he had been assessing. Only he knew which one they were going to do, for now they were safe from capture, but it unnerved him. Already they knew of the high street garage. In future, they would have to be more careful. He was feeling a pressure he had never had before almost like someone was watching all the time. He shrugged it was impossible he told himself. It was unlike when they had first started, the Police did not have a clue at the time so they did not have to worry about where they were based. Over time, inevitably even they could work out who was responsible, so each time the preparation had to be that much better, tighter and slicker with no clues left behind.

He admitted to himself, they had become so confident he had set up a coding system as an arrangement with the Police. It served three purposes, allowing friends to carry out robberies with the Police looking directly at them unable to prove anything. They would also get away with the odd robbery themselves because the Police has gotten used to him owning up to the prospect a robbery could take place by code at times they never gave them one. Lastly, it helped raise their own game giving them an edge. Lately he had stopped alerting the Police, they found out anyway.

They moved into the high street garage in the centre of Tonbridge where he felt they would be away from prying eyes, but he knew the Police were onto them so he chose the industrial unit. His trust in his own brother Ron and his adopted brothers Trevor and Lawrie was absolute together they were solid.

Someone else had to be involved outside, helping the Police. Lawrie's brother had tried to tail Sergeant Rainbow she was being too clever, but generally went into Maidstone to a block of residential apartments and business offices combined. She always went to an organisation called FMPC who dealt with missing persons. The owner was a man named Michael Smith he also had an apartment in the same block. Lawrie had taken over from his brother and followed the man to Ashford where he visited the William Harvey hospital. Lawrie lost him in the maze of hospital corridors and departments but not before taking his photograph. The research on him turned up that he had been the man who had been involved, injured in a gas explosion at a scrap metal yard a few months back on the banks of the river Gerry remembered reading of it. The man had spent a couple of months in hospital, no memory and no history he dismissed him as not having any relevance until he looked at the man's photograph.

It hit Gerry like a hammer, not only was he looking at the man who stared at him in the Police station sitting down by the kid in a wheelchair, while he was being booked out, this was the face that peered out of the back of the taxi cab at the gallery when they went back for the money. This Michael Smith, worked with the Police and had taken his money they must be laughing at them waiting patiently for the gang to ask for their money back, very amusing. They would never see it now, he took comfort from the fact the Police may have the money but still could not prove they did the raid. Gerry would never know Michael never handed the money back to the gallery or into the Police.

"Sophie you need to find out anything you can on a Michael Smith, what's his involvement with the Inspector and our raids."

"Gerry you shouldn't be calling me at work, right now there's loads of activity and manpower being used determined to catch you, I'm not sure where this Smith fits in, he only seems to be the boyfriend of Sergeant Rainbow. He actually gives me the creeps he keeps staring at me."

"He doesn't suspect you of helping us does he?"

"Why would he what can he know, anyhow what I do know is ever since he's been around our success rate in missing persons has hit the roof."

Gerry figured if he was a professional owning a missing persons bureau he could also be a consultant to the Police.

"Find out all you can Sophie and keep me posted its important," worried he realised he may have to 'solve' the problem another way.

Later that day the others began arriving at the new industrial unit Ron and Trevor were the car men and spent their time making sure they were ready. Gerry decided not to mention to them or Lawrie about Michael Smith and their money.
"When and where Gerry, it's time we honed into a particular location and type of raid we are going to do," Ron appealed to his brother. "We're too split in our efforts and besides we need the cash."
"Haven't you had enough?"

"Ron's right Gerry, its make your mind up time."

"I know that Lawrie, but I'm not getting good vibes about any raid this time, we were almost caught the last time out, Police know about the four locations it's obvious when we turn up at them, we may easily give them the slip but they've always been waiting. The real problem is they may know of this unit which by now means whatever happens this is the only job we can use this place for." He looked at him frowning. "You know by now they have to know about the stolen vehicles meaning they could raid us at any time, if they followed any of us back here."

"I wonder why they don't," now Lawrie was sharing his concern.

"Isn't it obvious?"

"Not to me."

"The Police want to catch us in the act for robbery not car theft, which is why we have to choose our next job carefully."

"Why don't we just cancel and walk away?"

"You know it is not that easy we've all got commitments, how long do you think we'd survive going straight without money to protect us."

"I don't believe that applies now we've made tenfold for everyone, the family's needs, have to be satisfied by now they're lucky we haven't been caught."

"So you're saying we should get ourselves a different career?"

"Good God Gerry, I never said go straight!" The two men laughed as the great friends they were. "As to the cars that hasn't worried us before once the job's done the cars will never be seen again, if they are watching us they already know about the cars, I agree they want to get us for a bigger crime."

"That's true and they can't know about the security van and uniforms, we have because we've had them for months now. They could not link that to us three months ago, I also doubt Securias reported the van and uniforms missing." Gerry had previously talked the others into stealing an empty security van for future use, the company never made it known publicly, in part because of the embarrassment but it was the loss of faith in the company, which was more important to them. They'd hidden it and had to move it from the high street so they let the Police who were covering the garage believe they were in a rush to escape making them follow, meanwhile Gerry waited and drove the van to this new industrial unit, it now safely covered up inside behind a false wall.

On a totally unrelated opportunity, they'd also stolen four security guards uniforms and radios. With the technology in the security van and radio, they were able to monitor the frequency the security controllers used at the Securias Company.

Securias immediately tightened their own security around each van replaced the missing one and were confident in their protection on routes and locations where they picked up and dropped off large amounts of cash, relying on their sophistication why would they worry about an empty vehicle there wasn't any sign of for the past three months.

The uniforms were more of a concern because of impersonating security officers, after two months without incidents they put it down to stock errors and never would relate the two thefts.

Securias were even more confident when Detective Constable Sophie Mason called on behalf of Inspector Paul Wyndham of Ashford Police station checking on the routes and pick up times of their armoured vans for the following Saturday's football club and Lakeside Shopping Mall pick up's. Routine she told them so they could cover the sites assuring them of safety. She asked they checked back to the Police station to verify who she was and if confident to fax the times and routes, she gave them a number to use.

Gerry was patient and bided his time of their use. He was amused to note the security company was so confident in themselves and their procedures the company never even bothered to put a radio lock on either the stolen van or walkie-talkies and worst of all did not change the radio frequencies.

When Trevor brought in the lunchtime sandwiches, the four of them sat down together.

"I think we should reduce the targets to two what do you all think?"

"About bloody time Gerry you've never run this number for so long before now,"

"Shut up Ron, he knows what he's doing he always plans what we do."

"I know that Trevor but we seem to have spent so long fluffing about, it's had to increase our chances of being caught this time."

"I don't agree the only worry I would have is about the security van, the transit and the car are made so they are untraceable. We have resprayed and changed number plates on those. The security van has to stay exactly the same as those in service."

"Lawrie after this job all three will be dumped, I'm more worried about the Police tailing us and knowing about this place and I don't like to say this but someone is talking. There's no other explanation."

Ron immediately stood up by his brother in a show of solidarity.

"Sit the fuck down Ron it is not one of us we've

been far too successful to crap on each other now."

"Trevor's right, its outside of us four and what we need to do is examine what we've said and to who. Friends and families are solid as rocks you all know that Gerry, they've been questioned so many times if they were going to talk we'd be inside already."

"Gerry it occurred to me, maybe Sophie?"

"Unthinkable Ron, she would have too much to lose, her career for one and the other she's been our fifth member for us as long as I can remember, besides she would have the worst of it if she ended up in prison."

"I also agree with Lawrie but how did they know where our last job was combined with the loss of our money, what about the tails we all have now every bloody where we go."

"What are you saying Gerry we should call off all the jobs?"

"No Ron, because they cannot know whether we are going to do one at all, which one or where it is, that's still in my head."

"What are the two then Gerry?" Lawrie knew how they always operated eight to six to four and then to two.

"It's either the football club or the shopping complex. Both of them will be served by the security van we have"

Each nodded in agreement appreciating his foresight in obtaining it.

"Good, I didn't fancy Goldhursts Pawnbrokers he's a funny old bugger, I've heard he carries grudges to his grave. If he found out it was us I'd be worried about my legs at a minimum."

"You've always been shitless," laughed Ron at

Trevor, the others joined in.

"Bollocks I'm just stating facts, he's not worth messing with, that's all I'm saying."

"The arcade I never fancied much, coins mostly and not enough cash notes."

Yes you're right Lawrie but both were being used as decoys."

"So when are we going to do one of them Gerry, the family are waiting to get away on holiday?" The rest groaned.

"Gear yourself up for after next weekend, we have to make sure this place is cleared and clean of us afterwards."

"No point in trying them both, I suppose?" A thoughtful Lawrie suggested. "While we've got the van, that is."

Gerry's eyes lit up. "Now that would be a challenge."

Not until the next day Gerry realised the high street garage had been searched the signs of dust, papers and furniture not quite put back in the right places. It was lucky they relocated in time thanks to his own informant he only left some old diagrams and odd papers to pick up. He wondered how long their luck would run for this was the one job he was not comfortable with. The job or jobs themselves were ok to do watched so closely was like being in a strait jacket. Smiling to himself, he was considering doing both, although outside their normal patch, the both were within a few miles of each other.

Chapter 13

"Are we Ok Josey?" It was the first time for a couple of weeks they had been alone together.

He had changed, becoming more used to helping people find loved ones Penny had purchased a brown leather two-seater sofa for relatives to be more comfortable when asking him for help and this was where both sat together holding each other in his office.

"Oh Smithy, my feelings for you are very special, but we need to get this gang caught and I'm conscious you might feel I'm using you," she held him closer to her.

"How much do you know of Tom?" she asked quietly.

"You really mean how much do I know of his father Miles Broughton and why Tom came here in the first place."

"Yes I'm convinced Tom is not the novice he portrays himself to be."

"I've never had any doubts that Tom is quite an experienced investigator, too good for us, unwittingly from the moment I shook his hand, when I gave him the job I knew."

"Surprise me why on earth did you hire him? He could be dangerous Smithy, MI5 or MI6 with involvement in espionage, terrorism," she despaired worried for him.

"Well connected then," he joked.

"It's not funny Smithy," she scolded. "His father will want you to work for him you know that."

"I know and I probably will on my terms, I could find it interesting, but he will have to ask."

"You could find yourself dead," she wished she had not said that. "Be careful please my love I beg you, I don't want to lose you now I've found you."

Michael realised he didn't have the fears that age bestows upon every individual where as you gradually age sobriety kicks in and beyond youth we attempt unconsciously to lessen risk in everything we do. He had no base except what he gathered during the past three months, not any lifetime experiences of breaking or spraining an arm or leg, bruising, cuts even falling over drunk it just never happened to him as far as his memory was concerned, although he gained a healthy awareness of gas and electricity dangers.

When his mind opened up to him finally which he hoped it will one day, he would then have a point of reference. Right now, how people behaved to each other for or against he had no experience. If his memory returned maybe he would develop many fears or issues, his overriding concern has to be if his 'gift' disappeared he hoped not.

Not difficult for Josey to know all there was, is, about him, the night was for him, getting to know her far more.

By nine the next morning Josey was gone he realised during the night every now and again he would close his eyes for what he thought was a second only to find three hours had passed. His temples throbbed knowing this was the way he received 'updates' much like the infuriating updates on a computer when connected to the net. His thoughts went to the hospital monitor he shook himself determined not to get depressed recalling his hospital check-up.

What alarmed him he was not wearing the robber's items, he had forgotten them so began to put them on filling his pockets except for the crowbar which would not fit anywhere. Within literally a split second an impression came to him, he started to develop words he associated with getting awareness of the individuals involved. He was gaining a "fix" on each of the men as "pictorially" they entered his brain updated. Sometimes he wondered whether he was a human being or a robot, his brain behaving like a computer, he thought back to his earliest memory, it never budged he was in hospital and Josey greeted him as he woke, he remembered her softly, gently kissing him, that memory the best he has.

All four of the gang were at a place he did not recognise and there looked to be three vehicles he judged they had moved from the garage and moved to the industrial estate, unit 22 on the outskirts of Ashford.

He gave Josey and her Inspector Paul Wyndham the information who had also discounted two of the four likely raids, leaving the shopping mall and the football club. At the weekend both places would be full of people and traffic, it was late in the afternoon. Josey never understood why there was a third vehicle either they had accounted for all of them in and out of the building, but they had to make a decision which one to cover the club or the mall. She decided on the mall, on the basis too many people would be at the football match to challenge them.

The security van with Gerry driving, Trevor riding shotgun in the front passenger seat, Ron drove the car and Lawrie the small van. All drove out of unit 22 at 5am and made their way towards the M20 motorway at junction 10.

Mid-morning, Paul Wyndham was on the telephone to Michael. "Where the hell are they? Can you see them?" No realising how much he had gotten used to Michael's skill and taking it for granted.

"Three of the men Gerry, Lawrie and Trevor are in Epping, the other Ron is in Enfield, I'm not sure what vehicles are involved or where they are, the journey started from the industrial unit and stopped at a lorry park close to the 10th junction of the M20 motorway. Ron went direct to Enfield the other three have only just arrived in Epping."

"What the bloody hell are they doing there?" A frustrated Inspector spoke to anyone who was listening. "They were supposed to be going towards the shopping mall on the M25 motorway at Thurrock."

Kick off at the football ground is at 3pm, the ground closes at 6pm, the shopping mall closes at 8pm.

A number of assumptions were made by Paul and Josey, one being the football ground would be too busy with heavy traffic to be viable for the gang to rob and secondly the mall was favourite with the cash pick up expected after 8pm. They believed it to be the target as the offices back onto what would be, by then, an empty car park and getaway would be easier than the football club, it meant they didn't bother to find out the routes or pick up times from the security company. It proved to be a mistake, as did their assumptions. Sophie Mason had only passed the details onto Gerry Fielder and not to her police colleagues.

Josey just received word that the Securias Company confirmed their security van destined for the Premier League football ground had just left with three men on board. It was 4.15pm.
"They're early Paul."

"No matter just check in with Michael again would you Josey, I thought we had hours yet."

Josey unsure if she had made the right decision her team began monitoring vehicle X818 on the way to the football ground. The security firm's controller rang the operations desk of the club to say the vehicle would be delayed they were not in an accident, but were affected by one and were assured the delay would not be too long.

The security vehicle arrived roughly ten minutes late as expected made a quick pick up and were on their way within fifteen minutes.

Mentally, Michael kept a fix on all four members of the gang. Ron had been driving a car and had stopped in the busy high street of Enfield. Both Trevor and Gerry parked out of town outside Epping down a small country lane, soon joined by Lawrie in the small van left in the lane as they moved on.

Michael had spent fifteen minutes trying to get in

touch with Josey for an update when he finally got through, she told him the security van had been held up by an accident up ahead, but was now moving towards the ground.

"I've been trying to tell you Gerry, Lawrie and Trevor have just left the ground seemingly in the third vehicle I mentioned," not understanding he continued. "And Ron had been held up in Enfield town."

Inspector Wyndham at that point gave her the news that the security firm had informed them their security van is now on its way to the football ground, they were going to relay this information to the club.

They put Michael on their conference speaker telephone.

Josey told Michael as the Inspector spoke to her.

"What's the matter Michael?"

"For God's sake you pair," he said frustratingly. "Don't you understand what's happened Gerry and company have already left the stadium meaning the third vehicle is a bloody security van and more importantly they've just gotten away with raiding the football club."

Within minutes, the arrival of the second security vehicle caused the club to go crazy, they had handed all the day's takings to a rogue set of security guards.

"Oh Christ, what do we do now Michael they've got away again?"

"For God's sake you're asking me police people! Take down this address, it is just outside of Epping, it is a deserted lane. Ron should be there already and the other three are driving there right now."

"Paul wants to speak to you Michael can you stay on the line, I know we cocked up again, but please help us."

"Look I suggest you watch them go into the lane and shut off both ends or whatever you Police do."

Paul, they've got a security van, you'll have to wait for them to transfer to the small van."

"Josey get the team out there now, watch and wait this is our one chance if they leave the lane with the small van and car. They'll be dumped and God knows where the money will be then."

"Get going, for Christ's sake!"

When they got to the lane there was no sign of anyone, Ron had met them earlier than intended and took the cash from the security van and drove ahead of them fast towards the shopping complex. The same ploy was going to be used to stop another Security van from the Securias vehicle number X821 in traffic, meanwhile a similar message, will be relayed to the controllers. Unfortunately, because of a 6pm shift change of the controllers when the message came in from the real van suggesting lateness the controller relayed the message to the shopping mall without suspicion.

While Josey and part of her team were placating the football club directors over their cash loss no call came in to inform them of the likely X821 delay for the shopping mall, why would it the controllers treated it like any other day.

"Christ they're doing two raids," she phoned her Inspector who mobilised everyone possible. "And they're earlier than we anticipated."

Meanwhile the X821 stopped in Dartford because of a supposed accident. The Securias vehicle followed by the Police, with the traffic jam causing them to arrive on the scene by foot by having to leave their cars. Quick to arrive at the scene, having caused the jam Ron was already gone.

"Michael where are they now?" He was still on standby by conference call.
"They are at the shopping mall right now picking up the cash boxes, for God's sake hurry," they were too late.
Paul had directed as many officers he could to hit the industrial unit 22. When the Police arrived at the unit, there was no evidence it had been thoroughly cleaned, the uniforms were in the car but true to form, the security van was also clean with no trace of them. Lawrie was caught bleach spraying the whole van while the others caught with the football club and mall money forcing open the cash boxes to split the proceeds just before leaving the unit.
The gang were caught red handed the irony being if they had stuck to one raid they would have escaped, a matter of minutes and Michael had caught them out.

Paul invited Michael to view the interrogation through double-sided mirrors. He watched each of them who had previously been so sure of themselves now demonstrate their individual horror at being caught knowing full well they would spend a good deal of time behind bars, the sheer weight of thought when it dawned their lifestyle was over was enough punishment. Each member could not help but admit to the crime, they wanted to understand how they had been caught they would never be told, but Gerry suspected it had to be Michael Smith's responsibility.

Lawrie realised his family holiday would have to wait, probably for a long, long time.

Michael recognised the gang's departure from the other planned raids proved their undoing, they were not able to effectively, hide the money too much activity and too much urgency this time around.

Chapter 14

Michael, now the robbery case is over I need to talk to you!" Tom was leaning over the desk nervously twitching.

"Do you want to leave us Tom, the missing person's bureau I mean, we will be very sad to see you go?" Michael played with him, knowing he was trying to confess, he smiled to himself as he watched Tom squirm.

"No I don't, but there is something you need to know about me."

"Do you mean your father Miles Broughton and that you actually work for a higher security service rather than us or the Police, MI5 or is it MI6 Tom?"

"Yes, MI6 you knew?" He would never fathom the man out.

"Oh yes Tom and that's actually why you were useful to me."

"And why was that?"

"Because I'm guessing your father would want to keep a watchful eye on our activities in the hope of using me one day, he would also be protective towards his son thus, he would watch our backs."

"How long have you known?"

"Since the day you first walked in from the Job Centre, oh you made all the right noises and would've convinced anyone to give you a job, but you were too good and not forgetting I have the sort of skill that can check on anyone."

"Why didn't you say something to me?"

"To what end, I needed you to help with starting up the bureau, quite frankly I didn't see what MI5/MI6 or whatever had to do with me, I'm hardly in the James Bond league am I, just missing persons, so I just thought I'd let it play out and you'd tell me eventually."

"I'm so sorry if I've deceived you Michael, sincerely I am."

"Come on no harm done, you've done a fantastic job for me, I hope you can stay."

"If you want me to, gladly."

"How are you going to work for two organisations?"

"I want to leave MI6," knowing it would be difficult, as his father would try to stop him.

"Good that's settled then," he said not wishing to make it a problem.

"Will you see him Michael?"

"What will your father want from me Tom?"

"I think he'll want to explore your skill to the full."

"What does that mean all I do is try to find people?"

"I guess he'll settle for that to start with."

"Ok Tom can you arrange a meeting sometime."

"Would 2pm today be alright?"

"I am tempted to say no to see what happens how about that Tom?" his eyebrows raised knowing there was not a choice.

At 2pm Michael arrived at the Vauxhall Cross MI6 Headquarters, the young man who greeting him showed a keen interest in why he was there to see Mr Broughton as if his life would be assured once he'd given over the information to him. Michael told him the truth, he just did not know. The young man became very suspicious, but let it go. Must be this place paranoia had to be rife in this line of work. Michael entered a large corner office overlooking the River Thames.

"Thank you for coming at such short notice Mr Smith, we appreciate your time."

Michael looked around the empty office for someone else to join the 'we' together, he was amused already and wondered whether people who spoke this way actually realised how stupid it sounded.

Miles Broughton offered an outstretched hand taking Michael's in greeting.

Michael smiled subserviently almost as if he was in the presence of some king like person. The office full of light had to be the best position in the building with panoramic views across the Thames River complimented by modern furniture and technology strategically placed, Michael bet he had worked hard to obtain the illusion of ultimate power. Political heads are one thing for the media, this man Head of Covert operations made it work, a dangerous man to cross.

As much as Tom's father was seeking to create an impression of dominance, Michael took the view he had only been 'alive' the last few months he couldn't care not phased, by any attempt to unsettle him. Having just shaken the hand of the man who unwittingly had been informing him of his own life's journey as well as one or two of the world's secrets because of his very touch.

Miles Broughton an astute well-rounded man recognised this as a quality in Michael immediately and instantly became wary of the man he had just shook the hand of his son's employer understanding what little he knew of his gift. He judged the touch as a possible second mistake the first was inviting him here. Miles mind was in a dangerous protectionist place right now. He held his voice as calmly as he could.

"Please, please do sit down, may I call you Michael?"

"What can I do for you Mr Broughton?" he said coldly, he was aware of the thoughts as he touched the desk Tom's father was sitting at resting his arms on. It chilled his bones, at the capabilities of the man, able to hand out sentences of death, nothing fazed this man normally and yet Michael felt the man was, if not scared of him certainly wary of his capabilities, intriguing.

"Please call me Miles my intention is to get you to work for us Michael."

"Why would I do that I'm aware you feel threatened by me and can cause me much harm should you wish, you know with your son and others including the Police we have already created a missing persons bureau, it is all I need."

"Michael, I'll admit you unnerve me greatly I'm beginning to ……."

"Regret inviting me here," he interjected finishing his sentence. "I know."

"Your work its small league stuff Michael," dismissing his whole reason for being with one gestured wave of his hand in the air. "You should use your gift to better effect, for your country even."

Annoyed at the dismissal of his whole life's work and the patronisation, Michael was seething. "What do you know of me or my so called gift Miles?"

"We know you have a severe form of amnesia caused possibly by the gas explosion you encountered a few months ago," Miles noted his anger and felt stronger he touched a nerve but he would need to be careful. "And apparently since, you have become a depository of people's locations and from what I gather to great effect. The robbery case resolution was quite spectacular by any standards."

"You say my amnesia was possibly caused by the gas explosion what do you mean?"

"Michael it's our job here to analyse everything possible and that means looking at every angle including the fact you may have also been electrocuted without death of course."

"Do you doubt my amnesia?"

"No of course not, just the when it kicked in. look if you don't remember anything of your previous forty years, what makes you so sure you had a memory before the explosion, why could it not have happened to you ten years ago? God knows I'm in the business of making people talk, not just talk I mess with minds, so I have to explore the possibilities especially if I believe you could be useful to us."

"You're suggesting that I remember the last ten years and I don't."

"All I'm saying is your amnesia may not have been as a direct result of the gas explosion, it could have happened earlier and memory retention could be the issue."

"But I remember everything since I woke up in hospital."

"All I'm suggesting is its highly probable your condition happened earlier and the accident took you a step backwards."

"It hadn't occurred to me," he began to doubt himself. "Well perhaps that's not strictly true but I've discounted it, it seemed logical to link it to the accident."

"Why wouldn't you or anyone else for that matter. People generally put things in boxes mentally, for explanation or as you say a logical fit, but life doesn't work that way all the time, a lateral view is more in keeping with how we think here. What would you say if I suggested someone caused the explosion to make it look like an accident and to explain your condition."

"That's incredible it can't be can it?"

"It is unlikely Michael, but you see how we consider and we are always looking for demon's where none exist that's our business."

"Pretty scary."

"Sometimes, again what's to say you haven't always had your gift? Who's to say you're not mentally unstable and have just walked out of an institution where you've been kept because of your condition."

"I thought the hospital checked these things out," Michael was becoming concerned his stability and sanity was being called into question. "You're giving me a whole bunch of stuff I hadn't even begun to think about."

"Sorry Michael, don't get dragged down into our way of thinking as I said it's what we do here. For the most part, you have to see your condition logically the result of the accident, you were fortunate enough to survive from, you walked away with a talent for finding people. As long as it lasts you have to, must, use it to good effect. That' all I am after. Rest assured we've checked on you fully, there are no records of hospitals missing people, no prison or institutions mental or otherwise that know you or your DNA, finger or ear prints or dental records."

"You've done all that?" Michael was not convinced. "How did you get my ear prints without me knowing? I can accept the others because of the hospital's records, but ears?"

"You'll recall the dampness you felt before your recent MRI scan?"

"Thinking about it I do, that was about the need to sterilise my ears to use the protective headphones which have music piped to them because of the machine noise before entering the scans tunnel." It began to dawn on Michael.

"It was to make a cast of your ears without you knowing, it was the only test we hadn't done. We have to know what we are dealing with at all times. There are other possibilities." Miles looked at him carefully assessing his ability to cope with this type of approach he was adopting.

"What are they, the possibilities?" Michael mind was in a spin.

"That you've been produced, manufactured."

"What, I don't understand?"

"A foreign power has a programme for world domination, a terrorist could have had you brainwashed, a single word said to you triggers off an explosion in your mind and you cause the equivalent to 9/11."

"Good God, that's deep."

"It does happen Michael, believe it, a word a trigger anything could psychologically make you a tool for use, we just haven't found the answer yet or code, but what if someone other than the good guys have the answer?"

"To what end, surely there are enough people doing that now, why pick me."

"Oh that doesn't matter, it's about control, power being able to, that's the key always, only in the future comes possible benefits and you may never ever be used but we could never be sure."

"I hadn't thought of anything so far reaching."

"Why would you Michael, you're not in my game, don't forget I'm paid to think this way. I will admit although now discounted and I stress that we have studied you closer than you think, believing you could be faking amnesia and for some reason being fed information to make it look like you had a gift."

"What would be the purpose of that Miles?"

"To fool us, the country, me into getting you to work for us an elaborate plot, gains a person on the "inside" so to speak, in short a plant."

"Much too deep for me," he had a headache.

"But that's exactly why people don't get involved and leave it to people like me, it's exactly what this, my office is about. Impossibilities, the improbable and impractical."

"You'll be saying the world's not round next," Michael laughed attempting to ease his own tension.

"Technically it's not," they both laughed, the ice between them broken, Michael knew he could work with this man he liked him.

"What's the limit of your skill Michael?"

"I obviously consider this all the time and its variable, once I place people either by seeing them personally or a picture in any form TV, photograph or drawing I know where they are or live and I know something's about them as well.

"It could be different right?"

"Yes I obviously place you here, knowing you actually live in Surrey. When I touched you I found out what you've done for the job."

"Oh that's dangerous."

"Only if you judged so Miles."

"So you have a picture or whatever and then what happens to you personally?" Miles dismissing his thoughts in order to concentrate better.

"Well normally the picture is enough its crackly like old film footage. I place them where they are first and then secondly where they live and who with, mostly, it is per individual, but I get an impression of whose nearby 'sometimes' and this is not the exact bit invariably I know where they've come from and maybe what they've been doing, it is not an exact science."

"So let me get this straight, if I leave here tonight from this office and was travelling home on the train. With any picture of me at whatever age, whatever location you could place me at, say a particular railway station, know where I've come from and assume I'm going home because you know that already."

"Yes."

"Ok let's take this a little further, given the picture what would you actually get from that?"

"Where you were in the picture, how old you

were and sometimes, not always, why you were there, on holiday visiting people, business etc."

"All from a picture interesting, do you know where anyone's going?"

"No, this where I've personally started to adapt and do within my mind some detective work, assumption like you must be going home."

"What about groups of people in photographs?"

"Can be a bit fragmented, but I am able to work as I said individually through each person."

"So it's logical if you place a group of individuals in one place they're likely to be together?"

"Yes something like that."

"What's going on in your mind Michael?"

"Information comes to me like a ticker tape, bulletins repeatedly."

"If you put down the picture would you lose sight of them?"

"Yes, but if I have something they wear or any belonging, an item they use or have used it seems to help me to follow them around closely."

"But if you keep looking at the photograph it would have the same effect wouldn't it?"

"Yes it does but with the items I can start to plot a route, a path which they move towards, it helps as it did with the robbery cases with groups of people. Strangely, I can only pinpoint people one at a time with an awareness of others around. I need articles or items to pinpoint each member of a group together or each of them separately."

Miles laughed. "Something you find strange happening with your gift, my friend it's all strange. Again what's going on in your mind?"

"Timings help, if I consider a date my information moves or starts from it and then moves up to the present time and day. With the belongings it is like instead of ticker tapes, headline stuff, I'm getting pages like word documents, loads of information to sift through at times I can't keep up."

"I see, so if I've given you five people to pinpoint where they are, by the time you get to the fifth, even though you would have their home location, actual place where they are standing the previous four could have moved already? Thus negating the search for the group except that if you had a possession of each you could keep tabs on them all simultaneously."

"Yes that's exactly it."

"So where does knowing what previous actions, they've been involved in come from?"

"It's there on actual touch."

"Oh," silently Miles hoped he would not regret his involvement with Michael. "Wow, what about pinpointing objects like ammunition depots, banks, tanks or satellites?"

"Now most normal people would've asked could I find their car, bike or money even car keys. Either way it's a no, I believe, feel it's the mental connection with a human being rather than an inanimate object and no I haven't tried it with animals yet."

"I never said a word," an amused Miles shrugged. "Do the "victims" of your mental trace know you've found them?"

"I'm not sure, Gerry Fielder the gang leader in the robbery cases said he felt he was being watched, the others never mentioned anything. Is it important Miles?"

"Hmm, he's seems one to talk to if he has a heightened awareness. I'm just considering if it could be used against us."

"So how do you see me helping you and how safe will I be?"

"Are you happy about Tom and the deception Michael," purposely not answering him yet.

"There was no deception for me because I knew about it from the moment I met Tom, Josey feels differently of course, by the way he does you credit Miles."

"Yes I know I never get to tell him unfortunately, if you're happy with Tom being our go between and he can still work for you because I know he loves it."

"Yes we work well together and Josey she understands what I'm about."

"Michael she's in love with you and could compromise any project we get you to do, she's far too protective of you. However from what I gather she's a good Police woman, so if she's willing I'll get her seconded to my department and she can work with you directly at our cost."

"Thanks Miles I'd like that very much, I have to carry on the business though because I can achieve so much."

"Call it Consultancy when you do work for us, you can even charge us for your time that should keep Penny happy, let's say a thousand a day plus expenses," he noted Michael's surprise when he used Penny's name, he had to know all about his set up.

"Sounds good to me Miles." He knew he had to be wary of the man.

"Look Michael, I will be using your talents to the full and I cannot tell you that it won't be dangerous just as long as you don't let your personal feelings cloud the business end of what we are trying to do."

"What is the business end Miles?"

"Take a look at these five photographs." He asked pulling them from his desk drawer. "If nothing else I need to see you first hand in action."

"Are you testing me Miles?"

"No Michael I won't insult you, I know you'll be able to give me something I'm just unclear of the extent, but rest assured I trust you more than almost anyone." He smiled there was a test in the five he would gauge the reaction to it. "After all you always know where to find me." Seriously, he tapped the photographs.

Five A4 sized photographs spread out in front of him on the desk. Michael looked carefully at each as Miles pensively watched him.

The first one he looked at shocked him this was not any test for sure.

"What is it Michael please don't hold back run every thought you have by me."

"This man is dead, in a shallow grave," as Inspector Wyndham and Josey before him, Miles Broughton had to come to terms with the shock of knowing in an instance no luxury of planning a search, not succeeding and then becoming used to the idea the person, anyone could be dead. This was right now immediate answers, and like the other's he was not ready for it either.

"Oh Christ no! No! Good God man, where is he." Miles became nauseous he fought to control himself.

"Al Basrah, Basra province Iraq. Do you have a map?

Miles pressed a desk button opening a section of wall space to a computer screen he located the software via a keypad he pulled out from his desk and opened up the choice of varying countries regional mappings, he chose Iraq and clicked on the

Basra region.

"Locate the Shatt Al Arab waterway, the town of Al Qurnal is what I'm looking for Miles."

"There it is Michael, where now," Miles was stunned sickened to his stomach he had never reacted this way before it unsettled him.

Michael walked toward the screen and pointed to the exact location. "You'll find him just behind a petroleum station, looks like a sandpit."

"Do you know how he died?"

"No Miles that's beyond me."

"Excuse me Michael I have to pass this immediately to the military." Unknown to Michael as soon as Miles passed on the details of the find he stopped off at the washrooms and was violently sick.

The contact at the Contingency Operating Base in Basra assigned the task to Flight Lieutenant Andrew Donnell the deputy commander of number 34 RAF Squadron who in turn enlisted the help of two of his serviceman, such was the urgency and political nature of the request they left immediately for the town of Al Qurnal.

Michael hoped he had been wrong, but he knew this was part of his 'quirk of fate' he was never wrong.

By the time Miles returned, he had studied two more of the photographs. "This one is apparently a well-known terrorist and he is in Afghanistan, can you bring up the map's system again?"

This time Miles brought up on screen a map of the Afghanistan regions.

He's right here," pointing to Mazar–E Sharif. Michael noticed greyness had befallen Miles shaken by the initial results about the man in Iraq he waited on edge for confirmation. He had seen the same reaction in Paul and Josey.

"Yes you're right, we've known about him by way of the satellite overhead, unfortunately, he's heavily guarded and surrounded by civilians, so at the moment he's untouchable." Miles seeing Michael in action was staggered at the preciseness and speed of the results.

Michael pushed the next picture across the desk to him, holding onto his frustration at being tested, he half expected it. "This man's waiting outside your office right now and works on the floor below, my guess he's there to bring you the information you're waiting for," a knock at the door confirmed Michael's findings.

Sadly, the message was all too clear Michael had been right, the body of the man found to be in exactly the place where he described it to be.

"I sent him there only to gain information not to get involved, that's what we do, gathering so we can pass what's learnt on to help the efforts. I didn't want a good friend to die," he sat slumped in his chair a broken man remembering a friend.

"Miles we can do this later if you wish?"

"I'll be OK in a moment sometimes this job really sucks, let's go for a walk outside."

Michael noted the staff reaction as Miles told them what he was doing it was obvious he did not do this often. He became bombarded with what ifs, curtly telling them, all, whatever it was it would just have to wait.

As they walked through the main entrance swing doors of the building, the sunshine warmed them immediately. Michael noted two men joined them in step only six feet behind. They walked onto a private promenade towards Lambeth Bridge, gauging it to be only a few hundred metres in length with benches set apart at varying intervals. He mused here were meeting places for covert operations he looked around for anything remotely suspicious and felt decidedly foolish, telling himself it was somewhere for staff to go and eat lunch more likely, even he was getting a touch paranoid in this environment.

"Sorry Michael, I never realised the true effect of your gift. It really is special but immediate which was a shock and although it just caused me a great deal of pain and yes I put one in to test you, I can see you will be very helpful to us, have you had a look at the last two photographs?"

"Yes I have, the woman is also an agent of yours?"

"That, I cannot tell you."

"Miles that's bullshit, I see things, receive images, notes, flashes call it what you will but can find out without the secrecy, frankly if you cannot confirm what I need to know we won't be able to work together," he was annoyed.

"Alright, I apologise Michael I get so used to the subterfuge, yes she is an agent posing as a journalist and we don't have a clue where she is or if anyone's holding her."

"Well I do have a clue she is in Baghdad, she is being held captive but she is alive."

"Can you pinpoint her on the map like the others?"

"I'll do better than that, give me something of hers and I'll give you her precise location."

"I'll get it for you, what about the final one?"

"For a start it's a composite photograph, it has

parts of pictures and lots of individuals, but no-one clear individual. It's a good test Miles but I would hope from now on it wouldn't be necessary."

"You're right Michael, sadly I've seen what you can do let's walk back."

As they strolled back towards their building, Miles spoke quietly, but seriously in case of his being overheard. "We need to create a code name for you I think we'll call it TRACER.

Michael relayed the conversation and photographic tests he given to him by Miles to his son Tom, who confirmed the agent who had died worked and been a friend of his fathers for many years. Miles had sent him a scarf belonging to the captured journalist, Michael could still smell her perfume, strangely he recognised it, Lalique, he wondered why something from his past perhaps? The pictures and bulletins swam through his mind, the unfamiliar Iraq country, and its capital Baghdad pictured in his mind depicting each region. Somehow guided to the region of Al Andalas and further to what looked like crossroads. He searched for street names Al Fallujah and Al Mansur, noting a terracotta building, searching the pictures flashing before him, "The Union of Arab Journalists" ironic he thought. He found her in the basement holding her scarf as tight as possible she was tied to a bed, three men guarding her. He swayed with the effort it took.

Flight Lieutenant Andrew Donnell received another task.

Miles told him later the RAF Squadron had secured her release and terrorism had just gotten a new enemy they did not know of yet, he was grateful.

Chapter 15

Penny had been tearing her hair out she had so many appointments pending as a result of the new insurance contract and continued Police referrals, they were swamped with work the consultancy could not cope, they needed more staff and bigger premises, she had already hired her own typist and was rapidly assuming responsibilities as the office manager.

Michael loved her for it gave her a raise and confirmed the title she craved. She began organising everyone and everything even more than before. Tom, Josey, David and Michael had become so focused on the robbery cases, they forgot they ran a missing person's consultancy she scolded them repeatedly.

With Michael back, they all started to work through the lists provided by Penny's gofer her new typist Emelinda, a Philippine girl.

Several lists were created those missing persons specifically requested by the Police for Michael to look into urgently, these Penny quickly pointed out were freebie favours and no good to their business whatsoever failing to realise it was the other referrals from the Police that generated the income for their business. There were 6 he called them list A.

List B were those aged sixteen and under consisting of missing boys and girls 7 in all.

List C contained 17-40 ages there were 12, list D 41-70"s there were 32 and finally List E 71"s plus contained 13, seventy cases in all.

Michael then asked Tom, Josey and David to make sure any of the names on the list could be either removed, had been found already and were safe, sadly died or a Paul would judge stolen and abducted. There were just three possibilities.

He gave them lists B to E, divided between them, while he looked at the Police list A of 6.

Studying the list, there were two children, three women and one man. His obvious priority consideration focused on the two girls, but the man's picture seemed drawn to him immediately. He pulled open a map laying it down on the meeting table. The mental picture he had was of dense woodland, three days the man had been missing and had been the last to get on any of the lists.

He waited while he connected to Paul at the Police station. "Hi Michael good to hear from you, hope you're working on my list," he joked.

"Paul listen to me carefully I have bad vibes about the only man on the list 42 year old Kenneth Acton. He is in a woodland, take the location it's as near as I can get it. If he's been missing for three days he must have had an accident, Paul if you don't get to him soon he will surely die," no time for pleasantries Paul hung up the telephone.

Tom's list E were the 13 over 71's and he was able to remove ten almost immediately as just wandered off and found in the local hospitals or just gone on holiday deciding to find out how much the families missed them.

The eleventh found dead on a park bench apart from the cause being hyperthermia there was nothing suspicious about the death. He removed her from his list, leaving two men aged 74 and 75 who were apparently good natured people and were well liked in the community, both lived alone, no family ties, neighbours had worried they hadn't been seen at the local post office, shops and the village hall which held morning event clubs for the elderly.

The local priest usually assigned the fitter elderly ones tasks to do in the community, like making sure the notice boards in the village were up to date, the buses ran on time. Those less mobile would also get help alongside the odd hospital visits, all gainfully given their weekly tasks, but the two had not turned up for their weekly session. Two intelligent men who were firm friends, they seemed to have left everything behind and disappeared. Due to their limited resources before checking on their homes for any clue, Tom thought he would flag up these two for Michael to consider.

Josey had the biggest list D had 32 names for ages 41-70, Tom decided to help her 21 males, 11 females, having already reduced the numbers through her web browser access to the PNC system. 17 males and 9 females had been found not lost at all, once found, very often no-one bothers to inform the Police. This left 6, 4 men and 2 women. Without Michael, they knew it involved leg work a lot of it, they were all determined to try and find people on their own and only using Michael's 'gift' when absolutely necessary.

Tom and Josey sighed, FMPC had a near 100% success rate because of Michael, but these lists had built up because of his involvement in the robbery cases. They felt he should only be used as a last resort his 'quirk of fate' as Josey often liked to put it, saying it may not last forever and he won't always be there to use for them. Desperate in need of help, but who to get? They knew they had to stop wasting his valuable time and get people who could do the leg work.

Once referred to FMPC all cases were chargeable so they could've afforded the right help and somehow it was about who would fit in. They got started on this list by ringing each of the people's home addresses hoping to reduce the numbers further and as it had turned out a further three had failed to inform the Police of their return. This now left them with one woman and two men.

Josey began to wonder what her old team were doing they could have closed half of the files before the relatives were referred to FMPC for help.

So far between them they had five they needed to spend more time on, they both turned their attention to David's list he had taken Lists B and C. The B list, sixteen's and under with Penny's help they found five of the seven so far and had not touched list C yet. Both Josey and Tom set to work on C for the 17"s- 40"s, 12 in number. Tom was back to his cold phone calling checks and Josey searched the PNC. By the end of the day, they had refined all the lists ready for Michael, all feeling if they had the right resources they could do much more.

Josey, Tom and David presented Michael with four lists and Penny was taking the notes.

"Michael it's getting impossible not to bother you with these we need more room and more staff by that I mean people who have the intelligence to search out people and do leg the work involved. This is probably the fastest growing agency of all time, but we will never be able to keep up if we don't expand properly."

"Ok I hear what you're saying, Penny look into whether we can expand in this building I'd like us to stay here not least because I live here," pausing he had some thoughts on the type of people he wanted unfortunately he doubted whether Josey would appreciate it, he decided to stall them. "I'll have a think on expanding the team, let me mull it over."

"Let us get down to the lists then," Josey looked at him curiously, she wondered what he was up to.

They started with list B these were David's and Penny's it started out as 7 now whittled down to 2. Three had stopped over at friends and one had an accident and was in hospital with the other found attempting to run away from his foster home, he is back in care now. This left them with the two girls, both 13 years old and separate as cases. They stuck their pictures on Michael's notice board for him.

List C having four left to find, three men 28, 33, 40 and a woman aged 26, these placed on the notice board. List D the biggest challenge with 32 to find was now at the stage where only 6 still needed to be found, four of these men 48, 53, 65 and 69 the two woman aged 59 and 66. Finally they presented list E to him with strangely two men aged 74 and 75 listed as one case because of their friendship.

"Let me tell you of my six and as you know these were specific Police referrals," he watched Penny putting the faces of the still missing in order of ages and sex type. He counted 14 so far. "Children two girls, three women and one man, five females and one male, his voice deepened with overwhelming sadness. "I'm afraid five are already dead including the two children."

"Oh my God no!"

"Not quite what you signed up for Penny was it?"

She shook her head, tears making it hard to reply. David and Tom struggled to keep their emotions in check, Josey more battle hardened.

"The two children according to Inspector Wyndham had been reported missing by their school teachers initially for non-attendance, the Police as a courtesy call checked with the parents who told them the children were away on holiday with their grandparents."

"They, the two were of the same family I understand," Josey had already discussed these with Paul before he referred them.

He nodded. "Cousins and close friends."

"It took another three weeks before the teachers questioned it again, one girl aged seven the other girl her cousin aged six. At that point the Police passed the case to me as well as retaining sight of it for my help," he paused attempting to put into words his feelings to the group. "Let me say there is something about my "gift", my "quirk of fate", he said looking at Josey a wry smile on his lips. "Which I have to dislike and that's finding so many deaths of course, but it's also never knowing what actually happened to them and why."

"Oh Michael, you cannot be responsible for societies ill's you'll drive yourself crazy with the thoughts, I know I see bad things people do every single day which never fail to surprise me," she looked at him with understanding and genuine love for this kind man. "Michael know you are making such a difference, God knows how many would be dead if you hadn't intervened, believe your gift and what you do is very special."

"I gather the Police are currently demolishing one of the parents newly built wooden garden shed," he looked at the group whom he knew were heavy in heart as he was. "It's where I know the two are buried beneath the concrete."

"What of the other family?"

"What do you mean Penny?"

"Well there are two sets of parents."

Michael shrugged he couldn't help however he suggested Josey would be able to find out.

Penny ran from the room screaming, even hardened Josey burst into tears, leaving both Tom and David blowing hard to keep their emotions in check. It was time for a break.

An hour later, the group reformed to listen of the other four cases he had, Penny sat pale and silent holding Josey's arm with David and Tom stealing themselves for more possible bad news.

Michael worried for Penny wondering how much she could take, she had purposely attempted to divorce herself from the actual business end of the consultancy by throwing herself into the administration, but like today, she could not entirely escape the results forever.

"Quickly then," he looked at the group. "The three woman, missing during the past ten weeks , two had been involved in accidents genuinely and died as a result, the problem was that no identification could be made at the time," He looked closely at Penny. "I take comfort in the fact the families can now be at peace." Penny seemed to appreciate his comment.

"The other woman decided to end her life by jumping off a channel ferry on its way to France," he noted the stifled cries of both Penny and Josey still close to their edge of emotions.

"Surely there were checks, immigration, and customs?"

"It's simply check on, check off, no count Tom, no-one being left on board it becomes an error a figure adjustment not to be concerned about."

"Have the family been told, Michael?"

"Yes they have David the problem though is I cannot actually prove her death although I know she's in the English Channel."

"No body?"

"Absolutely right David," at least for the families" sake he knew she was laying on the sea bed twenty fathoms down no-one would be able to retrieve her body.

"You said five had died that must mean the man is still alive?" Josey asked attempting to change the tone.

"Yes my love he is," he spoke to her fondly understanding what she was trying to do for the group. "I immediately felt a connection to this man, clearly living and found him lying in a wood, the sort of place where you can lose yourself, miles and miles of forest. I understand the man loves to walk and wander by himself he had slipped on one of the paths and had been knocked unconscious by his fall. When he came to in the darkness, he became disorientated, he was found a very weak man and taken to the nearest hospital he's in intensive care and the signs are he will make a full recovery," Paul told him a few hours later. Michael touched Penny's hands and said to her. "It will have it is plus points sometimes unfortunately, it is likely the majority of our cases will not have happy endings, it is why they are missing, sick, old, people doing harm, running away, whatever it is at least wherever possible we can put the families minds at peace or bring justice to them properly."

"You're such a good man Michael," a resounding cheer joined Penny in her comment.

"Look you've all been impressive, we started out with lists of 70 people and now were down to 14 that's pretty good work considering I'm supposed to be the one with the skill, well done to you too." He clapped the group openly they decided it was time to go home for the day.

Everyone wasted no time to get away and be alone it had been a pretty sombre one, he heard Penny reassured by David as his taxi cab arrived first, Josey kissed and hugged her Smithy and left for the train station with Tom.

Finally, he heard Penny locking filing cabinets he walked out of his office to her reception area. She was putting her coat on getting ready to go.

"Are you ok Penny?" he noted her eyes reddened with sadness.

"Pretty harrowing today," she breathed in deeply.

He took her in his arms and held her tightly kissing her forehead gently.

"Off you go now, try and get some rest," she leant her head on his shoulder and whispered.

"Thank you," she left, the tears welling back into her eyes.

In the early hours he left his apartment and wandered in slippers, pyjamas and dressing gown to open up his office, he appreciated the darkness and silence. It was cold and quiet, he walked in the dark to his personal office, street lamps and passing cars lent their headlights providing an eerie glow invading his space he shuddered switching on his desk table lamp.

Coffee was the first thing he needed, curling his hands around the hot mug he viewed the notice board with the 14 faces looking down upon him accusingly, making him feel guilty of not giving them the attention they probably deserved.

There were 9 males and 5 females listed downwards on the board for some reason according to age. He decided to look at the youngest first, in particular, two 13 year old girls but had nothing of theirs to link to so he could only rely on the impressions and pictures entering his mind as he studied them. There was no dark feeling, he was sure they were both still alive, treated separately but he had the feeling they were linked, coffee mug in hand, he moved toward the board and looked closely at their pictures.

What came to him is they are friends, good friends and missing for a few days one for a week, one for a few days. It appears one set of parents set the alarm bells ringing after a couple of days and once in the news the second came to light a week after she was missing making them separate cases no one linked the two until now. They had been travelling to Devon, no onto Cornwall. Messages ticker taped across his mind, they had followed two boys, twins, who had gone on holiday outside of school term with their own parents who had taken them to St. Austell to stay at a caravan site.

He guessed, because he really did not know that the girls had told the boy's family that their parents had agreed they could go with them and stay. The real reason was one girl's parents could not care and the others just never understood their own daughter. He would give them this night and tell Paul in the morning to tell the parents. Meanwhile the boys being young themselves, luckily did not really know what to do with young girls, he judged they were safe with the boy's parents looking on protecting them.

Keeping to the ageist process, he picked the next woman at 26 and the next male of 28. These were truly separate, again he was pleased no darkness, he told himself they could not all be dead although he half expected the worse.

Just an address flashed at him for the woman, she simply moved without telling anyone and did not care either it was all he was going to get. The man getting married and had been missing since his stag night, when the 'lads' performed a prank, instead of keeping to the bars of Ashford they became quite the worse for wear. He was half-stripped and drunk when they took him across London into Essex and tied him to a post in Chelmsford in full view of a kebab shop. He has been missing for three weeks and had already missed his wedding, his fiancée frantic, as were his family and drinking pals. Michael laughed aloud, the man Peter, had been rescued by an Essex girl, a waitress working part time at the shop and he's been staying with her in Chelmsford ever since, they intend to get married very soon. What fate can do, he thought.

Drawn toward the two oldest men 74 and 75. Again laughing, they had no ties neighbours had not seen them for a few weeks, because they were living a life in Las Vegas spending their savings and winning too he noted, it was easy for him to picture them having fun.

He used a black marker pen making notes and commenting under each picture on the white board for the others to see and deal with the fall out among relatives.

Six down, eight to go. He decided to even up the ages and looked at the next three men 33, 40 and 48. The 33 year old man was described as having Down's syndrome and had walked from his care home one morning two months ago he was currently presumed dead according to the file.

The message he gained was the man/boy had simply stayed on the bus instead of getting off at work where he helped make furniture at a woodwork shop. Unfortunately he got on another bus which took him into another county, he was enjoying himself so much he hopped on another, he ate his packed lunch on the bus and spent what pocket money he received that week on the travel.

Originating from Ashford by the end of the day he was in Cambridgeshire, it was doubtful he knew how, along the way he'd lost any identification dropped out of his satchel when searching for his daily sweet bar he only knew his first name, he was, is, a lovely man but couldn't answer about where he lived. Once lost he began to panic and was directed to a Police station, the local council placed him in a similar care home where he's been waiting to be collected ever since. No one bothered to check the sewn in labels to his clothes containing his name, address and numbers to call. Very sad he considered but alive nonetheless.

    The next two men 40 and 48 both left home one because of debt and could not cope. They didn't know the man only lived about ten streets away and had a single room in another house, he watched his family constantly from a distance ashamed of the state he'd put them in. The other had been living with his parents and had a mid-life crisis wanted to see the world he was currently in Malaysia, Sibu to be precise.

    He updated the white board with his marker.

    Five left, 3am in the morning, he topped up his coffee. Female 59 and male 53, the woman had walked away from the home she shared with her live in partner where she had been for 35 years, she tired of his apathy to life, snoring and lack of any romantic feelings, lazy with never any ambition in life he'd become a lump she barely tolerated. Anything was better, simply she had spent months engineering her move a couple of hundred miles away she was enjoying life on her own now and certainly did not want to be found.

    The male lost for three years, darkness formed on the edges of a picture of the man diving off a cliff. Believed to be mentally "challenged" he had committed suicide. He too, like the woman who committed suicide from a ferry was at the bottom of the English Channel they were approximately nine miles apart from one another.

Three to go now, a female 66 and two males 65 and 69, he was relieved not to see any darkness loom upon him, luckily these were easy all three were subject to people being worried for their safety and two had Flu and been bed-ridden and the other the woman of 69 was in hospital having a hip replacement. Simple detective work, he wondered if he had made Paul's team lazy with his success. Done, writing on the board, in the morning he would update the team so they could inform the families. A good night's work it was 6am. His dilemma should he sleep.

His mind made up by an attempt at someone unlocking the main office doors, he heard a familiar squeak realising David and his wheelchair entered the offices.

"Hi David," he said peering around the doorway of his own office. "What are you doing up to so early this time of morning?"

"Hi Michael, I'm in earlier because I needed to upload some data I've been playing with at home," David clearly surprised to see him.

He noted the mystery in David's voice.

"Come on, what are you up to David, spill them?"

What came next even Michael was prepared for.

"Michael I love you like a father, brother, friend I've never had and I don't want to change my life one bit from now but I'm scared…" his voice trailed off.

"For God's sake David what is it, what's the matter, tell me!"

"I'm scared for you Michael," a serious David peered up toward him he moved to sit back down at his desk he followed.

"What do you mean for me, I don't understand?"

"I know about the money."

This hit Michael with such force it stopped him in his tracks, he actually had forgotten about it, his eyes looked automatically towards the filing cabinet where he placed it on the night after he took it from the wall opening down the alleyway alongside the Praetown Gallery. He had not even counted the money it was still in the holdall bag reading in the newspapers there was at least two million pounds in used notes, untraceable and still not found. With the robber's namely Gerry Fielder adamantly telling everyone it was nothing to do with them they never had the money. No one of course believed them except for one person him and he thought only he knew now so did David, how? He asked himself and attempted to bluff.

"What are you talking about, what money, not sure what you're talking about?" He blustered.

"Please Michael don't treat me like an idiot, I was looking for a place, the cabinet, in here to hide passwords to the systems I have access to and …."

"You do mean all the systems you've access too?"

"You knew?" It was David's turn to worry he was beginning to wish he had not come in so early now.

"David, tell me who is Gerald Robbins?"

"Ah do you really need to know?"

"David you hide the codes, keys whatever, but the information you give out sometimes suggest there would be very little chance of getting it without you breaking in. You would call it hacking into some such system, the output is your enemy and what you do with it, not your access, besides I've only to touch your wheelchair to know what you're up to."

"I keep forgetting why didn't you say something?"

"I figured if I needed to know eventually you would tell me, why my cabinet?" he relaxed knowing he could always trust David.

"I was going to pull the fourth drawer of it out and stick the details underneath it, except."

"Except you found the holdall."

"Yes."

"Did you look inside?"

"No."

"But you guessed it was the missing bag and money from the Gallery robbery."

"Yes, I figured you had to be the only one that could even a clue as to what happened to the whereabouts, especially with Gerry Fielder and his gang denying having the money suggesting the Police could have taken it. Going through your likely movements and opportunity coupled with the Police reports highlighting the empty hole in the sidewall of the gallery, which had to be to store the proceeds. I realised if the robbers denied it, the only other person who had the opportunity after the robbery," he paused. "Was you Michael."

"If you think that way would Paul or Josey realise it?"

"Oh I doubt that, it is the very last thought they would ever have about you."

Acknowledging defeat, he suggested they lock the doors and start counting. Michael unzipped the dark blue bag and up ended its contents onto his desk in front of them.

Silently they sorted the varying notes into denominations and together came up with a figure of £900,000 a far cry from the two million the gallery had claimed was stolen, the insurance company would pay heavily.

"Sorry Michael I still don't understand why."

"To be honest I guess I started to panic, I had become a success within three months of being born. I feared that one day I will look at a picture and it will be me and my life will suddenly change forever. I love what I do, but what happens to me when I wake up."

So you took some insurance."

"Yes I know it's wrong but somehow I justified to myself."

"And I don't blame you either, besides Gerry himself has his nest egg in his own Italian account."

"Does he," he was surprised. "How much?"

"Several million Euros so somehow, we've got to salt away the money as well so it's untouchable and no-one ever knows."

"Will you help me do that David?" He looked closely at him. "Why do you not judge me?"

"Michael you are the one person who has given me a lifeline, treated me as an equal and certainly never judged me over my past. Who am I to judge you?"

"Thank you, that means so much to me, what can you do for me David?" he felt his voice shake in emotion, if he ever wished for a son he would want it to be him.

"I can set up accounts anywhere in any bank across the world the harder part is getting the cash into those accounts, a physical transaction and not a technical digital number transfer which might just take a little longer."

The main office doors began to rattle people were arriving for work they heard Penny's voice opening up.

Michael scooped up the cash and put it back into the holdall, dropping it into the fourth drawer of the cabinet.

"We'll work something out Michael don't worry," David wheeled himself out of the office towards his own.

Watching David go, he wondered if he would ever come across himself and what would he find, if he could consider taking this money what else had he been capable of. While he lived in hope of a return to a normal life whatever that could be, it also scared the hell out of him.

The level of business in FMPC was growing in direct proportion to its success rate and during the following three weeks Penny negotiated additional space within their own building, the firm was growing rapidly and needed the space it was making a lot of money, the missing persons business was very lucrative, especially with a success rate of 100%.

Penny assumed control and pretty soon the space three extra floors gave were allocated in categories, the format they decided upon followed the previous listings in age groups which had been a successful way of operating the business, she hired the right people some of whom were ex-Policeman and even ex missing persons bureau people. They were providing a proper missing persons service without Michael now, with only ever the difficult cases being referred to him and there were plenty of those to keep him busy.

Unconsciously, the firm had been working on a rolling one hundred missing people but now had extended this to two hundred and fifty. Josey, Tom and David were now full time, fully paid employees and were directly responsible to him, Michael hadn't taken up Miles offer of paying for Josey, all others were responsible to Penny who had withdrawn from the work of actually involving herself in finding MP"s. She couldn't take it, she admitted the work was too harrowing with many downsides instead she took care of everything else from accounts to hiring and firing making sure everyone in the now 25 people strong business had everything they needed including the right technology through David.

With the business growing as it did, Michael felt it was time to make changes, he wanted to secure all their futures so he called David, Josey, Tom and Penny to his office.

Penny arrived flustered as if her time could not stand the interruption and was impatient for the others to arrive.

A squeaky wheel heralded David's arrival, as did Tom and Josey joking, being called into the headmasters study. Penny suggested someone purchased David some oil for his wheelchair for the hundredth time. They all kidded him about having a ball bearing loose he noted they all got on so well.

"What's the matter Smithy?" Josey's affectionate term for him still tugged at his heart and it showed her concern for him. He loved her as much today, as when she kissed him the first time in his hospital bed.

"I suppose you can call this an official board meeting of FMPC," he walked slowly toward his office door he rarely closed this was such a time.

"Wow that must make us all directors," each laughed at Tom's foolishness.

"What's this organisation's most valuable asset?"

They chorused his name.

"No, no, It is each one of you not me."

"Rubbish Michael, we wouldn't be here but for you."

"But don't you all see, I'm only here because of you."

"Ok, now we all love one another and this place is about all of us, what is the point?" David was becoming frustrated he had better things to do. "Oh God Smithy you're leaving us aren't you?"

Everyone laughed at David's use of Josey's nickname for Michael.

"No David I've no intention of doing that."

"Then what is it Smithy?"

"I've decided to offer you a partnership in FMPC."

"Well done Josey." Tom, David and Penny clapped in praise of her.

"Hold on you all misunderstand me. I'm offering each of you a partnership."

"What you really mean all of us?" Penny asked disbelieving what she was hearing especially that she could be included.

"Yes an equal partnership 20% each."

"Michael some are more equal than others and apart from me, you for instance."

"Shut up David," Penny scolded him.

"David my dear friend, I mean it truly you all have what I need as people, my family and each of you have the skills that make this business work. Please, please all of you say yes."

One by one, they shook his hand in agreement, except for Josey who kissed him and whispered in his ear how proud she was of him at this moment.

Josey had decided to leave the Police force with the reluctant agreement of Paul knowing since she first encountered Michael she had only ever been interested in him and the missing persons operation. Now she had a partnership in the business she did have some security although she would have liked a different type of partnership, Michael would have to sort his head out first before that happened. She showed a skill for the work that he certainly could not deny. She was pleased to see Michael friends with everyone and as part of the deal in using him for the more serious of missing person's cases, Josey and FMPC retained the browser rights to Police records for any searches they needed. The three never appreciated, just how much access they had, David had it all without their knowledge.

Tom admitted to his father that he loved working with both Michael and Josey. Michael had offered him a partnership in the business. He asked and surprisingly received his Fathers blessing to leave the service, but to retain contacts that could help the consultancy.

Tom had begun to have real feelings for Penny since they worked on the lists of names she had organised. He felt she was right to concentrate on what she did best. There were many downsides on those original lists with only a few they laughed about, like the two old men of 74 and 75, Michael placed them now in Benidorm, Spain, they moved on from Las Vegas they were having the time of their lives and both never intending to return to England. With such cases rare, he fully supported Penny's stance of divorcing herself from that side of the business, she was of more use elsewhere. Tom's fondness of her grew with each day. Unfortunately, she never showed any interest in him, it was his very dear friend David whom he had grown so fond of that she loved he would just have to live with it.

For a while now, the gang of five as they referred to themselves were doing very well.

Josey in charge of overall research, Tom was the people contact, Penny was all business processes, David the technology guru and systems access anywhere and finally Michael who did what he did and wanted to do, mainly getting involved when needed either by the team or especially by the Police. Life was idyllic. Michael still fretted about what his past was like, but they were all settled and comfortable.

Just as it seemed today would be like any other Miles Broughton telephoned Michael and on reflection this call shifted the business to a different level, a more dangerous level, giving them all a reality check. We were no longer dealing with people who were missing, they became, committed to saving lives.

Chapter 16

The second floor restaurant overlooking the Thames with its balcony above the private walkway opening itself up to the panoramic views up and down the river. Three young men laughing and joking in the fresh air on their lunch breaks from their busy office routines within the MI6 Victoria Cross building, they all worked for the organisation in some capacity.

On the surface, their laughter appeared harmless, except that if decoded, their laughing and joking spelled out very clearly the information gained so far while infiltrating the services of MI6. The highest ranking of them being Garvesh Pashwa the personal assistant to Miles Broughton, a senior officer without portfolio, another, Shorroco Bonjani worked in the technology department, fixing desktop computers and finding missing electronic files and folders throughout the services, more to the point he had full access to every file across the organisation unless kept personally.

Finally, the third young man Denz Rajal, worked as a Junior Liaison Officer who knew or heard about most of the cases at any one time. All three's task was to supply information to whoever would buy it outside of the terrorist networks they worked for to gain favours, funds and friends of their particular cause which was essentially to create chaos in the western cultures and try to destroy the way of life.

For several months, they had been drip-feeding information out to foreign services, liberation fronts and various activists groups, through an intermediary an organisation called FLA who had enlisted them and subsequently arranged their jobs in MI6 and paid handsomely for their information. Ethics, politics or conscience did not enter into it all three were having a good time.

Chapter 17

Prison life didn't suit Gerry Fielder, his brother Ron, Lawrie Berger or Trevor Cole, when they were caught they owned up to the football club raid and the shopping mall the audacious double raid plan didn't come off, the rest for which the Police had no proof they would never admit to. This meant they still had the proceeds from the other raids, because if they admitted those they would have been accountable for paying back the monies. At the end of their current prison sentences, they face further arrest for previous robberies with a likelihood the jury would, on probabilities, convict them despite a lack of proof.

  In prison as armed robbers they had notoriety and absolute credibility inside with money as well as the four residing within the same prison they gained a lot of influence, no-one dared to challenge them, the 'heavies' Trevor and Ron saw to that, both of whom had been inside before. Gerry and Lawrie regarded themselves far too intelligent, never having been in prison before this. Gerry always planned each robbery to the finest detail they knew who in the Police were working on their cases both Inspector

Paul Wyndham and Sergeant Josey Rainbow. He had them both followed and his cousins wife supplied the inside information, Sophie was a diamond. It's why they had never been caught, if they had heard of any likely suspicion over evidence she would remove or destroy it before they even investigated the likelihood. Now all they had to do was escape from jail Sophie could not help with that and Gerry could not see how.

Inside prison, inmates knew who were the Police responsible were for putting the gang away, one day at a mealtime Gerry was approached by two notorious robbers doing time for murder. They made Gerry cringe just being near them. Menacingly they questioned him on his capture causing Ron, Trevor and Lawrie to move closer to Gerry in protection.

The pock marked scraggy face of Joey Sawton shook with rage when he even considered his capture, which was right now in Gerry's face, his bad breadth oozing up Gerry's nostrils making him nauseous.

"Look lads me and Reece here aren't looking for no trouble are we?" his head turning to his companion a pronounced boned dirty faced man peered from behind him and shook his head.

"We hear you're in here as a result of Inspector Wyndham and Sergeant Rainbow that right?"

"Yes," Gerry eyed them both suspiciously he knew of them, they were dangerous hard men never caring about anyone if in their way, they were already suspected of two killings since they had been in Maidstone prison.

"They had to have help," he stated as fact. "Is that what you think?"

"Yes."

"Well man who? Do you know? Tell me and I'll owe you," favours worked for everyone in prison so he could not turn the offer down without reprisals.

"Michael Smith, get Rainbow followed and she'll lead you to him, I'm sure it was him who helped them." Whatever way he gained revenge Gerry not bothered, he owed the man nothing.

"Thanks I'll get it checked out, if you're right he's done for," the threat loud and clear, Joey Sawton and Reece Evans walked off.

"Gerry was that wise?"

"I don't care much Ron."

Gerry hated prison with a passion he had to get out fast. The cold brick walls painted with cream or green job lot paint all over the prison and bars mostly painted the same everywhere, bloody bars and thick concrete walls, it all served to drive him crazy, somehow he had to get out. He needed to understand how he ended up in this dog pen.

Both he and Lawrie wanted revenge, they had dismissed the one thing that had altered in the tailing of Rainbow and Wyndham and that was Rainbow's continued relationship with a Michael Smith, research revealed he'd been a victim of a gas explosion, had spent months in hospital. He had no history however, a firmer relationship had developed between the sergeant and him and noted Wyndham had become a firm friend of his.

Michael Smith appeared to them harmless enough but they realised he was all they had to go on, so from their prison cells they arranged for him to be watched very carefully, despite whatever Sawton and Evans did. If their incarceration turned out to be because of him, he would suffer the consequences. Gerry Fielder prided himself on never being caught in any raid until now, he vowed someone would pay and right now the only one in the frame seemed to be this Michael Smith, a man without a history at the moment and maybe there wouldn't be much more. He didn't know why he was responsible, just that he felt he was.

Chapter 18

Michael was silently distressed he had no memory, no recall since apparently the gas explosion planted him in hospital. There seemed a void of time behind him that he could not grasp, gone, what he was, who he had been, he never had a clue. He did realise that in place of a memory his brain appeared to be acting like a database, a register of people, their homes, addresses and physically the exact location anywhere should he ask his mind for the information. He felt spooked by this knowledge himself, he had to be careful who he shared this with. He wondered if ever his memory returned whether he would lose his 'gift'.

He was worried that his newfound skill was beginning to define who he was as a person because had no comparison. In some way, it felt exciting, a power he quickly adapted to and realised no one else had, but each person needs a point of reference, one that can tell who they really are and what their root beginnings are. If only for a measure of who they could or have become now.

He started to yearn for the gap in his memory as far as he was concerned he was born a forty-year-old man with worldly knowledge, an ability to communicate but without a history. Not for him the learning to walk, talk, to go to school, to know a family a father and mother possibly more, once in that lost forty years he must have had it all, where was it? Where has it all gone? Sometimes the torment of not knowing proved unbearable. What frightened him more if it did return the likely implications, with his 'skill' he realised for now, it would help him belong but there was an open space behind him mentally where life had once been. He desperately needed to know what, yet resigned himself to be reconciled to the present.

David appeared at the door of his office. "Are you busy?"

"No come in."

"Michael I need to begin taking cash from the holdall and paying in relatively small amounts just as Penny deposits from time to time because of our cash paying clients. I have been going with her on occasions to the bank on the pretext of her safety, although quite what she expects me to do in this thing," he banged the arm of his chair. "Run the person over I expect anyhow, I have created a current account for you as, you've guessed it Gerald Robbins with a fictitious address where I'm having the mail forwarded to my own address in Allington."

To pay in what I am going to do is give the slip and cash to Penny who will pay in without suspicion. A further two accounts have been set up one in the Bahamas and one in Liechtenstein both offshore bank accounts, both of these are kept away from scrutiny by anyone such as the taxman or any newly divorced wives which don't apply in your case of course."

"Come on David anymore?" Michael pressed him.

"Or of course previously robbed bank raiders."

"Funny."

"I try."

"How do we get the money from the English account to them?"

"Electronically, I will access the banks records and create a transfer process so nightly a large percentage of the cash will be transferred to each alternatively."

"How did you manage to get the account set up in the first place, don't you need some identification."

"Easy through the births, deaths and marriage systems I changed a birth record to produce a certificate for a Gerald Robbins who is now forty years old allowing me to apply for a passport," he showed Michael the result.

"This looks like a deathly me, how did you manage…"

"Oh it's an old photograph of you in hospital I needed it to be a bit vague as a picture so I could make out it was me when I set the account up."

"It can't be that easy can it?"

"Everyone trusts the wheelchair man," he suggested laughing. "Keep that for whenever you need to get the money out of the off shore's you'll need it, here's the account numbers as well, keep them safe. Gradually all the money will be gone I'll close the English account and later I'll remove it from the banking systems altogether."

"You're a genius David you could've taken some for yourself."

"No I'm happy enough with what I make here now especially as you've given me a partnership," he considered his next comment carefully. "Michael you didn't feel you had to give a partnership because of the money did you, I would never betray you."

"Good God David, never think like that, I gave you the partnership because you absolutely deserve it, I completely trust you over the money."

"Well I didn't want you to feel you had to."

"David you are full partner and above all my friend, I wouldn't treat you that way."

Thanks Michael just thoughts, spent too long in this wheelchair I suppose."

"It just occurred to me that to get the money at some point I would have to fly there. I've never done that before."

"How do you know you haven't Michael?"

"That's true."

"Besides I can transfer your funds anywhere."

"I bet you can my friend."

Chief Superintendent Miles Broughton turned out to be the first visitor to their new revamped offices Penny's assistant Emelinda showed him into his office.

"Reorganised very well Michael and very business focused."

"Hello Miles, what can I do for you, the telephone call made it sound urgent," Michael was in no mood to be patronised today. He had lost his memory and survived with a thriving business, a new love in Josey and had a special gift, which Miles wanted to make use of, he felt life's balance was in no small way shifting towards him.

"First of all Michael, I thank you for the partnership you've given Tom, I'm very grateful and pleased he's found something by himself."

"Well merited, I can assure you Miles."

"Nonetheless, because of it whatever happens I will support your operation here and help in any way I ever can."

"Gladly accepted Miles, now to business what can I help you with?"

"Two aid workers, women, have been taken in Burundi."

"Where that Miles?"

"Central Africa borders Rwanda and Zaire; it has not been made public yet, purposely. They were running a small school word has it they fell out with the local tribe over some part of the teaching, war histories I believe. We'll never know the full details so I need your help to find them and yes I did remember what you said about clothing, here's t-shirts and underwear wasn't sure what you could work with."

"I won't ask how you got underwear Miles," not smiling.

Michael looked at their pictures two vibrant women both with rose complexions, sporting African dreadlocks as a marked uniform of many aid workers attempting to fit in locally. Their t-shirts in the pictures emblazoned with Greenpeace messages, their cause was to save the world. The still photographs obviously taken at the beginning of the latest campaign, they both bore the smiles of young girls out to make a difference in the world clean in their shirts and khaki shorts, even their boots looked new. Miles told him their travels had taken them across Africa for two years, only in the past six months have they been working on a building project with others like a commune to build a village or tribal school.

Four weeks ago the builders all men from across continents had finished and opted to move to a similar project in another region. The two girls decided to stay behind to teach and develop the locals learning. Very soon, it was evident once the protection of the many volunteer men had disappeared the tribal leaders began asserting their authority on the tribe again imposing their will. Unfortunately the girls did not call the particular aid agency they worked for to help them, which they could have done by radio. The leaders tested their strength towards them with arguments and threats until finally shutting down the school and removing both women from the site.

Michael listened carefully as Miles told the story and asked. "So who has told you all this?"

"A tribe member who has been working with the aid workers on the builds to learn the skills he had only gone home to his family for a visit. He made the men he worked with aware but their searches had revealed nothing. Michael we need to find them, it has been two days without contact, dead or alive. The government wants to send a short sharp message to both the tribal leaders and their government. Interfering with aid workers amounts to acts of war. Unfortunately, we cannot do that until we know whats happened to them. Please help us," he begged.

"What will happen if I say the girls are dead?"

"Simply the tribe responsible will be obliterated."

"Isn't that likely to cause humanitarian outrage across the world Miles?"

"The world won't know, the media will be gagged and the government threatened with likely sustained conflict and total restriction of aid," he said coldly leaving Michael in no doubt as to the seriousness of the situation, despite his own misgivings in being able to keep it out of the public gaze, there were too many people involved.

"Sounds like murder to me Miles."

"And what of the girls who are the victims they have been supporting the tribal community unwanted or not and yes they had a choice whether to be there or not, but, there can be no excuse for them to die. If you tell me the tribe's leaders condemned them to die, I'm afraid it's an eye for an eye in spades."

"That's brutal."

"Absolutely Michael what planet do you live on, there are thousands upon thousands of good hard working souls doing their best for people our western governments let starve, despite what anyone's politics in the country, we are not one of the leading political nations in the world without action seen or not and others recognise this. So my question to you Michael is will you help us and are they already dead?"

"My answer is yes and no do have you a map of the area?" Miles unfolded a map he had brought with him, he learnt of Michael's needs quickly.

"They're here," he provided a pointer to a particular region.

"And?" Miles sharply questioning.

"They're not dead, Miles, but they are held captive, by a breakaway faction of the Tutsi tribe." He touched their clothing and seemed to drift off considering his next response. "Here, that's exactly where they are right now," he pointed to the Runubu National Park on the outskirts of Mutumba in Burundi.

"Bloody hell, and bloody great Michael," he emphasised. "You're even better than the satellite can you tell if they've been harmed?"

"No Miles pictures only remember, location, dead or alive that's my limit." Miles not listening he was on his mobile phone.

The reaction was immediate, no attempt at negotiation all the kidnappers were killed. Although the girls rescued, Miles prediction that the media would not hear about it proved false. They had a field day about the lack of negotiation and causing an extreme level of deaths. Threats to reduce aid kept the Burundi government quiet and more to the point it sent a message to all country's about what will happen if they interfere with aid workers.

The women would go home to decide whether they wished to carry on trying to save the world they needed a break it would take time after seeing their captors die. For a while the British were called bullies, forgetting the women had been kidnapped in the first place, the unseen spin off was the rapid reaction of the British forces, pinpointing within two days exactly where they were being held captive. By destroying their captor's it sent shivers across the terrorist world.

Quick reaction by the British was unheard of, they normally acted only after much deliberation and normally through negotiation albeit hard and only when these have been fully exhausted and or the death of an individual warranted it. A process of huffing and puffing threats normally ending in a back off by all parties then only to wait after much pleading for any release if the terrorists decide they wanted to do it. If the USA told them not to or Russia and China made the particular country an ally describing any intrusion into the region, as an act of war, normally a diplomatic back off would occur followed by more negotiations for releasing of prisoners, months or even years may pass during which time people except relatives and friends forget.

Miles stressed the next point to Michael as he was telling him, even after all this bullshit politics, the British rarely ever move in without a 90-100% guaranteed success. They would have had insider information to act so fast whoever it was could be dead within a couple of weeks. The reaction tamed for once. The British people, without condoning the killings, felt the government had acted decisively.

"When it happens a second time the worlds groups of terrorists will take more notice," Miles assured him, he looked forward to it.

The early evening television channel broadcasts interrupted by a simultaneous message across the globe by liberation army representatives, Afghan freedom fighters insisting everyone should release their own jailed terrorists around the world. Six hostages currently held are American embassy officials, apart from three male Americans these included two women both French and an English man. The terrorist broadcast not saying which group they belonged to, Miles called Michael immediately.

"Michael for God's sake turn on the TV, help us please, there's a live broadcast going out," surprisingly Miles hung up.

On call back, he said. "Miles the broadcast is not live, I know where they are being held or at least where these people are speaking from in the broadcast which is not necessarily the same thing," he talked him through the details.

The swiftness by which Miles responded astounded even Michael. The late evening broadcasts reporting that terrorists had been killed and captured following earlier television reports of terrorist demands all six hostages were alive, well and safe and have been speaking to their families. It was a triumph against terrorism and the whole world knew it. Miles expected there would be a backlash.

Terrorist sympathisers were contacting each other through networks set up to trade information they wanted to find out how the authorities knew of the locations. Something was different terrorism was being confronted head on, by their nature each group operated separately although they traded arms. Not the expected negotiation battles and threats, these were direct elimination hits. Only one or two had allegiances with each other, but because of lack of trust fiercely divided it appeared the governments were more and more joining together to fight them.

One man outside of the terrorist network suspected he knew who was involved in the raids he watched on the news channels being fed to a felonious group within his prison walls, but a little more investigation by his friends on the outside should bring him enough of the leverage he needed. Gerry Fielder expected to be a free man very soon. Time he checked in with Sophie.

Miles Broughton was becoming more and more powerful unfortunately, he was starting to be a known face in the media, which he did not care for, no one knew how he was getting the information and gradually every hostage found and released. This also caused several to be automatically killed, Miles had a policy that not one terrorist was intended to survive it gave a threatening message.

Very quickly every one of the groups knew there would be no negotiation simply death, many despite having a cause to die for, never actually wanted to. This had the effect of terrorists walking away from their hostages and gave more thought to the business of whether capturing them in the first place was such a good idea at all.

The varying organisations through their intelligence network realised Superintendent Miles Broughton was the key. Inside knowledge needed so unknown to him the pressure began to build on his own personal assistant Garvesh and his two accomplices.

The recruiting FLA, Front for Liberating Activists, had been borne originally out of India, with so many organisations, nationalists, liberationists, Basque separatists, IRA, Bader Minhoff, mercenaries to fight the wars no-one wanted involvement in, infiltrators, information carriers a whole industry of observers and followers of people designed in secret to support the relevant cause for cash. Supplying headhunting services getting the right individuals for any cause, governments including the British, USA, Russia, China while none of whom could be seen to support terrorism each promoted a lucrative trade in weapons, as an information network the FLA just did not have sufficient skilled manpower.

The organisation conceived by a British envoy Ralph McIntyre, who had himself negotiated the release of several hostages around the world on behalf of many countries. He created the idea of payments from each of the countries and terrorist groups for which the countries paid him to negotiate releases for returned activists.

The terror groups paid handsomely especially if the individual countries paid for getting the hostages back, this also would have a knock on effect for keeping the hostages and imprisoned activists safe from harm. Each side would then treat them as commodities, goods that could be bartered with, every so often a rogue group of terrorists and even a government would not wish to fit in with his methods, his double role was testing as each side believed he was working solely on their behalf.

It led to him gaining automatic credibility among every group whatever the politics and because he was able to negotiate releases being well respected by Governments and terrorists alike. Naturally his bank balance legitimately grew in direct proportion he actively encouraged the process to increase his own wealth.

What was worrying him, Miles Broughton started taking immediate direct action without going through him as the discreet recognised conduit and felt in danger of losing face and not being able to control every angle. What worried him more Broughton seemed to have developed a greater insight than he did, it could ruin him, if governments started turning to Broughton and not him for solutions. He supplied infiltrators to the varying groups so he knew who was where and he recalled three within Miles Broughton's own MI6 building. One as his personal assistant. It was time to exert pressure for information before ordering a resolution to the problem.

Chapter 19

Paul Wyndham visited Maidstone prison at the request of Gerry Fielder who requested a private discussion that would likely be of benefit to all parties. Paul hated visiting prison it made him uncomfortable, ok to put criminals there but it was not for him, his admiration grew for the warders locked up themselves each day, most Policemen, felt the same and had the recurring nightmare of being locked in with no one believing they were law officers.

"Hi Jack how are you today?" speaking to a familiar face.

"Slumming it I see Inspector, who've you come to see this time?"

"Fielder, Gerry."

"Follow me then Sir!"

Paul noted the extraordinary thing about prison was its noise, not warders or prisoners but bars, in the compound in every prison each second bars clanging open, clanging shut. Jack appeared oblivious to the sound, after a short walk across an empty parade ground a metal barred gate unlocked from the inside where another warder took over from Jack he didn't know him.

"Far as I go Sir," Jack waved and headed back toward the main gate not waiting for an answer.

He followed the new warder through varying barred sections wincing as bars opened and shut including on close up the further noise of keys jangling, he had the beginnings of a headache. Following along the lime green coloured brick walls, bare and cold, no pictures to highlight any reference to another world on the outside, he was led into a bland room, he was sure it was once a broom or a store cupboard it was that small.

He sat down at the bare wooden table and waited for Fielder, the sunlight of the window shone into the room his only company, the barred window too high for him to see outside, he loosened his collar and tie beginning to feel claustrophobic. From the quiet, he heard voices, distant at first then becoming louder to match the bars and the keys sounds. The door opened and in he came, thinner than he remembered, slightly older, less confident, he had stubble growth, Paul wondered whether the man was letting himself get dragged down into the despair of capture, he looked an almost beaten man. Paul waved to his jailer to wait outside.

"Hello Gerry how's life for you," Gerry noted a hint of smugness in his voice. "You sent for me?"

"Sorry about the room, I see they haven't laid on tea, I shall have a word." Attempting to get some parity with the Inspector.

"So why have I been summoned here Gerry?" Not wishing to accept comedy from the robber.

"Come on Inspector, you know I politely asked if you would come, I'm hardly in a position to demand anything am I?" He decided he would try to negotiate.

"You are being treated properly Gerry?" He sensed although tired looking there was strength of purpose and confidence in the way the prisoner spoke.

"Yes I'm fine, thanks for asking Inspector but I, we could do without being here at all."

"Ah, such are the spoils of war Gerry," Paul began to relax the grim conditions forgotten in conversation. "I don't do sympathy."

"Suppose I gave you something big enough to enable me to negotiate my, our release from this Godforsaken place?"

"Frankly, I couldn't believe anything to be as big as that, possible reduction in sentence maybe, however it largely depends on what you have for me, but I have to reiterate it would have to be pretty special, hard to imagine anything that could make that happen in a million years."

"But you would consider it for all of us under whatever conditions if it were that big," he felt his voice croak, he tried to control his nerves, this was his one chance he had to roll the dice and hope he did not blow it.

"Is this a fishing exercise Gerry or have you got something real for me?" he was becoming tired of this exchange.

"Michael Smith," Gerry let the words hang in the air gauging the impact it would have on the Inspector, who barely moved apart from a twitch above his right eyebrow, he tugged at his left, 'gotcha', Gerry thought now let's play the game.

"Who's that then?" Paul decided to play for time while he collected his thoughts, how on earth, did he know about him.

"Come on Inspector we both know you or Sergeant Rainbow wouldn't ever had a chance of capturing us without his help, let's not play games," he was of course and intended to keep the bluff going guessing Smith was the key.

"So it's the name of one of the people who helped us solve the robberies you were involved in," he tried to be calm and particularly careful about what he said, he needed to understand just how much Gerry Fielder knew.

"So you do know him, strange how you couldn't get near us until he came along," again he bluffed. "Don't insult my intelligence Inspector, let me spell it out for you, Michael Smith has a special gift and honestly I don't know quite what it is yet and how he does what he does, but he's been able to know where people are."

"You mean he knew where you all were, I've got news for you we know where you are now!"

"Oh ha, very funny Inspector, but I know quite a lot, you'll find."

"Go on Gerry tell me what you think you know."

"We have been finding out about his FMPC business, unusually, it has a 100% success rate for a missing persons bureau that's good, no I'll rephrase that, it is bloody incredible by anyone's standards. It doesn't take much of a shift in thinking to realise because of his involvement with ex-Sergeant Rainbow and his friendship with yourself you used him to catch us."

"My, my, you have been busy, so what," annoyed by the intrusiveness. "You've wasted your time and money, most if not all is largely public knowledge or could be if someone chose to look for the information like you have done."

What you don't appreciate is our attention wasn't only focused on you or your Sergeant, it's also been on Michael Smith."

"And just what is it you believe you know?"

"He's developed some interesting links with the British Government specifically MI6 hasn't he?" Gerry immediately noticed a darkness cross Paul Wyndham's eyes, he immediately regretted this bluff he knew Smith had only been followed into the building he didn't know why. He felt for the first time a measure of fear he never encountered before. He stuttered his next few words in an attempt to recover the situation annoyed with himself at his loss of composure and stupidity.

"Look Inspector all we want is to be free, released," at that moment he decided to add. "And to help the terrorist effort in any way we can, we have no wish to talk about this to anyone after all we can all see the success on TV."

"And where does terrorism come into this?" he asked pointedly.

"Strange Smith is seen at MI6, next thing you know hostages are found released and a group of terrorists are wiped out."

"Pure coincidence Gerry two plus two makes five." Paul was getting edgy this was not good.

"Could be viewed that way I accept," Gerry was moving in for the kill his stomach knotting. "If you couple that with the phenomenal success of Smith's missing persons business, even that could be a coincidence, but when you also include our capture and there are others I know of who are in here as a matter of fact, it begins to stretch the imagination a little too far."

"Very clever Gerry," he was struggling to counteract his findings. "You're playing a dangerous game Gerry, make no mistake, there's walking free and free in a box, you don't know what you're dealing with."

Gerry noted that dark cloud veiled over Wyndham's eyes again.

"Seriously Inspector, you're right I'm not sure yet, I just want to use my brains, fair cop my old career is over, surely you can use us all for your own benefit?"

"So what do you intend doing with this so called information?

"I don't know yet, we just want to be freed and we could help you."

"I obviously need to talk to others about this," he considered his next comment carefully. "I hope this is not a threat or a try at blackmail, make no mistake Gerry, if you speak to others of this you will get out of here but in a pine box."

Paul Wyndham had heard enough indicating they would talk again.

Not until later when Gerry alone in his cell mulling over the conversation in his mind did he realise that last sentence of his probably saved their four lives, the fear returned with a tight knot in his stomach again he was uncomfortable, he needed to visit the toilet block urgently.

Miles Broughton was none too pleased when Paul Wyndham called to tell him common criminals were interfering in his operations and his instinct when Paul first discussed the situation with him was to have them killed which would be very easy as they were in prison. He would not be blackmailed Michael or no Michael it made no difference to him it did of course and that was the problem.

Paul received the brunt of his anger he was not going to let a group of petty criminals ruin his march on terrorism when through Michael he saw the potential to rid the world of the menace completely.

He arranged a meeting with Paul and Michael to decide what to do.

Michael loved his life and currently working for Miles brought him a sense of danger keeping him careful, it added an edge to his life, the way he viewed it. His love for Josey was for him, as real as his limited background would allow. He adored her and counted himself lucky to be with her. His thirst for knowledge over his own background was becoming obsessive. Whenever he could he would sneak off to walk along the path of the River Stour where the now boarded and fenced off flattened scrap metal yard replaced by housing foundations still haunted him. The faint smell of scorched rust and burned upholstery mixing with the rivers dampness still hanging in the air embedded in the bark of the trees nearby.

Every time he passed the site it brought him more pain always expecting something, anything to jog his memory, the majority of times just walking sometime jogging or running, for moments he would stop and stare at nothing in particular hoping for something, it never materialised. Yet in his world, he could pinpoint anyone else, perhaps that was the price to pay. He was at least thankful as he would never have known his Josey but at what cost to his past he doubted he would ever know. Back at the office two urgent cases awaited his attention, one from Paul and one from Miles.

Tom and Josey were working on the endless cases received by Penny from the insurance company along with two they flagged for Michael's immediate attention they were getting cases from almost every missing persons bureau across the country. Some of the cases had even begun to come from Interpol through David's access intervention, identifying those where we could help, no longer were the Ashford Police's missing persons unit able to control what came to them anymore, it was a full time job as Penny was realising just to control the numbers they received. Both were protective allowing him his space and only presenting him with the really worse cases so he wasn't overloaded, they all had this thought of surviving if his "quirk of fate" didn't last forever, there was always a sense of urgency.

They told him they were unsure what Paul or Miles wanted except he needed to meet them urgently preferably at Miles office. They also needed more help.

Before Michael left for London he decided to take a look at the two files from the insurance company, a husband missing for just seven years allowing his 'widow' to claim his death and subsequently receive the pay out on his considerable life insurance policy.

Michael looked carefully at the couples photograph together, a happy event on holiday it seems. A shadow appeared above the man's head imperceptible to anyone but him with an impression of great sorrow enveloping his wife, he believed this to be a genuine case. He studied the man closely picking out his name Terry Windash from the file, searching for a clue to his whereabouts to put him finally at rest and end his wife Emma's torment, he waited for information to arrive in his mind as he was confident it surely would.

In the meantime, he looked at the other case where an aged couple had been involved on a holiday flight crash to Dalaman airport in Turkey. On landing the airplane the two side engines on the right wing caught fire which displaced some of the metal puncturing the passenger area on the inside. While the majority of holidaymakers survived to enjoy their holidays, it left a couple who did not make it the man because of the carbon inhalation with his wife suffering a third and fatal heart attack one too many due to the shock of the crash.

The issue for the insurance company is they gave each other as next of kin on their forms no other relative traced by the company or Michael's own team. They wanted to pay out but who to was the question. This time Tom had enclosed the man's watch and his wife's rings. Michael read the airports local hospital mortuary were awaiting pick up of the bodies by relatives.

Michael recognised information coming to him about Terry Windash his mental pictures taking him to Castle Vale Centre Park in Birmingham about six miles out of town in a residential area. Terry had gone for a walk alone, late afternoon winter time, the evening's darkness descending on the light of the day. His body literally gave up clutching his chest in agony, it was sudden he dropped to the ground a dead soul.

With night approaching, his body lay there for several hours just a mile from his home, a gang of youths happened upon him realising he was dead took his wallet with identification and ripped his clothes as a game and threw dirt over him as he lay there.

When light came the Police were called to a vagrant dead in the park, happens all the time the minimum checks were done with no effort to find his family. After the required public notification for next of kin which his wife Emma would never read believing him to be still alive somewhere, a funeral company which provides free service to the county on occasions such as this buried the body and registered him as a John Doe within six months of him going missing. Michael wrote the details in the file so his wife could claim him and register his death properly.

Finding the couples dependants or next of kin who were both in their sixties was proving problematical, his mind sifting through two lifetimes. At last, he found an estranged daughter who had left home some forty years earlier. Both Terry and Emma did not approve of their pregnant daughters partner so she decided to leave never to return.   After their third child together her partner decided to disappear, she now a pauper and on benefits had struggled maintaining a life for her two sons and daughters where they were in and out of social care because of her general despair of existence. Her thanks being now all grown up with families of their own they disowned her. Perhaps the large pay out would provide well for her, give her the last laugh and make her happier in life, somehow he doubted it. He updated the case file.

"Look Michael we may have a problem and it concerns Gerry Fielder and his pals," he stared out of the window absentmindedly following a tugboat pulling a houseboat along the Thames River below.

"What is it Miles?"

"I'll let Paul fill you in on his conversations with Fielder and you can give us your thoughts," he carried on watching the houseboat wondering about the people who owned as it pulled under Lambeth Bridge journeying down river toward Westminster Bridge, wondering where they would berth.

Michael listened as Paul word for word related the discussion with Gerry Fielder in Maidstone prison and the implied threat of exposure to the terrorist organisations if not released.

"Do you believe he was serious Paul?"

"Personally I believe he was bluffing Michael but I really wouldn't want to test it, they seriously want to get out of prison and this is their smart attempt at doing just that."

"What's your opinion Miles?"

"Michael I feel the same as Paul but for his last comments about their careers being over and they'd want to help us. Frankly, they would be dead by now, so it gave me an idea. Gerry Fielder is clearly an intelligent operator along with Lawrie Berger and they could help me in my efforts against the groups engaged in terrorism, I would also have use for his brother Ron and Trevor Cole as strong arm men."

"So you're advocating releasing them."

"Tell me how you're intending to use them Miles, I'm concerned they'll abscond the moment they get out of prison, I have to have justifications."

"Paul, I'm not sure I should tell a member of the Police force. I'm being watched so I'm not sure who I can trust in any event I would certainly use them to look after me."

"And you believe they could be trusted?"

"Certainly not Michael but, and here is where you Paul need to close your ears, they'd be under no illusion this is their last chance if they fail they won't be going back to prison they'll just disappear," his message crystal clear.

"So what are you going to use them for Miles?"

"Observation, protection clearly they trained themselves in that art, details in helping find the terrorist's sources of arms supply, rob them and finally I need some muscle outside of the service to get things done that are not palatable to the establishment."

"Sorry Miles I don't understand, finding the terrorists source what's that?"

"I can answer that Michael, we have long suspected that a network exists solely to supply the terrorists with anything from anywhere at a price of course." He looked at the pair as if he were talking to a pair of children about to learn adulthood. "This network encourages hostage takes, supplies information so the varying government forces can catch activists and then sets itself up as mediator so a hostage gets freed for an activist."

"Why would they do that Miles, its perpetuating the problem?"

"Oh Michael skilled but so naïve, money my friend it's that simple, chaos costs. As Paul said, there is a network but not a terrorist one as it suggests all the groups would have a co-ordinated approach but that is impossible because most only start with a specific cause and the others use it for their own ends. For example, suicide bombers are indoctrinated on the basis of their doing particular God's work but we all know, at least in the west the reality is, it helps those wishing to create chaos, some for chaos sake and to be high in the pecking order of terrorists. Right now its Al Qaeda, it used to be the provisional IRA or Badar Minhoff, remember their Olympic tragedy, each train everyone at one time or another. It is mostly about gaining prestige hardly ever the cause but if they can free like-minded individuals they do it," he paused not sure if they were still attentive, they were he continued. "However none started with ready-made armies or people who want to die, except the kids of course, so each turn to a supplier the source it is that network I'm after."

"And you don't know who this is?

"No, we have, based on the recent help you've given, two of the recently freed captives have confirmed the likely existence based on what they'd overheard, somehow we need to find and destroy this network otherwise the success we are having will be short lived."

"Michael I intend to use Gerry & co to infiltrate this service and flush out the plants even in this building and at the same time they could work for and protect you as well."

Michael liked the idea, but he was not going to show it just yet. "I'm amazed how both of you readily accept Fielders terms," he looked at Miles and Paul for an explanation.

"We have to be practical, they are intelligent resourceful men which we can use I accept the situation is not ideal." Paul conceded.

"They're criminals who are blackmailing us, that cannot be acceptable."

"Michael, so if they talk we'll have half the criminal fraternity after you as well as most if not all the terrorist groups baying for your blood, great, is that really what you want," he looked carefully at Michael. "Or perhaps you'd like me to get them killed, because I can and that's exactly what it will take."

"Why so drastic?"

"Because even if we say no, call their bluff and tell them to rot in prison, one day they will get out and a few drinks with friends later you'll have a bullet in your head, not mine, not Paul's. If you want to wait for that day we don't," he saw that Michael got the message. "Far better for us to control them in a subtle way of them getting to know you becoming a colleague with you working together maybe if not actual friends that way at least you'll be protected by them."

"It makes sense Michael, you know it does," added Paul.

"Ok, so what happens now, because in case you've forgotten these guys are armed robbers not spies and they currently reside at her Majesty's pleasure, just how are you going to affect their release?"

"Easy Michael, I'll get them a pardon."

"Can you really do that Miles?" He was astonished.

"He could probably do anything if he called it for Queen and country," Paul assured him.

"They've been convicted of a crime and have been sentenced surely you cannot release them just like that can you?"

"Frankly, Michael yes, although they were armed luckily no-one was actually hurt and we can really use them and their skills."

"They could get themselves killed by helping us surely Miles?"

"Yes they could but that's the price of their release, it doesn't come with choices," Miles nodded to Paul who touched Michael for effect.

"Look my friend you need protecting without realising you've become this country's, if not the world's biggest asset, your gift would be widely sort after or dependant on your point of view deemed expendable, if you were found by the wrong people."

"How much will you tell them Paul?"

"Everything, it won't work otherwise and the choice such as it is has to be for them."

"When will you ask them?"

"Tomorrow and if necessary I'll release them at that point."

Chapter 20

Garvesh Pashwa noted the meeting held between Inspector Paul Wyndham, Michael Smith and his boss. Normally there was a subject reference registered against meetings, but he saw it marked as a private appointment in his calendar.

Miles Broughton was causing mayhem among the terror groups his recent successes were of real concern to Garvesh's employers and they needed as much information as possible about his activities especially who his next targets would be. There was an implication if no useful information was available he would need to be eliminated, his instruction was to take care of it.

Garvesh knew he would never be 'in the loop' as far as information gathering was concerned he felt Miles Broughton suspected him already so he would have to be careful, it would be up to the three of them to carry out the murder. He had not signed up for killing they were enjoying life just obtaining information when and wherever they could and passing it on. They were not supposed to be assassins, but knew if they could not get information for them to use, he would have to kill Miles Broughton, if not it would be done by someone else and then they will be killed. His only option was to delay the inevitable for as long as possible because they did not have a clue how yet.

He generally obtained information without arousing suspicion on Broughton by looking at his current activities, his colleagues the liaison officer had monitored most of the operations, on a new satellite was being configured to orbit above Afghanistan. There is an investigation into a suspected rogue ambassador in New York, but nothing related to any terrorist group. He didn't bother passing this on, his technical colleague had been sifting through all the computer files, especially those marked hidden from view and the best he could come up with was the budget value of two billion was allocated for the fight against terrorism. He worried what he could provide was of little value to his employers.

He turned his attention to the Police Inspector, but he seemed caught up in normal policing of day-to-day crime, missing persons and managing his own team of officers. The only real focus he had gained for the moment was his visits to Maidstone Prison in Kent where through a bribed prison officer they learnt he visited a convicted robber again. He felt this had nothing to do with terrorism, he assumed the Inspector was trying to gain more information about previous or other robberies they or others had committed. He decided to dismiss this as irrelevant to his terrorist employers. Finally there was Michael Smith, a strange one, he ran a small organisation called FMPC which is a missing persons bureau and it appears to be very successful, unusually so. The disturbing fact is, he could not trace the man's history. He been followed several times walking by a river in Ashford being the place where he had the accident the purpose unclear.

The real issue was to understand what his connection is with Miles, the Police yes it was obvious for a missing person's bureau but his boss less so. He was determined to concentrate his efforts on Mr Smith, if he didn't provide something to his masters very soon they would expect results or he would be accountable with his life, which he had no wish to do.

Chapter 21

With the necessary paperwork from Police Commissioners, Judges, government representatives all signatures were in place for the pardons signed by the Home Secretary for four prisoners currently serving sentences for armed robbery.

The prison in-mates selected were essential for the continued stability of the United Kingdom, The prison governor Broderick Hawton was furious this was setting a precedent for others to attempt the same they are dangerous men. It was only luck they never killed anyone evidence of their tactics of control among the prisoner population, suggested they would kill without hesitation. By their actions, he doubted whether they would bat an eyelid if threatened on any of their robberies to kill, luckily for them it was not his decision. The Home Secretary signed the paperwork for the prisoner's release.

"Sir they were only convicted of the one robbery, well a dual one anyway, with no previous record only minor GBH for two of them."

"That's bullshit Inspector and you well know it, half the in-mates in this prison have worked with them on their many robberies in some capacity or other and they demand loyalty to a point of terror itself. How come they are so valuable to you Inspector?" Governor Hawton enquired.

"That I cannot tell you, enough to say they can be useful to us and part of the pardon conditions will be they work with us exclusively."

"And if they don't you'll fluff about begging and pleading, they'll claim rights because of being pardoned and we'll all be a laughing stock, at best you'll put them straight back inside where I'll have to pick up the fall out."

"No Broderick that will never happen"

"Do you believe they will accept your terms Paul?"

"Quite frankly they have no choice, all I can say, they hold vital information which could be useful to terrorists themselves."

Hawton laughed realising what was going on. "Their holding you to ransom you're being blackmailed that's it isn't it, bloody hell it must be something really special for you to work so hard getting them a pardon. What if they don't agree or more likely run out on you once free?"

"That will be the end of their usefulness to us."

"Meaning?"

"Governor Hawton were grown up's here we cannot ever allow the information they've learnt to be made public. It will automatically cause the death of others."

"I see."

"Governor, I sincerely hope you do, as I said they will never come back here once they choose to work with us," Paul looked coldly at him surprised at the steel in his voice. "If it doesn't work out they will be dead."

"Ah, let us just hope they see things your way," the prison governor's anger dissipated, not convinced they would conform so justice would be served he expected. "I'll take you along to see them now."

Paul expected after four visits to Gerry in Maidstone prison this would be his last.

For as long as he could remember since he started this process with Inspector Wyndham, he felt scared. The other three didn't have a clue what he'd been up to, he saw no point debating the merits of the plan with them and certainly didn't want them to put doubts in his mind the problem would come if they didn't agree for he knew he'd signed their lives away. This was a gamble, he'd heard Michael Smith's name related him to their capture his photograph reminded him he'd seen him at the Police station then in the taxi cab at the gallery. Further linking him to the news with the terrorist hostages release successes, it was total bluff it worked he hit the jackpot he saw it in Wyndham's eyes and once done he knew there was no turning back.

He must have been right because it had worked there were no denials forthcoming from the Police Inspector just a veiled threat to keep what he knew to himself. He was blackmailing the establishment, the Police, Government whoever, at worst he told himself they could all die but instead of rotting in this dump, it had to be worth the punt he told himself, he was afraid of being out of his depth, robberies, villainy no problem, spy's, terrorism, killings a different league not his bag at all. If they said no what then? A longer sentence for blackmailing, treason perhaps life, his thoughts were running away with him, he'd end up putting himself on the end of a rope, he would never tell what he knew if they called his bluff he'd be sunk or dead.

Enough people in this prison that would cut you for a cigarette let alone money, what price would their lives go for. He felt sick, helpless he threw up into his cell's cracked porcelain sink he sat on his bunk just staring at the walls and at the skylight barred window to the outside world, wondering what he had done.

It jolted him when his cell opened and the prison warder beckoned him to follow, he tried to dismiss this feeling of impending doom but could not shake it as he followed meekly behind. He was shown into a caged room closely followed surprising him by Lawrie then Ron and finally Trevor, it was the first time they'd all been together properly alone without a warder or others prisoners milling around listening since the trial two months back, each looked worse for the prison experience.

"What the hell's going on here," Ron's voice booming out deafening everyone. "I was exercising."

"For God's sake Ron shut up," Gerry had his index finger to his mouth.

"Do you know why we are here Gerry?" Lawrie noted his hands were shaking.

He nodded and before he had a chance to talk to them the door to the room opened. They watched as Inspector Wyndham entered the room and waved away any form of warder protection. He looked closely at them all as the door sealed behind him.

"Good morning gentlemen, please be seated."

"I'm going to give you a smack; it's your fault we're in here."

"For Christ's sake Ron, sit down now all of you," Gerry hid his fears, but only just, he did not want them to make the situation any worse.

Paul noticed the sweat beading on his forehead and decided for his own benefit to play the fear card with them by the look of Gerry it was already working he had never seen him so nervous before.

"I'd listen to your brother If I was you," looking at him squarely. "You haven't told them have you Gerry?"

Gerry shook his head.

"This is what's going to happen, in a few minutes you will all be given your belongings, as we speak your cells are being cleared out. Then you will each be processed for release into my custody," by now the other three gang members were beginning to get Gerry's reaction who was shaking uncontrollably. "Please don't try anything stupid when we leave the prison, there will be an armed guard surrounding us and you are still legitimate prisoners."

"Can someone tell me what the fuck's going on?"

"No Trevor, not at this time, but make no mistake all of you," he said looking directly at Gerry. "If you attempt to escape you will be shot."

"You are fucking kidding?"

"Gentlemen your release I can assure you is no joke."

"Our release but how why?"

"You wouldn't shoot us surely," Lawrie disbelievingly looking at Gerry for assurance, his eyes were rooted to the floor.

"I'm deadly serious, step out of line and you'll be dead every one of you," Paul felt he sent the right message, each shivered under their bravado.

"For Christ's sake Lawrie, all of you," Gerry begged. "Go with the flow, were getting out of prison aren't we!"

"You've got some fucking explaining to do!"

"Yeh, and at what cost that's what I'd like to know."

"And you will understand very soon," Paul bowed to Ron and Trevor. "For now I suggest you take the lead from Gerry who started this process on your behalf."

Disbelieving they each glared at Gerry as if he were a spy in their midst. Gerry shrugged his shoulders and they fell into line. They trusted him completely.

Once processed the single blacked out stretched limousine held the four of them and three armed guards two in the back seats with the four facing out to the right side by side, the third guard sat in the front by the driver clearly visible to all the partition dropped. Once through the main bar gates they positioned themselves at the final checkpoint between the bars and the high arched wooden gates which led out to the outside world.

Apprehension on their faces with Gerry was sweating profusely expecting any moment to be shot and dumped from the vehicle his body language not lost on the others a final sweep of the vehicle took place.

With the formalities over the outside facing wooden doors of Maidstone prison opened inwards and the limousine carefully slipped through the opening and turned left out onto County Road to an audible sigh of relief from three of them,

Only Gerry considering the implication of something going wrong, he looked sideways at the others then to the machine guns the guards were holding and couldn't help feeling they had all just left safety.

Joined by more guards in a navy blue Volvo and to the front of their silver vehicle and a black Daimler to the rear housing Miles, Paul, Josey and Michael.

An office just outside Ashford at the Orbital Park Industrial Estate on arrival more guards waited to usher the limousine through the open entrance to the unit, the other two cars parked alongside. The guards gestured to the four men to climb up the metal staircase to the mezzanine floor above the parking bays. The four watched as the shutters closed noisily down on the unit sealing them in. The guards prodded them with their guns to move them along to a separate enclosed windowless room.

The room contained three large sofas, four armchairs with plenty of food and drink on a back wall table.

"What's this the last supper," each wondered whether Ron could be right.

"Might as well help ourselves," Gerry gestured to the food.

"Are you going to tell us what's going on Gerry, I want information not a bloody sandwich?" Lawrie was getting angry and had begun to feel the fear oozing from Gerry. He had never gotten this feeling from him before even when they served in the army together.

At that moment, four people walked into the room, the guards clearly minding the exit.

"Now will somebody tell us what the fuck's going on?"

"It's Lawrie Berger isn't it perhaps Gerry would like to enlighten you all?"

Gerry already noting the presence of Michael Smith and realised, perhaps his punt was not as bizarre, as he had first thought he finally stopped sweating.

"Before I do Inspector, how about making some introductions?" he was growing in confidence.

"Certainly," unexpectedly Paul turned to his own group. "Here we have four convicted robbers firstly Gerry Fielder he is the one I have had most dealings with, never before been caught by the Police but known specifically to have masterminded and had a hand in some twenty robberies at least and considered to be the brains of the outfit. His brother Ron here," he offered pointing. "Is what's known as a strong arm man and gofer the same as Trevor Cole although he is useful with technology and both have done time for petty theft and GBH, which leaves Lawrie Berger who joined the team after serving in the army with Gerry where they committed their first robbery together in Italy?"

"Never proved," offered Lawrie.

"Anyhow they work specifically as armed robbers and fortunately for them they have never actually harmed anyone apart from the odd broken bone," he looked at the four one by one his tone of voice cold as ice. "If they had of done they would not be standing in front of us now."

It sent a shiver down their spines again including tough old Ron the implication very clear.

He continued, directing them to sit down. "For me I'm Inspector Paul Wyndham of Ashford Police as well as head of the missing person's bureau for the Kent district and you all know me."

"Chief Superintendent Miles Broughton, Head of Covert Intelligence Operations MI6, I have to say he is the reason you are here today," Miles bowed to the group. "Some of you already know ex-Sergeant Josey Rainbow, the main instigator of your capture," she bowed toward them. "And finally, Michael Smith of FMPC Finding Missing Persons Consultancy."

"What's our release got to do with missing persons?"

"Shut up Ron." Gerry not in the mood for his brother's hysterics.

"Come on Gerry, there's plenty of time for us all to get to know one another better but you'd better explain to Ron, Lawrie and Trevor what you've been up to during the past few weeks and how we all came to be here today." Paul was enjoying himself immensely watching Gerry squirm. "Please help yourselves to refreshments gentlemen while we listen."

"Mmm, not sure where to start, while not admitting to anything I was surprised how both the Inspector and especially the Sergeant here swarmed all over us within minutes because of the Praetown Art Gallery robbery and appeared to have an inside track on timings and exactly how it had been done."

"But you did the raid the four of you, no question," Josey pointed out.

"Not proved and beside the point, what I will admit is us being aware, involved in a number of robberies where you haven't had a clue, only for the gallery one you seemed more certain and we didn't understand why."

"Are you about to admit every robbery you've done Gerry, for the sake of our working relationship moving forward you understand?" Paul Wyndham asked cynically.

Gerry felt the shifting unease of his own gang unsure of where this was going.

"Gerry for Christ's sake what are you up to?"

"Don't worry Lawrie I'm not about to jeopardise our freedom so readily, anyhow I noted our friend Michael here when we were being released, that's one. The second time I saw him," he stopped short of speaking about Michael in the taxi cab at the gallery as he would have to explain why he was there now wishing to incriminate himself.

He never noticed Michael's face redden.

"Er, the second time I saw him was in a photograph which Lawrie had taken of you Michael outside at the William Harvey hospital entrance," Gerry looked directly at him.

"Why were you following him?"

"We had to find out what had changed to affect your approach to the robberies Sergeant and, Michael had been the only change," he would not tell her of the information Sophie had supplied to them. "This then was linked to the publicity surrounding his accident in the news on a river bank in Ashford. He was then followed to London and to the MI6 building which I now assume as the reason being to visit you Chief Superintendent Broughton?"

Miles knew he had made the right decision to release these men Gerry was very clever.

"What happened to the galleries money Gerry?"

Gerry shrugged his shoulders giving Michael a cursory look not meeting his gaze.

"How do I know Inspector we are innocent," he had no wish to accuse the police of stealing the cash.

Michael realised it would not ever be mentioned again.

"To continue, when we were caught for the football club and shopping mall I always felt we were being watched closely and again with all due respect to you Inspector and Sergeant you had to have had help, so Michael once again came into my mind."

"You had no real proof though did you?"

"No we didn't but one day during a prison recreational session, the TV was reporting how MI6 were making great strides in dealing with terrorism. I began monitoring the quick wins that seemed to be occurring where even I with limited knowledge knew dear old Great Britain took an age to get off their arses, let alone take the fight directly to the terrorists, for me the difference had to be again Michael."

"Very astute of you Gerry."

"Thank you, that means something coming from you Miles," he took a deep breath with the group noting his use of the MI6 man's Christian name.

"Anyhow it was worth trying to engineer our release on the basis because the Police had kept Michael under wraps in the background, I was pretty sure MI6 would do the same," he looked towards his brother and two lifelong friends. "And the result is us being here today is as much of a surprise to me as it is to you all, which is why I never bothered telling you. I still don't bloody know where we stand despite the fact the Inspector and I must have met four times but all I know it brings us to this point out of prison and that to me feels good."

"Oh yeh, dead good," Trevor cynically suggested.

"Did you ever think it could get us all killed?"

"Yes Lawrie my friend I did, but I felt the risk was better than spend our days behind bars."

"Did it not occur to you we would have liked to know if you've signed our death warrants?"

"Not really Trevor, don't be so dramatic," he admitted.

"Taking the leader of the gang just a little in the extreme don't you think?"

"Perhaps yes Lawrie."

"We would have got out eventually."

"No Ron we wouldn't they would have taken us on over the others, how many did you say Inspector twenty robberies. I doubt if any of us would've seen daylight again."

"Personally I think it was worth the punt Gerry."

"Thanks Trevor I appreciate that." He looked to the Chief Superintendent who cleared his throat to speak.

"It seems you do appreciate how close you and your band of merry men, partners in crime came to being, let us say eliminated?" Miles stated coldly, intending the others to appreciate the severity of Gerry's actions.

"Bloody hell Gerry is what I think he's saying right, you really could've got us all killed without us knowing it, for fucks sake you might have told us, me your own brother," Ron had just gotten the implication.

"What's your problem, were here aren't we, out of bloody prison and still alive."

"Oh yeh, but for how long?" Chorused Ron and Trevor.

"What's the payback that's what I want to know," Lawrie added.

"I think you find that comes under my remit gentlemen, Gerry has opened a path of no return and I suspect he already knows that."

"You're suggesting we have no choice about what we get involved in, because if we don't then we are not going to return to prison either."

"That's about the size of it Lawrie," Miles confirmed. "However we wouldn't have brought you here without a reason and before we go into that, I believe Paul has some paperwork stuff that needs clearing up, one of it is the signing of the official secrets act."

"Thanks Miles, OK chaps let us get to the positive stuff for you, do you all agree to work for the British Government, Police or any other agencies we so deem you to?"

Reluctantly, like lambs to the slaughter they each agreed and signed the paperwork placed in front of them by Josey, leaving just their final signatures required on the pardon documents.

"Here's the deal, a full pardon for all of your crimes and not just the two you were caught for. This translates into several life sentences should we continue to pursue the investigations and convict or alternatively, find a good place for the four of you to rot without release or parole ever," Paul let the implications sink in before continuing. "Gerry is right when he said you would never ever be free again, you would die in prison. Also this pardon covers all proceeds you have gained as a result of previous actions you will not be required to return any monies at all."

Every one of them raised their eyebrows, the deal not so bad after all.

Gerry looked closely at Michael who had not spoken at all so far. "Do you have anything to say about this?" He said pointedly at Michael.

"Nothing except I disagree with letting criminals loose," he said coolly. "Especially those who resort to blackmail."

"Good job that it's the Chief who has the say then," Gerry was sneering at him, almost dismissing him as irrelevant to what was happening. It was a mistake.

Miles cleared his throat. "Gentlemen please once again, be under no illusion it is precisely because of our need to protect Michael and us all feeling you could play a part in that you're here. Should Michael ever suggest you are no longer useful to him, it will mean you are no longer useful to me, do I make myself absolutely clear?" The sneer left Gerry's face immediately and he looked at Michael in a completely different light.

Gerry went grey, he felt sick, he couldn't believe what he'd done inside the prison.

Michael noticed.

"Gentlemen the deal is you are free to walk and go anywhere but you work for us, well Miles and Michael actually without question and do their bidding, it is likely to be dangerous and you could get killed for your country. No matter what they ask in return you may just like the work and be free men, in fact untouchable." Paul paused for their reflection.

"How long is this for?"

"As long as we deem you are useful to us Gerry," Miles softening towards them. "You will all be paid handsomely for your work, the caveat being what you learn stays within this group alone, we know already you do this with the four of you, together you are a solid unit trusting no-one else including family, this time it needs to extend to eight of us. It also means you will have equal say within this group and that is important, we all have roles to play.

"Some are more equal than others though aren't they Miles?" Gerry explored.

"Only for now while trust builds its up to you, so what's it to be gentlemen, will you sign the pardons on the basis of your agreement to the terms?"

"We surely don't have to point out that failure to comply with the official secrets act or you do not comply generally the deal is considered a treasonable risk which will result in us shooting you anyway," Paul started to grin. He'd made his point and said finally. "Of course, you always have a choice of returning to prison and await whatever fate befalls you there. I'd guess you'd like to discuss the options you have, but I stress you must all agree."

"And what if we don't all agree?"

"I suggest the deal then becomes unworkable," Miles unspoken threat clear to all.

The four nodded to each other accepting they were without any bargaining power and anything was better than returning to their prison cells, even their journey so far had given them a taste of what freedom can mean. Gerry's relief overwhelmed him and he found he needed to steady himself even though he was sitting down already. He spoke for them all.

"Where do we sign?"

Josey passed around the varying documents to them and as she did so she felt part of an elite group she felt would work well together. She winked at Michael.

The documents signed, Miles placed them in his briefcase.

"Can we go home we all have families you know?" Trevor who posed the question to no one in particular.

"Absolutely, but I'd advise against any celebrations, too much attention would cause too many questions which we cannot or will not answer to the risk of our operations. Although pardoned you are all still convicted felons. The best way to put it behind you is to operate on a low-key basis.

"I suggest you take the next few days to acclimatise yourself again to being in the outside world. Funds have already been placed in your individual bank accounts, the cars will drive you to where you wish to go and after your break they will pick you up and take you to Michael's offices which will become your base in Maidstone." Miles looked at them all. "Welcome aboard all of you, when we begin to work together, you will start to learn of our worlds and be able to ask any question you wish. Gentlemen let me assure you, the right decision has been made."

"So you knew we would sign anyway?" Lawrie suggested to Miles.

"No brainer, we took a calculate guess you didn't want to die," he looked at the four one by one smiling. "Were we wrong gentlemen?"

The four shook their heads muttering as they left the room to Miles amusement.

Michael purposely shook Gerry's hand.

Gerry, Ron, Lawrie and Trevor once at home, discussed their loyalties to each other, backed into a corner; this was infinitely preferable to a prison cell and with a feeling of respectability and were part of the establishment. Not one of them really understanding the likely cost to them, feeling this was all about them being at risk, they vowed to ensure above all else to watch each other's backs no matter what.

They had an air of expectancy of being completely free, each in their hearts felt it would come at a price and knew they would never rob anyone ever again for their own profit, they marked the notion one career had ended. Nevertheless, they agreed to transfer allegiance and trust of each other to the other four, besides they all agreed while Paul Wyndham played it tough, Miles Broughton seemed a real cold hearted bastard and wouldn't think twice about killing them. Their next few days, taken up with spending time with their families explaining as best they could no more criminal activities or monies would be forthcoming and all talk about them should cease, low key was the message.

A few days later saw the four's arrival at the FMPC"s offices, the attitude among the eight was of complete cohesion if not harmony. The overriding question, Gerry had to know was how they were caught in the first place.

Michael went through with them how he came to be there, the explosion, loss of memory, "quirk of fate" and finally how he was able to pinpoint their individual locations. He ended with an apology to Gerry.

"No Michael, it was a fair cop as they say, Paul or Josey would never have caught us without your help," Gerry became serious toward him. "I know you don't agree with what's happened to us and I accept that 99% of the country would feel exactly the same but we will give it our best shot and hopefully prove to you it was a good decision."

"Just as well otherwise you couldn't use those same skills for our little venture, you have to appreciate eventually you would've been caught," Miles was enjoying seeing Paul and Josey squirm having to work with criminals. "At least Michael has provided you with a get out of jail free card."

Everyone laughed together cementing the bond, which would last for a long, long time.

"Let us get started, Michael has told you of his beginnings and how he turned his skill into real practical stuff for finding missing people and he bowed to the four. "For catching bank robbers, but I wanted to take that skill to another level and we've done that already with some great success," Miles looked carefully at all of them to make his point.

"It's why we have increased our numbers by you four, because Gerry was astute enough to connect all the events together. We need this type of intelligence and loyalty you all displayed when planning, executing robberies and toughness under interrogation. The worrying thought is if he can do it so might others and that shortens the window we have for action."

"What you're saying is Michael could be a target, who needs protecting, although to be fair we were coming from a different angle Miles." Lawrie had already assumed partial responsibility for Gerry's actions.

"Absolutely right Lawrie, our first and foremost concern must be to preserve our main asset because without Michael we've just been playing at hunt the terrorist and we might as well pack up and go home."

"Depends what you regard as home of course," offered Trevor lightening the mood, thinking of his prison cell.

"You have immediate concerns though don't you Miles?"

"As I said we have to protect Michael so I'd like to assign both Ron and Trevor to work with that if you agree?" Miles saw both were ready. "Naturally there will be other tasks I will be requiring your services for," the personal assistant back at his own office came to mind.

"Gerry, Paul and I will work on finding the source network who are the suppliers to the terrorist groups."

"You may only find these once you manage to capture one and get him or her to talk."

"You're right Lawrie and that's exactly what I need you and Josey to do, perhaps with the help of Ron or Trevor, I'm convinced my service has been infiltrated, I'm sure even in this building, Michael's unique gift would help flush that out. So each of you have complete authority to go anywhere within my building at Lambeth and to question anything in the guise of carrying out a security audit."

It amused Michael that Miles looked on MI6 as being his.

"Paul handed each of them their security passes."

"God Gerry these look real for once," joked Lawrie, something was wrong with him, he touched and nodded to him, a signal asking if he was ok. Gerry made a slight left and right gesture with his head they needed to talk urgently.

Miles continued. "All heads of departments have been made aware of your audit credentials and will naturally have a healthy suspicion on what you are looking for however, it justifies your presence perfectly."

"Miles what am I meant to be doing, everyone else has tasks to do?" With a slight pang of jealousy, Josey and Lawrie would work together.

"Michael you have to be free for us to use at any moment, but you are too valuable to take a prominent role in our investigations, your background is a mystery and is more likely to attract attention quicker than someone whose record can be traced."

"I understand that Miles but I'm not keen on just sitting around and why can't a background be conjured up for me?"

"Michael I doubt you'll be sitting around very much and yes once over we can consider creating a past for you," Miles dismissal angered him. "Right let's get started, you Ron and Trevor have been given your own office within the technology department at the MI6 building, here I'm not so sure."

"That is my concern Miles," said Michael coolly making him aware he is not in control of everything.

"Quite, there's always some project or other reviews going on in that area so it shouldn't create suspicion. Miles noted Michael's frustration with him, later he thought, later. "There's an office directly connected to mine next to my personal assistant Garvesh's office, it makes sense that Gerry and Paul work with me from there. Lawrie and Josey you'll have desks in the open area, a corner with at least some privacy in the liaison office."

Miles looked at the new group of four. "Gerry, Ron, Lawrie and Trevor you are all used to working with each other tightly and I want to use that relationship by each of you working in each of the camps, I've set out so each of you can help co-ordinate our efforts more effectively. While each pairing can meet up whenever, no one must see the whole group welcome all of you to the payroll.

For the rest of the day Gerry followed Michael around interested in how he worked and how FMPC worked.

"Are you happy Michael?"

"Yes I think I am, I get frustrated having no past, but I have to live with it and my work really gives me a buzz, being different has its benefits."

"How do you work, could you explain?"

"Let me show you Penny has left a couple of new insurance folders on my desk and as I usually get those the team cannot solve I have to bring my skills into play," he considered carefully the explanation to give. "There are a vast amount of grey areas with this gift of mine but essentially two main attributes come into play, one is when I view a picture or an image of a person I get many pictures in my head, which tells me about where the person is or could have been but never where they're going. Secondly, with an item belonging to the person although not always needed, I start to get ticker tape time messages which provide me with enough information to make deductions on who, where and the why people are where they are. Notes, lots of them are all jumbled I have to work through them with the pictures and make judgements. I've found as I have been doing this for a while I can generally do the assessment quickly."

"Wow, I'm truly impressed."

"Help me with these two folders."

He opened the first one and was puzzled, apparently the person looking back up from the picture a male was missing and had been for several years a charity was waiting because of his will bequest for the insurance company LEP Life Enhancement People, to pay the money out to them as the beneficiary. Penny had passed this to him because Tom and David could not find the person or his family on any system, even though to create the insurance, certain documents would need showing to obtain the life cover in the first place.

"The insurers have passed this to us as it is a substantial sum and normally they would pay these straight away because a charity is involved, but now they have a contract with FMPC it is another check. There is a note on the file that the charity has been paid by six other insurers against missing people and twice by LEP themselves."

Gerry read the file. "Don't really have any choice but to pay them but its suspicious, looks to me like a scam, a long term scam but nonetheless a scam. I see the charity checks out, it's just the person and if you can't find him there is no choice."

"Trouble is Gerry this is not a person, well technically it is, of six actually."

"I'm not with you."

Michael pressed the intercom linking him to Penny's desk. "Penny, can you and David come in here please."

"The familiar squeak told him David was moving toward his office, Penny joined him.

"What's up boss?" He nodded to Gerry.

"Here are six names which are the composite part faces in this photograph can you run checks on them I would hazard a guess they are members of the charity stated in this file." David turned and wheeled quickly out of the room.

"Have you had a chance to look at the other file Michael," she asked noting the reaction of his guest he introduced her to Gerry.

Michael opened the second file a woman stared back at him she was 53 in Tunisia and had been there for the past .eight year's. Husband she left was claiming against her life policy suggesting she was dead. He gave Penny the address, it was a good result and she was pleased the claim not be paid'

David wheeled in. "Michael you're right it is a scam, I've phoned Paul he's going to deal with it.

"Thanks David well done."

"I know you don't I?"

"Gerry Fielder."

"Ah yes I remember your picture you're part of us now welcome." He turned on his wheels and left the office leaving Michael to explain about David his skill and his partnership.

"Michael I'm impressed, you could tell all that from a picture and a folder, fantastic," he became serious. "I hope one day you will trust me as much as you seem to trust the people around you."

"Gerry I'm sure I will, but there is just one thing."

"What's that?"

"For the sake of our blossoming relationship I won't tell Paul, but I suggest Sophie Mason which is her maiden name or should I say Sophie Fielder your cousin's wife actually asks for a transfer from the Ashford Police. She has probably out lived her usefulness to you and I doubt you'll want to jeopardise your new position either."

"Shit, how long have you known?"

"I've been aware of her for a while in the background apart from watching her once and David telling me about her when he was in Paul's office, when I connect to you, I get she talks to you on the telephone, it then becomes a matter of putting two and two together."

"One other thing you'll need to sort out Gerry."

"What's that," he was becoming defensive.

"Sawton and Evans, they know of me don't they."

"Oh God yes," he' forgotten about them, nausea swept through him again their new life could be at risk because he opened his big mouth in prison.

"Use Miles, you'll find he can be very helpful in such matters."

"I'll deal with both Michael thanks, wait a minute aren't you supposed to have something of mine to help you tap into me," attempting to recover himself.

"Yes I suppose it's time to give you back your Skagen watch," their laughter heard down the corridor.

"Please, why don't you keep it with my heartfelt gratitude?"

Gerry found it strange for once in his life being legitimate, he had only known from an earlier age nothing else but thieving, it had been a family thing for generations.

Chapter 22

Gerry was in awe of his surroundings the plush offices, bright and airy populated with plants and water dispensers and a restaurant for good measure. A week or two ago he would not have dreamed he would be part of the government establishment about to be doing legitimate work in an office, getting paid well and working for MI6. He could not have wished for better.

He was excitedly suspicious when Miles Broughton's personal assistant Garvesh Pashwa offered his help to Paul and himself as it was clear by his manner he hadn't been told about their use of the office next door to his. Constantly interrupting and finding an excuse to stay with them attempting to extract every morsel of information he could, suggesting he knew exactly what they were doing there and of course there to help them.

Instead of backing off as they attempted to push him out of the office Garvesh asked them directly for their plans and progress so far so he could update Miles and help set up meeting arrangements and be their project administrator, his eyes darting searching any ounce of paperwork he could pinpoint.

Garvesh made his mistake by telling them Miles had suggested they include him, they knew it to be untrue but had not Miles specifically told them of his suspicions it would have sounded plausible coming from the Chief Superintendents personal assistant, they gauged this was how he'd already acquired information about MI6.

Gerry from that moment felt himself watched, he advised Paul not to leave for view any papers. He intended to watch Garvesh right back.

Miles, Paul and Gerry began by collating any information they could get their hands on reading about the varying activities of the terror groups and looked for ways of linking them, hostages, threats and likely locations of any such group. Gerry decided to look at video footage to determine although masked the numbers in gender and age of each terrorist group member, he put himself in the role of assessing the resourcing needs of each group.

Paul concentrated on the aims of each, were they attempting to free prisoners held with an implied bomb threat, hold captives or kill individuals. Miles was getting together the raft of information and shared insight across all intelligence sectors, the world over.

It turned out as a bonus, Trevor was a technical guru, he'd lost count the amount of computer equipment he'd stolen and rebuilt to use for hacking into systems to change security codes and alarm sequences, a given if your business happened to be robbing banks and the like. It lent some credibility to their guise of being auditors. Within days, Trevor knew every system the service had with its files structures where all the information is and who was accessing what.

Trevor became agitated he called FMPC and asked Penny if he could see Michael alone, he travelled to the Maidstone offices arriving an hour later.

"What's the matter, Trevor?" he hadn't had much opportunity to speak to him before and was glad to see him.

"On viewing the systems at MI6, I noticed someone hacking into the systems."

"Great our first positive lead then?"

"Unsure but I traced the hacker to this building, this business in fact," Trevor wondered, whether the risks to Michael were closer to home.

Michael stifled a grin, and pressed a button on his intercom. "Can you come in please?"

They both looked at the door Michael hearing the familiar squeak, new to Trevor. In came a young man, who noted Trevor frowning at him not understanding.

"Trevor may I introduce to you our resident hacker of the world in David, I believe you two need to get to know one another," he grinned at the confused pair.

Michael quickly realised Trevor had a complimentary set of technical skills to David and they immediately took to one another, he saw Trevor providing the help David needed. Ron on the other hand just looked surly, unsure of his role. He decided to look into and watch people at the Lambeth building and one person in particular caught his attention who tried to latch onto Trevor as his "mate" fortunately Trevor was no fool and played the game carefully with the information he gave once he got back to MI6 from Maidstone.

Shorocco realised he could learn a lot from the auditors arrival, he would help the Trevor character who seemed to know his stuff he will likely get information from him as well. There was pressure brought to bear on Garvesh to deliver.

Josey and Lawrie sat by a young liaison officer called Denz and he talked at them as if his mouth would run away if he didn't speak. He knew everything that went on he told them attempting to promote himself as being important and the one to talk to in the organisation. The way he worked telling them proudly, he told everyone what they needed to know, what he had found out and in return whatever they could tell him he could pass on as a sort of fuel to the fire, everyone in the organisation was up to speed.

Lawrie and Josey soon realised others barely tolerated him, he was like a rash, an itch, forever interfering in what they were doing and most felt he should have been dismissed long ago. Unfortunately, no one knew who had employed him and were not going to the bosses about him in case he was there to snoop on them. Both of them recognised the con, his information was total rubbish. Denz gave out false snippets of information in the hope of gaining real stuff. Invariably he got it, definitely one to watch.

Ralph McIntyre was not happy, the three men he'd supplied to work within the British Covert Operations at MI6 had not delivered, this had occurred several times before, his plants had gotten used to the pay and the lifestyle and when that happened they invariably forgot there was a mission. He assumed because of the lack of information forthcoming from them they had been compromised. These three were full of promises and enjoying themselves, but without any substance coming forward, they were useless to him. What they did tell him was Miles Broughton had two people working with him one a Police Inspector nothing unusual there and another likely to be an undercover agent, with talk of some kind of internal audit being carried out on operational activities, this happened from time to time. Frank decided to get tougher, if they didn't supply more information particularly on Miles Broughton's current activities within the next five days he must be killed by one of them. If not they must expect to face the same fate.

Chapter 23

The gang of four sat in the conservatory at Trevor's home, their wives chattering and children playing in the next room. "How are we doing my friends?" Gerry asked, it was the first quiet chance they had to talk together without interruption from family, friends and their new work colleagues being around.

"Jury is out for me as to whether you sold us out Gerry."

"What did I do which was so wrong I'd have done anything to get out of prison, I assumed you would too surely?"

"Blackmailing the British Secret Service was hardly the best way of going about it though was it?"

"I saw no other way but it worked Trevor didn't it?" he grinned sheepishly.

"We were bloody lucky I say," Ron added. "Trouble is we're locked into this deal we have with Broughton, God knows for how long and I wouldn't want to cross him."

"I admit I was scared shitless especially when they took us by armoured car to the industrial unit, I thought we were goners," Gerry mused. "I expected them to stand us up against a wall and shoot."

"Personally," Lawrie spoke seriously. "I think Gerry, it was a stroke of genius, for the first time in my life, I'm not looking over my shoulder waiting to be nicked and I'm so enjoying it."

"No, waiting to be shot more like."

"Shut up Ron, that's not helping, I agree with Lawrie, for once I feel bloody useful."

"Thanks Trevor, look we all signed up for this covert lark, surely we can see it through can't we?" They all nodded agreement.

"Firstly we need to consider how we approach our end, it's alright Miles saying we need to look after Michael and yes we do but it's no good if were working in London and the problem is …."

"You're thinking more of Miles aren't you?"

"Yes Lawrie, with Michael kept under wraps in the background the obvious target has to be Miles."

"So we need to protect both or at best our own meal ticket."

"I wouldn't have put it quite so eloquently as that Ron, but you're right."

"That means we as this group need to come up with some sort of risk analysis."

"Fuck me Trevor, how long have you been working in that technology department."

"Bollocks Lawrie," while he did not see the funny side the rest collapsed with laughter.

"No, no Trevor's right, what have we so far?"

"I'm not sure of a lad named Shorocco wants to know everything going in and out of a gnats arse, boasted to me that he has access to every single computer file, in fact, every piece of information ever written down or typed in MI6.

"Yeh, I've got one like that Trevor, my lad's named Denz he's a liaison officer and lies through his teeth to gain information, no-one likes him but they tolerate him as he just may be useful to them no-one knows who employed him or who he's supposed to work for."

"Thanks, Lawrie believe it or not Miles personal assistant Garvesh is high on my list. A complete know it all, likes to make you believe he's more connected than he is."

"We could get rid of all three, they could be dangerous."

"No Ron, let's watch them all closely, do it by the book for once, just for a short while anyway and see what they do, collect evidence so to speak."

"Oh that bloody makes my day, you even sound like a fucking copper Gerry."

This time three of them chorused for Ron to shut up and even he laughed.

"One thing to find out is if they know each other, how the information is passed to one another and if they are employed by a terror group who are they working for and how they pass the information to them."

"Sounds like some friendly persuasion is needed to me, doesn't it to you Ron?" who nodded.

"Trevor we're in a more sophisticated arena," he grinned. "Instead of guessing we will make sure and then provide our friendly service."

"Gerry it may need more than that, are we allowed?"

"I think you're right Ron, whatever it takes. If we each provide Ron with any information we can on the three lads, where they meet if they do, addresses, hangouts and we'll let you decide what's needed, is that ok Ron?"

"Fine by me."

"We have a problem, well two as it goes."

"Come on Gerry talk."

"They know about Sophie, well Michael does at least."

"Christ Gerry, how on earth did he find out?"

"It's what he does, there's more. We're supposed to look after Michael yeh!"

"That's right."

"I told Joey Sawton and Reece Evans in the Maidstone prison a few days before we left."

"Sorry Gerry just what is it you told them?" Trevor and Ron had the same question as Lawrie did.

"They know about Michael, he helped Paul and Josey catch them as well as us."

"They'll have him killed, you know that Gerry."

"Yes Ron I do know that, at the time I didn't care we were locked up too and the information was for favours."

"Shit now what the fuck are we going to do now, we'll end up where we started thanks to you."

"You're all heart Trevor, what about Michael does he know?"

"Yes Lawrie he reminded me."

"How."

"Again it's what he does," all but Gerry were confused.

"I don't understand what you mean Gerry it's the second time you've said that."

"Let it go for now my friend."

"What are we going to do brother," emphasised Ron interrupting.

"Michael told me to talk to Miles."

"Then do it my brother," for the first time Ron was disappointed in Gerry. "Do it now."

Chapter 24

"I called each of you for a meeting because you needed to see this video of a latest broadcast directed at the German's in particular," Miles pressed play on the recording as the screen in his office dropped slowly down from the ceiling, as well as the eight person team Tom had joined them.

"An eminent scientist working on China's space probes has been captured while on home leave in Berlin and is now being offered for ransom against those suspected of terrorism in a Berlin jail," the background shot was of a suburban apartment building in the Charlottenberg district on Paderborner Strasse 10, it was the scientists family home. A masked terrorist pictured by the side of the hostage who had a newspaper pinned to his shirt depicting todays date.

The implication clear, Michael needed to go to work they had twelve hours then the hostage will be shot, Miles noting this would be the first time the whole of the new group saw Michael in action, he asked Ron to check the outside of his office for any eavesdroppers.

Suspiciously, he noted Miles assistant scurry back into his office, one to watch mused Ron thinking Gerry was right. He nodded to Miles the all clear.

Gerry had spotted something on the recorded clip and needed to investigate further.

"Michael I cannot get you anything from anyone involved, what can you do for us?"

Three of the four new members did not understand what was going on and Lawrie asked. "Sorry what can Michael do alone we've surely got to plan what we're all going to do about this and assess the risk of releasing the captured terrorists haven't we?"

Josey put her fingers to her lips indicating for him to keep quiet and to watch and listen to Michael, she had been through this so many times and it had never failed to amaze her.

Michael spoke slowly and carefully. "I have trouble pinpointing he is not out of Germany, not even out of Berlin, but is currently travelling to the Kreuzberg district. There are three other people with him in masks, two men one woman I cannot see their faces. Miles can you roll back the recording, I have the presence of a woman sitting beside him as well as one of the gunman, I don't see the third person, but I feel this is the second man who is possibly the vehicle driver." Miles made the calls.

"What the hell was that?" Lawrie was confused. "How did you get all that from the clip?"

"It's what Smithy does, that's his 'quirk of fate' his gift," Josey enlightened.

"Smithy?" Lawrie was even more confused.

"Her nickname for Michael, can we get on," Paul was losing patience.

Gerry also saw what he needed from the clip. "I also have a lead I think, Miles if you could run the clip again, there stop it, you'll see a solitary badge on the masked terrorist, I believe I've seen that before in other clips you've shown Paul and myself."

"Mmm, I had read in some of the papers about your heightened awareness Gerry, well done."

"What's it mean Gerry?"

"I don't know yet, I'm going to need those pictures as stills and blown up, I'm convinced there's a connection."

"If you can get me one, we might be able to place the source."

"Hold on I have an update?"

"What do you mean," Trevor too was confused. "You've just been sitting there."

Again, Josey put her fingers to her lips the group fell silent and looked at Michael.

"They've stopped they're still in Kreusberg but they've gone into Checkpoint Charlie Museum, the one created to mark the building of the Berlin Wall in 1962."

"Got an address Michael?" Miles picked up the desk telephone.

"Friedrichstrasse 44."

"Is what I'm seeing correct are you mentally charting the terrorist's movements on the basis of a picture on the screen," Ron looked at Michael in amazement. "This cannot be real right?"

"That's his business Ron and it's how we were caught," Gerry enlightened them.

"Bloody hell."

Miles mobile pressurised him to answer, he interrupted them and turned the TV on to live television where a news flash appeared on screen, the commentator speaking.

"We have just learnt following an earlier broadcast in respect of a person being held by an unidentified terrorist group, during a Police raid at a Berlin Museum the captured hostage described as a late forties male scientist, who is believed to have been on his leave from working for the Chinese government in their Space probe programme has died. Sadly he was killed in the crossfire when the Bundespolizei counter terrorism force, who were working with the special operations force of the German Police linked together to apprehend the terrorists involved. The three terrorists who were involved believed to be two men and one woman were also killed no terrorist group has yet claimed responsibility for the act." Miles switched off the television.

"It also means because they shot the terrorists it's not much good to us in our search for the resourcing agent."

"Miles I think the answer may lie closer to home," Ron gestured towards the door.

Miles Broughton was once again, privately credited with the capture of the terrorists, the Chinese government were grateful to the British for their swift action. The scientist's information died with him, it was unfortunate the German forces were so heavy handed in apprehending the terrorists. They were able to retrieve a badge worn by one of the terrorists, apart from this clue, but no DNA and the badge simply read in Arabic language and translated into English the words "Run, Time is now".

Miles gave the badge to Gerry when they all met back at Michael's offices a few days later.

"What's it mean Gerry?"

"I've spent hours going through TV footage covering the past two years and what I've noticed every time a group demanding whatever appeared on the news, at least one of them wore one of these, not all of them to be noticeable but at least one, Gerry took his time to consider his next statement. "Now we know there are varying groups of terrorists and none of them work together but each time one has a badge."

So you're saying there's a loose connection, perhaps it's the badge of the source network?"

"Correct Lawrie, so I guess this must be a form of communication maybe even advertising?"

"Michael, I can't begin to tell you how confused I am seeing you in action especially last time, but I wonder how you are with objects?"

"I'm generally only able to detect people specifically although given an object belonging to the individual I may find out where they are, it's not an exact science Gerry the findings change, I work on what's thrown up in my brain."

"Will you at least take a look at it to see what you can get?"

Michael held the badge tightly in his hand, closing his eyes feeling the room sway, a whole raft of images flash in his mind's eye, the silence in the room deafening.

"Ok the badge belongs or has been handed out by a man called Ralph McIntyre, currently he's in New York, has an organisation called PDO, Project Development Organisation. I think it is a legitimate business, you'd have to check that Miles but I get the reason why the badge is significant it's a front for the FLA whatever that stands for. Great work Gerry for spotting it in the first place and recognising its value."

"Fucking hell Michael, you're good," Gerry applauded him.

"Good God I actually know the man," a shocked Miles relayed. "He's our British Envoy to the USA and I know what FLA stands for, Front for

Liberating Activists, sorry Michael please continue."

"The badge itself is as Gerry said an advertising tool for what's called "Resourcing United"."

"That's the Run part."

"Yes Paul it is, the rest "Time is now" is simply translated into a number 291591112 obviously derived from the English alphabet and acts as a contact number, I'll leave you to work out dialling area codes."

"I should get you to work for our cipher department," Miles mused.

"Bloody hell" Michael, you're not just good are you, you're fucking brilliant."

"Thanks Gerry, glad to be of service," bowing at him.

"So by giving every terrorist group one of these to wear McIntyre was advertising his services, as a business card and that's how his organisation has evolved."

"Quite right Paul, after all not only do the public watch the broadcasts so do the terrorist organisations."

"Let's go get him Gentlemen," Miles giving a clear message to Ron.

"There's still the question of the infiltrators."

"One step at a time Ron and yes we will need to take care of them as well."

"Will do Sir," Ron was enjoying himself in his new role, the others shuddered shutting out the implications in their minds.

"Miles I need a word."

"Certainly Gerry, let us go outside for a walk on the riverside."

Gerry suggested Paul came along he told them both about the conversations he had with Sawton and Evans and what he knew they were capable of and told them Michael knew and suggested he spoke to Miles. Paul spoke of why they had been in prison because of the boy thrown onto the railway track and hitting first the train and then spiked by the tree. Paul explained when Michael had told him about them for once he bent the rules and it was a wonder those two survived through the battering they took from his colleagues. They would never live on the outside because of it. He suggested this could be their way of getting revenge.

"You don't know they've done anything with the information yet."

"I guarantee they have the time and the inclination to do something about it especially if we're not around."

"He has a point Miles they have to be dealt with."

"Ok Paul," he considered for one moment only. "Gerry I'll make a call and then," he looked at Paul. "I suggest you forget about this conversation, come on we must get going."

Back at his office, he made a discreet call to a fixer.

Miles and Paul left the room hurriedly with Ron and Trevor in their wake, the others decided to get back to Maidstone.

Chapter 25

It was a few days before most of the prison in-mates realised Gerry Fielder, his brother Ron, Lawrie Berger and Trevor Cole, were missing from the prison.

Word fed down from the Governor's office suggesting they had been taken away to be questioned over previous robberies. Soon the warders talked of the black limousine taking them away.

Joey Sawton was thankful of the information given him by Fielder and had already arranged for Michael Smith to be followed, when he gave the word Smith will be killed. On the next update, he intended to make it happen. Next day when it came and he gave the instruction to his own brother to carry out the elimination. His brother Patrick was the only one on the outside who could be trusted and capable he would sort it for him.

Two days later, Reece Evans was outside of his own cell block at the vegetable area tended by the many in-mates as it was easy work one of them, shoving into him causing his cigarette to drop from his hand to the ground. He swore loudly and the inmates moved away from him afraid of his reaction. When he bent down to pick it up the butt his face was pushed hard into the dirt, as he tried to break free a freshly sharpened kitchen knife slit his throat from ear to ear, the blood soaked up by the earth surrounding the growing tomatoes as his body hunched kneeling, his face resting between the plants. An hour passed before someone noticed he had not moved.

Simultaneously, Joey Sawton reading on his bunk with his cell door open received two visitors. Gagged and tied hands behind him struggling furiously, his feet were bound by his own sheet, then used to wrap around the bars on the high cell windows with the cell door pushed closed. Joey breathing hard fought for his life knowing if he didn't death would be near he attempted to break free, but the knot joining two more sheets together pressed hard against his windpipe he tried to scream as his neck was pulled by the sheet towards the last light he would ever see, his neck snapped under the pressure.

Three prisoners the next day were transferred to another prison their sentences would be drastically reduced no one added the two incidents together. Prisoners left all the time, prisoners died all the time. It was prison life.

Unknown to Miles and Paul the risk to Michael was still alive.

Chapter 26

Through Ralph McIntyre's networks word filtered down to the three India nationals in London, to ramp up their efforts or kill Miles Broughton, unfortunately for Ralph, he would not get to see the results, everywhere he went in New York he was followed.

When the two FBI investigators appeared at his PDO offices in an attempt to charge him on terrorist counts, Ralph McIntyre demanded, he be allowed to make a private phone call the officers believing he could be contacting his legal representatives or relatives, the two men waited outside his office door after securing any escape route he may have had.

His first call was long distance and he spoke just three words. "Kill him now."

His second was to his lawyer who asked to speak to the FBI investigator in charge. As he listened, the officer began waiving his men away realising he would have to come back another day to arrest this man officially. With the FBI men gone, he decided to get some air and walked out of his building toward his favourite coffee stop in the Rockefeller.

In this business he accepted the risks realising it was only a matter of time until he was caught, he believed he had tied up the loose ends in ordering the hit on Miles Broughton, it was now time he cut and run, moved on. Later, under the Rockefeller Center in full view of the ice skating rink he sat by the Starbucks Coffee outlet, he liked to watch the bright coloured clothing of the many skaters circling the ice rink it took his mind off his operations making him feel normal, one of the crowd, it helped relax him, he wouldn't finish his cappuccino. A scream rang out as a young girl with her baby in a pram joined him at his table the man in front of her a deathly grey, the pool of blood dripped steadily to the floor underneath his chair, from the barely noticeable puncture in his neck performed discreetly as a passer-by disappeared among the shopping corridors.

His first call traced to the offices of Superintendent Miles Broughton. Miles wondered if he had enough time to wait for Ron and Trevor to return from their 'holiday' in New York, he decided not and put contingency plans in place.

Another lunchtime and all three men continued as they did before laughing and joking as friends in London's MI6 building passing carefully coded information. To the trained observer they would have noticed their underlying fear. They had not signed up to kill anyone, now told to and Miles Broughton was the target. What made them more nervous was the fact they should have done it 5 days ago and unknown to the three, their employer who ordered them do it had since been eliminated himself his resource network broken as a result. The ordered killing of Miles Broughton weighed heavily on them unfortunately the three had no way of knowing their employer from the source network was dead with the implied threat to them removed.

A trained observer was indeed watching them eating their lunches she had her own mission, which she expected to carry out during the next 24 hours.

The implications were clear, the terrorist groups around the world had gotten used to the McIntyre network, it had the element of cohesion, they had been used to giving RUN a requirement and almost immediately the resource would appear, now they were being challenged, terrorism had become that much more dangerous for the terrorists themselves, it wasn't meant to happen. Up to now, they were always in control. Miles considered how he could engineer a replacement to McIntyre it had its merits for increasing his dominance, control and to continue maintaining the network, it would become a vehicle for control of both governments and the terrorists alike.

Denz was choosing between a patterned red or blue crossed tie, when the department store assistant offered her help, she suggested the red one and promoted the deals they had on offer such as trousers and shirts that could compliment the tie, there was even a free cufflink and tiepin set. He could not resist her stunning bright blue eyes, she was so helpful and after choosing a new shirt and trousers for him she ushered him into the men's changing cubicles and suggested he change to see if they would fit him while she went for his free cufflinks and tiepin.

His thoughts as he changed, were on the beautiful assistant he would suggest they could meet later, he felt sure she would agree.

"Hello I'm back," she called out to him and opened the curtain of the cubicle. He noted her name badge read Gemma she giggled apologising as he zipped up the fly on his trousers. "Take the cuff links for your new shirt and I'll do the tiepin for you.

"Ouch that hurt," Gemma Harpham pricked him through his tie and shirt into his chest, he heard her apologise. He would ask her for date, perhaps later, right now tiredness crept up on him, struggling to sit down on the bench of the cubicle. Somewhere he heard her distantly say she would just get him another pair of trousers, he did not understand why the new pair he had on fitted him perfectly, with the cubicle curtain closed, darkness swept over him.

Following the group meeting in Miles office Garvesh had spent most of the time eavesdropping trying to learn its purpose, he felt Miles was having him watched so had to be careful especially now the Police Inspector and Fielder were in the next office. He had certainly learnt Michael Smith was the key to Miles Broughton's current successes in fighting terrorism. Garvesh was worried, McIntyre's direct call had unnerved him and their own terrorist network contact had simply disappeared, it was impossible the network had closed down so he concluded their time was up believing his contact had deliberately given up on him, he had to do something. Deciding the way to get the three of them off the hook he knew Smith was the one to kill.

It was the following morning when he spoke to Shorroco, he already heard Denz had been killed nothing escaped anyone working in MI6, poisoned in a department store. He'd been left in the changing rooms, a dark haired woman posing as one of the shop assistants had been spotted on the stores CCTV camera's and deemed to be the suspect, they hadn't caught her and were unable to trace her through other camera's in the street outside the store. Shorroco warned him to be careful.

They both believed Ralph McIntyre had begun to take steps to remove them permanently Shorroco was beginning to panic and believed they should get as far away as possible. Garvesh reiterated his plan to kill Smith he believed it would save them both.

The first thing Garvesh needed to do was get the gun a 9mm Browning from Miles office, he spotted it when he was searching his desk for information it was underneath a stack of folders he already read in one of his desk drawers. He was out leaving him free to walk into his office, the desk drawers were locked the keys under the chair seat inside a secret pocket used for this very purpose. He cupped the cold metal in his hand, checked the safety and chamber, the magazine was fresh full with 15 rounds, he put it into the inside breast pocket of his loose corded jacket. He locked the desk and put the keys back into the chair pocket. He searched the address file Miles kept on his desk and found the

Maidstone address for Michael Smith, it was time he paid the man a visit he touched the Browning.

On his arrival, he checked the population board just inside the glass and tubular steel framed building, FMPC operated from the top four floors on the left side of the double fronted six floor premises. The right side were residential apartments and Michael Smith had one of them on the sixth floor a short corridor walk between his apartment and business.

From the river walkway across the road he watched and waited until the second day he spotted them leave the building he followed Smith and Sergeant Rainbow walking arm in arm and eat lunch in a Thai restaurant in Week street, it was very public and difficult to take aim with the risk of being recognised and be caught. He had an impression, something else, on the third day he realised what it was.

Garvesh had noticed someone else following the man and assumed he served as a backup protecting him from such an attack as he was planning it added to his risk of exposure. He began to watch the watcher and saw he was practising his own line of fire, taking aim on occasions as if he would be shooting the man. The sunlight glinted off the man's sunglasses it was how he spotted him in the first place.

Patrick Sawton was beginning to come to terms with his brother's death in prison and did not believe in the suicide theory the governor had been suggesting. An ex-army sergeant he was used to people around him dying and what caused suicide,

Joey never fitted the pattern, his time in Iraq made sure he had gotten used to death around him, but his own brother's death he wasn't expecting, a bastard yes, dead no, he couldn't take it.

His last request to kill Michael Smith took on more significance and too much of a coincidence, he felt sure it was related even though he was no killer he would carry out his brothers wishes and avenge his death at the same time, he never needed to know why.

Garvesh needed to take away the uncertainty of not having an exit once he had dealt with Michael Smith. He saw his opportunity when the man took a break from watching the same building. He followed at a distance as the man walked like an army soldier along the Maidstone riverbank eating a pre-packaged sandwich. The opposite bank fronted by a sports club went out of view the longer he walked under the overgrown trees, which lean over the footpath on to the water's edge of the bank. Taking a deep breath Garvesh sucked in nervously the cool air of the river breeze and ran behind the man calling for him to make way and let him pass.

Sandwich in his mouth, packaging in his hand, the man relaxed to let the runner go by. The moment stood quietly still for Patrick Sawton he could hear the water rippling over the bank. He knew, no felt as he took another bite of his sandwich it would be his last.

In slow motion, Patrick Sawton stepped aside to let him pass, the runner turned back toward him, he saw the gun and the bullet fire at his throat and worried about dropping the sandwich starting at the noise of fire only to take in the warmth of blood oozing from the hole in his neck. He dropped the packaging to the ground in favour of raising his hand to his throat attempting to stem the flow of blood gushing from the wound. He dropped the cloth wrapped weapon he was concealing. Too late, he too dropped like a stone onto the pathway, dead before hitting the ground.

Garvesh had never killed anyone before and was panicking, trembling his whole body as if on fire. His clarity of thought precise and full of purpose, he had to get rid of the body, he still had to get to Michael Smith but wrongly assumed he shot Smith's bodyguard and now nothing stood in his way to kill Smith. Holding the gun tightly caused his hand to cramp, he dropped it instinctively.

Looking through the trees across the river no one had noticed the sound at the sports club opposite. For quickness, he rolled the man into the surrounding bushes covering him with broken branches taken from the overhanging trees, kicking the sandwich and packaging and the man's cloth covered rifle into the river. He ran fast back up the riverbank from where he came towards Michael Smith's FMPC building. Seconds later, he was backtracking realising he dropped the Browning on the path where the bodyguard lay.

Retrieving the gun he heard the sound of voices coming down the path in the opposite direction, dog walkers chatting, animals barking and playing enjoying their walks together.

He turned and ran fast back up the path toward the building deciding he needed to find somewhere to hide. Looking around he spotted a cinema complex on the other side of the rivers bridge and made for it. Inside he slowed himself down sweating from his run realising he had actually killed, purchasing a fizzy drink he checked the board for what was showing. A new Disney film was displaying about to start. Buying a ticket, he hid himself along one of the back rows on the end of an aisle out of sight in the darkness. The hairs on the back of his head prickled, having this feeling of being watched he looked around and saw only teenage children with presumably their mother sat just behind them enjoying the film sitting in the first half a dozen rows at the front of the auditorium. He shrugged and relaxed intending to stay for a while.

His mind went over the screams he heard as he ran away from the dead body they rang out far louder than the gun shot had. The couple attempting to stop their normally placid dogs from going wild after unearthing a dead body due to the sickly scent of human blood. Police arrived quickly in response to their mobile call, taking over and cordoning off the crime scene.

Two hours later Garvesh left the cinema to watch from the riverside opposite and spotted Michael Smith with the Rainbow woman. Laughing together arm in arm he knew he would have to be quick if he were to act they were about to walk up the steps to the building entrance and once inside Smith would be protected again. It was now or never without thought he started running across the road traffic to the sounds of irate motorists on the double lane highway he pole vaulted over the pedestrian barrier rail shouting at the same time as he pulled off the gun's safety.

"Smith, Michael Smith stop!"

Surprised Michael looked directly at the man running shouting at him, he was familiar, Miles personal assistant registered, in a flash he worried something had happened to Miles himself, he turned to Josey as she too recognised Garvesh.

"I wonder what's gone wrong, Miles must be in trouble," disbelieving he watched Garvesh pull a gun from his pocket and held it in his hand, stop, aim he fired at them.

Michael's thoughts were to step to his left to protect Josey by his side it saved his life.

Garvesh heard the Rainbow woman scream understanding what was coming next before he began to run from the scene he saw Smith drop to his knees immediately buckling over to the ground the bullet catching him high on his head. He had not allowed for the gun's recoil in his rush to get to his victim, it altered his aim but at least he hit him and watched him drop pleased the task was over, Smith had moved but he got him. Blood poured from the wound like a sickly mess into the hands of Josey Rainbow as she held Michael's head his eyes closing, his body limp she continued to scream as loudly as she could for help.

Listening to the screams Garvesh panicked and ran back over the road down onto the walkway of the riverbank careful to go the other way and avoid the crime scene where the Police were still assessing the murder.

Walking hard but trying not to attract any attention until he was far enough away to take a breather on a nearby bench, looking around no one was following him. In the distance, the sound of emergency service sirens were blaring out, he guessed an ambulance to attend to Michael Smith.

One thing Garvesh realised he could not go back to MI6 as Rainbow and Smith had recognised him. He never planned for that, he would make sure he took care of Broughton outside of the service now.

Josey in tears, her screams ringing out she had brought the office and apartment block alive, several people coming to her and taking charge. The ambulance service and the Police called and Penny crying, bringing with her a blanket for Michael's head to rest on as Josey cradled his head in her lap, she sat on the cold ground with him waiting for help to arrive.

He was barely breathing, eyes closed with blood oozing from his head's gunshot wound those standing around her began questioning the time the ambulance was taking, forgotten with the distant siren sounds telling them it was getting ever closer.

Garvesh became aware of a blonde haired woman, red high heels with a short tight skirt, her leather red jacket open revealing a figure he could die for, he smiled at her expecting her to pass, lovely he thought but now wasn't the time. She sat down on his bench, surprised he automatically shifted along the bench away from her she spoke to him.

"What's up honey not interested?"

He checked the gun in his pocket hidden from view. Moving closer toward him, not now I need to think, work out what to do next, the sirens had stopped blaring. He noted the quiet of the river running gently past him, three swan's in the distance following the current of the water in chevron format as time stood still for him, she was right by his side, he smelt her perfume, intoxicating it filled his nostrils.

"Won't you be tempted," she asked, he looked deep into her beautiful bright blue eyes.

"Er, no thanks, er not just now," he was shaking, barely controlling his nerves, the sirens began to sound again as if panicking to get away, he guessed hospital bound, a fleeting thought came into his mind, Smith could still be alive.

"Someone sounds to be in trouble don't they?" She looked at him for a reaction he was trembling. "Oh well better move on if you're sure I can't interest you?" Standing up she leaned back down toward him, her fragrance mesmerising, her lips brushed against his ear. "Goodnight my dear."

The shot rang out loudly causing the swans to take flight strangely toward the sound she placed her preferred Kahr cw45 lightweight, using only one out of the 6 round magazine back into her handbag. She felt his jacket finding found the Browning, crude and heavy she thought, doing up her jacket she walked back down the riverside toward the

Maidstone town glad she finally got her man having been following him for two days. Obviously, stalking Miles friend Michael Smith, she watched him shoot another man who she did not know nor did she understand why and shrugged not caring, two down one to go she thought.

Garvesh's head leaned against the lamppost next to the bench, at a distance he could have been mistaken for a sleeping tramp, a small round black skin burnt hole open at his left temple.

Miles looked for Garvesh the next morning out of habit and realised his desk was cleared by personnel, as had the bright Junior Liaison officer Denz Rajal the day before. His department were told he had been fired, profound relief swept the department with varying comments of 'thank God' 'good riddance' and 'about bloody time' were recorded, no one wishing to seek out his opinion.

She had been busy Miles thought he realised he may have found his new terror network leader. The telephone rang informing him Michael had been shot in the head and initially been taken to the Somerfield Hospital nearby in Maidstone and hadn't woken since the shooting, The Police had insisted he be moved to the William Harvey Hospital in Ashford where they have treated him before and knew his case better.

Miles guessed Paul Wyndham had a hand in the move and expected Josey to be by his side already he would call in later right now he had other business to attend to. He placed a call requesting a meet immediately.

Lambeth Bridge in the midst of people crossing, with traffic racing across it was always busy and a perfect place to have confidential discussions, the noise drowning conversations. Miles had used the middle of the bridge many times for meetings such as this.

"What happened Gemma, what went wrong?" He could die for those blue eyes he hoped he would not have to.

"Nothing," she replied affronted at the suggestion, she was after all a professional. "From my end Denz Rajal has been dealt with."

"Yes I saw that on the TV."

"And Garvesh?"

"I followed Garvesh Pashwa from here to Michael Smith's building and another person was also targeting Michael Smith, Garvesh killed the man and ran from the scene, for a while I lost him because the Police were everywhere. I waited near the building."

"But Michael was still shot by Garvesh, you were meant to eliminate him, that's what went wrong Gemma."

"I'm sorry where I was watching him from, I had him covered only unpredictably he suddenly dashed across the road and shouted something at Smith I was guessing he was just going to talk to him," she looked at him squarely. "I didn't realise he'd be carrying."

"What?" His voice rising at the implication.

"This," she handed him the Browning discreetly.

"Hell this is mine."

"Great security," making him aware of his own mistake.

"But it's dealt with, yes?"

"I became distracted by the woman screaming for help."

"You lost him?"

"On the building stairs just behind the crowd gathering I asked a man if he'd seen where the gunman went, he pointed the way exactly, he said he was about to go after him and I told him not to," she described the man to him.

"Yes is the answer, but I haven't dealt with Shorroco Bonjani yet," she offered coolly.

"Don't worry about him, I've got another job for you," the network would be safe in her hands he thought.

An hour later, when Miles returned to his office he sent for Trevor.

"Some extracurricular activity needs to occur Trevor."

"Cut the crap Miles who do you want us to bump off?"

"Shorroco his usefulness is at an end," Miles updated him on the events of the past 24 hours.

"Bloody hell I'd better let the other guys know,"

"Trevor, it would be best you do this alone," he handed him his Browning.

"I meant they would like to make sure Michael is ok,"

"Oh yes of course," embarrassed realising he had been in this business too long to remember such niceties.

Back in the IT department, Trevor watched Shorroco and realised he would be missed as a technician he proved his worth. Trevor suggested to him he was going to check out a new computer store in Oxford Street near Selfridges and did he want to come.

Together they walked to the underground tube station of Lambeth North a Bakerloo line station. Their aim to get to Marble Arch, Shorroco plotted their route to change at Oxford Circus to then pick up the Central line direct to their destination, which would be the nearest to Selfridges.

The platform at Oxford Circus as usual was heaving with underground passengers being the main connection not only for the Bakerloo line but for the Victoria and Central lines as well. It was as far as both would travel together.

There would be severe delays this day on the underground due to a passenger accidentally falling on the Central rail line just as an oncoming train entered the Oxford Circus station, Trevor would not need the Browning. No one knew why the person was travelling on the underground this day. It happened all the time too many people on the platform at any one time, the underground staff continually attempted to control the flow of passengers, however the level of abuse they received because of it meant they rarely controlled the crowds properly.

Trevor switched platforms and caught the last Bakerloo train line for several hours back to Lambeth North. At his desk, he selected four numbers on his digital phone pad and spoke softly.

"It is done," he replaced the receiver, he would return the Browning later.

No one really questioned too hard the disappearance of a colleague in MI6 especially being in the type of business they were.

Gemma caught the next flight to New York from Heathrow airport.

Chapter 27

Riding around a hospital's car park looking for a space was not exactly Miles favourite pastime nor, hunting around the many corridors looking for the Kings ward, when finally found he noted the concerned faces of his group outside of Michael's hospital room. Gerry, Trevor, Ron, Lawrie, Tom, Paul and two more people, he hadn't met the chap in a wheelchair he believed to be David Forrester and the pretty young girl Michael's Office Manager Penny Whitmore, although he knew of them both, he guessed Josey was inside the room with Michael.

"Any news folks?"

"Not yet Father, he's been in a coma for nearly two days now and has only just begun to wake up, the Consultant Mr Broadacre and Sister Jocelyn are in there right now with Josey by his side of course."

"That's good isn't it?"

Miles looked through the wire meshed window of the door panel and Michael was obscured by the nurse, he did notice the monitor beside the bed, amazingly it was behaving erratically he heard of this from Paul. He watched the consultant switch the monitor off the readings were likely to be useless to him.

For a moment when Michael woke, to him the past six months had not happened his Sister Jocelyn was fussing over him like a mother hen, he loved her dearly and could think of no one he would rather see looking after him in hospital. It felt strange being back in the hospital, familiarity washed over him as if it were his home, Josey was holding his hand, she looked tired.

"How long have I been out?"

"Nearly two days about thirty six hours, once again you've had us worried," his dear Sister answered.

"You gave us quite a scare Mr Smith and the monitor has been behaving true to form, can you remember what happened to you," his consultant Geoffrey Broadacre's voice boomed around the room, everything seemed louder, but smaller in his presence.

This time he could recall what had happened, Michael relayed how he and Josey had been out for a late afternoon meal and on returning just outside the building. He heard a shout, his name, they both recognised Garvesh the next thing came the pressure he felt on the side of his head, his legs gave way, no control passing out dropping to the ground as he heard Josey screaming.

"I expect the Police will want to talk to you Michael."

Geoffrey Broadacre looked out above his half rimmed glasses at him. "And how's your memory old chap, any change?"

"No memory I'm afraid Geoffrey and I think outside you'll find I've my very own Inspector of Police," what he didn't tell him something was different he was trying to determine the extent of the difference while his memory of his past was still the same, lost it seems forever, he felt his brain had expanded with increased information.

"Good, good, well you should be ready to leave us again in a couple of days, no lasting damage the bullet scraped your temple causing the blackout and that should heal in a couple of weeks, Sister will change the dressing before you leave us."

A bullet, he had not realised Michael touched his chest, the scar of another life still there.

Michael thanked him, Josey embarrassed him by kissing and hugging him, he coughed to clear his throat as he left the room to a sea of visitors.

"Don't stay too long people, he needs his rest," A satisfied Geoffrey Broadacre marched out of the main Kings ward.

"Hi Michael," the group chorused as he recognised the familiar wheelchair squeak with the rest standing around his bed jostling for space his room not that large to hold twelve of them including Sister and him in his bed.

"We might as well have our meeting as we are all here together," Miles suggested raising his eyebrows asking if it was ok with Tom, David and

Penny in the room, Michael nodded to him to continue.

"Well I have work to do, don't you dare tire my patient," Sister Jocelyn winked at Michael and left them to it.

"Will someone tell me what's been going on?"

"I'll pick that one up Michael, first let me say thanks everyone, especially to Gerry for pinpointing the network source through the badge the person Ralph McIntyre has been dealt with and for the moment the network is broken."

"Really Michael should have the credit he gave us who and where."

Michael laughed. "I've only been doing what comes naturally to me."

"Seriously though, I would like to thank you all, we have what I can only term as a "work in progress" for the ongoing destruction of terrorism and I certainly would wish for this team to stay together in some shape or form.

"Miles do I detect you intend to revive the source network."

"Ah Gerry very astute, that's a covert question I cannot answer."

"That's a yes then folks," the group laughed at Paul's suggestion, he tugged at his eyebrow.

Miles spoke about the three men who had infiltrated his operations and what he put in place to remove them being as honest as his position allowed.

"One more thing Gerry, you'll remember Joey Sawton and Reece Evans."

"Yes Miles I understand they met with accidents."

"Indeed they did unfortunately not before Joey Sawton enlisted his brother Patrick to kill Michael."

"Christ what do we do now?"

"Josey it's been dealt with."

"Are you sure Paul?"

"Absolutely," he looked directly at Miles for confirmation, who nodded.

"My personal assistant took care of him in what we believe Garvesh's own mistaken belief was that Sawton's brother was there to protect Michael from his kind of threat so luckily for us he decided he had to be eliminated first."

"Who killed Garvesh then Miles?"

"I can't answer that Michael."

"Miles you know I could find out anyway don't you?"

"Yes I do, but personally I have no intention of compromising one of my operatives, it is up to you what you do with the information should you bother to find out," there was a hint of menace in his voice.

"You said three men one Garvesh, what about the other two?"

"We gather, Denz who worked in the liaison office where we were assigned," Josey looked at Lawrie and switched her gaze toward Miles. "We gather he had been poisoned in a men's changing booth of a department store. Odd that don't you think Miles?"

"I'm sure it happens all the time," he shrugged his shoulders.

"And what of the final man?"

"I can answer that Michael, Shorroco was the lad I worked with in technology, I was with him when he accidentally slipped and fell in front of an oncoming underground train."

The whole group stared at Trevor in silence.

"Happens all the time I'm sure," suggested Miles.

"What do we do now?" asked Ron. "I've actually been enjoying myself."

"Well FMPC will take up a lot of my time, but I'm always willing to reform back into this group at any time.

"Like Michael, I too will be involved in FMPC, but I would also like to still be involved in the future."

"Thanks Josey and you Michael, how about you Paul?"

"Sorry Miles, I'm back to fighting crime and putting villains behind bars," he suggested looking at the gang of four. "No offence meant chaps."

"None taken I'm sure, what happens to us now?" Gerry posed.

"Gentlemen, in your own way each of you have made important individual contributions whether it be major or the smallest detail. For example Ron helped us in New York to address the McIntyre problem, Gerry led us with identifying the badge of the source network and Trevor lent a hand with Shorroco,"

"More like a push," offered Gerry unhappy that he did not tell him.

"But I haven't done anything yet," Lawrie interrupted.

"When I said the smallest detail I meant it Lawrie, do you recall a young woman ask you a question when Michael had been shot?"

"Er yes, she asked did I see where the gunman went and I told her."

"In fact you told her exactly because you were concentrating," Miles looked directly at Michael and asked. "Do you remember what she looked like Lawrie?

"Blond I think, with stunning bright blue eyes, why?"

"A small detail Lawrie, which may just have saved my life," Michael nodded to him understanding. "So in answer to your question Gerry you are all now truly free. However should you wish to continue in my, our employ, we would be happy to have your intelligence and support."

"And you can turn up all of you for work at our place right now, there's plenty for you to do," Michael held Josey's hand tightly. Trevor, you and David work well together on the systems side and he does need a partner in crime so to speak," the group laughed, he thought it would help prevent David becoming overloaded, winking at him. "Gerry, Lawrie and Ron you'll all be welcome to help Josey Tom and myself keep Penny from nagging us to get more staff. The FMPC business is certainly big enough for us all to enjoy."

"All of you we thank you for believing in us, you have given us an opportunity to prove to ourselves and helped show us we can do more than just thieve, I speak for us all in saying we would like to take you up on your offer Michael and you Miles of course."

"Grand, very grand." Miles preened himself at Lawrie's comments.

Sister Jocelyn came into the room to point out it was time they departed each took this as their cue, with the meeting over they began to say their goodbyes as she stood guard in the doorway ready to usher everyone out.

Josey bent down to him at the side of the bed where he lay and gently kissed Michael's lips and whispered in his ear how proud she was of him and would be back later on.

With Josey, each went their separate ways only Michael and Miles left in the room. Miles helped him out of the bed so he could look at them leaving from his window above the car park, Michael stood looking up at the sky, his hand touched the bullet hole in the centre of his chest, he had become aware of it since awaken from his latest coma. Two bullets in two lives he wondered if it meant something.

"A few people have died because of my gift Miles."

"Necessary I'm afraid Michael, be assured its immeasurable how many lives you have saved in our fight against terror, criminals placed behind bars and how you've improved individual lives and saved countless families from extreme torment," he paused to reflect. "Michael you've woken me up in my career and given my son back to me, I'm very grateful and you have provided me with a circle I truly call my friends."

"I was aware of the dangers of course, you made that clear, it surprised me to be targeted by both terrorists and criminals."

"Yes we need to be more discreet in future using your skills."

"Nature of the job is that it Miles?"

"Well perhaps we could change your identity."

"Oh yes I know how about from Smith to Jones?" He grinned at Miles knowing he was right about the friendships gained he truly had a family.

"It must be difficult for you knowing who and where everyone on earth is and not yourself Michael?"

"Yes it's very frustrating and amazing at the same time." He said still looking up at the sky.

"How are you really feeling, I noticed the machine playing havoc before it was switched off, that was normal, at least the same as last time wasn't it?"

"I'm fine really, only," he looked straight at him.

"What is it Michael please tell me?"

"I'm not quite sure but there's been a further development in my brain."

"Have you mentioned this to the Doctor's here?"

"No, no, it's to do with the information I hold and my skill generally, only right now I'm unclear how I'm going to put it to the test."

"For God's sake man speak English."

"Since this latest 'accident', not only do I know where everyone on earth is Miles."

"Oh shit," he too looked up at the skies.

-o-

Books by the same Author

Alan Baulch

Finding Bridie

As a young teenager in the 1960's Bridie London develops the life
Threatening Meningeal Tuberculosis.

On Medical advice and because of risk to her siblings and his greengrocery business, her father Desmond London delivers her to a mental asylum offering the isolation she needs.

Unwittingly he gives up his parental rights consigning her to a life in an institution. At last there is an opportunity to release her from the mental torture after fifty years, with siblings unwilling to help, Desmond finds someone who can.

The corruption found by Haydon Robbins would shock the nation, with the real B

ridie missing he must find her before it is too late.

Love, Life, Fantasies & Poetry

A thought provoking first volume of 30 Short Stories, Tales and Ramblings with 20 Poems spread across different genre's.

From Love in New York, A Scare in the Dark to Something Crazy, Asylum Seeking, The Pain of Redundancy, Spine Chiller and a Spirit of Hope.

With Poems on Time, Friends, Work, Teenage Angst and Human Values.

A Collection to Enjoy.

The Tracer

A gas canister explosion in a scrap metal yard leaves Michael battered, an Amnesiac without a past.

By a 'quirk of fate', he is left with a unique gift his mission is to trace the missing.

Struggling with his identity, he enters a world where kidnapping, murder, rape, robbery, hate and great sorrow are normal.

Single-handedly he offers the solution for driving terrorism into extinction while providing the answers for solving crimes across the globe.

He has to be stopped, the only question who will get to him first?

Mind Trap

Samuel Thornton arrived as a patient at the Berkshire clinic direct from Shanghai. The grip on his mind total. More patients arrive the grip on their minds the same pure evil.

Without out the help of David Bareham an ex-priest they will all die and be used as tools for the pleasure of Kali Ma herself.

Friends rally and a group with David is formed. They have to tackle the spiritual evil attacking them.

The group are taken on a journey following past lives, death and business corruption. Their experiences cause them to fear for their very souls.

Death beckons, they become trapped in a fight they couldn't possibly win alone.

-o-